...am Lincoln: Vampire
...wrote Tim Burton's recent film, *Dark*
...e lives in Los Angeles.

Acclaim for Seth Grahame-Smith:

'Even bookworms are in love with Seth Grahame-Smith's
ingenious "mash up" fiction'
Sunday Telegraph

'Grahame-Smith has forsaken neither graphic gore nor gleeful
historical and religious revisionism . . . Great fun'
Washington Post

'Wickedly well-researched'
SFX magazine

'Scholars think it's a bloody travesty, and the fans
agree – the bloodier the better'
The Times

'Not just the Lincoln biography we've all been waiting for.
It's also the funniest, most action-packed and weirdly well-
researched account of the Civil War you'll probably read in a
long time. Grahame-Smith could be poised to become the
Howard Zinn of vampire-related alterna-history'
Vanity Fair

'Dismiss Seth Grahame-Smith's historical romp
as nonsense at your peril'
Sci Fi Now

'A lively, fluent writer with a sharp sense of tone and pace'
Time

Also by Seth Grahame-Smith

Abraham Lincoln: Vampire Hunter
Pride and Prejudice and Zombies

Unholy Night

Seth Grahame-Smith

BANTAM BOOKS

LONDON • TORONTO • SYDNEY • AUCKLAND • JOHANNESBURG

TRANSWORLD PUBLISHERS
61–63 Uxbridge Road, London W5 5SA
A Random House Group Company
www.transworldbooks.co.uk

UNHOLY NIGHT
A BANTAM BOOK: 9780857501509

First published in the United States by Grand Central Publishing,
a division of Hachette Book Group, Inc.
First publication in Great Britain
Bantam edition published 2012

Copyright © Seth Grahame-Smith 2012

A CIP catalogue record for this book
is available from the British Library.

Addresses for Random House Group Ltd companies outside the UK
can be found at: www.randomhouse.co.uk
The Random House Group Ltd Reg. No. 954009

The Random House Group Limited supports The Forest Stewardship
Council® (FSC®), the leading international forest-certification organisation.
Our books carrying the FSC label are printed on FSC®-certified paper. FSC is
the only forest-certification scheme supported by the leading environmental
organisations, including Greenpeace. Our paper procurement policy can be
found at www.randomhouse.co.uk/environment

Typeset in 12/15pt AGaramond by Falcon Oast Graphic Art Ltd.
Printed and bound by CPI Group (UK) Ltd, Croydon, CR0 4YY.

2 4 6 8 10 9 7 5 3 1

MIX
Paper from
responsible sources
FSC® C016897

For Gordon, who wouldn't have believed a word of it.

'Do not be afraid. I bring you good news that will cause great joy for all the people. Today in the town of David a Savior has been born to you; he is the Messiah, the Lord. This will be a sign to you: You will find a baby wrapped in cloths and lying in a manger.'

—*Luke 2:10–12*

Go tell that long tongue liar,
Go and tell that midnight rider,
Tell the rambler, the gambler, the back biter,
Tell 'em that God's gonna cut 'em down.

—*Traditional Folk Song*

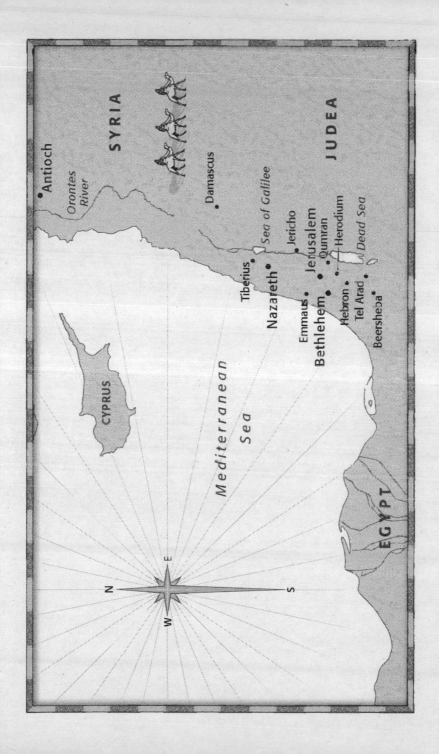

2 BC

The magic of Old Testament times is coming to an end.

Great floods, mystical beasts, and parting seas have given way to the empires of man. Many believe that God has abandoned the world – most of which is ruled by Rome and its new emperor, Augustus Caesar.

One of many Roman provinces, Judea (in modern Israel), is ruled by a cruel puppet king named Herod the Great, who – although sickly and dying – fiercely clings to power through murder and intimidation. And he has reason to be paranoid, for the Old Prophecies tell of the imminent birth of a messiah – *a King of the Jews* – who will topple all the other kingdoms of the world . . .

LAST STAND OF THE ANTIOCH GHOST

'No king is saved by the size of his army; no warrior escapes by his great strength.'

—*Psalm 33:16*

I

A herd of ibex grazed on a cliff high above the Judean
Desert – each of their tiny, antelope-like bodies
dwarfed by a pair of giant, curved horns. A welcome
breeze blew across their backs as they searched for what
little shrubbery there was here in the great big nothing,
each of them pushing their hot, cracked noses across the
hot, cracked earth, gnawing at whatever succulent bits of
green had managed to push their way through.

One ibex – tempted by the sight of a few lonely blades
of grass on the cliff's edge – grazed apart from the
others, closer to the bone-shattering drop than even they
dared go. These blades it now pulled at oh so carefully
with its teeth. Its cloven hooves clacked against the loose
rocks of its perch as it shifted its weight, sending the
occasional pebble tumbling hundreds of feet into the
valley below. Ten million years of geological aspirations
undone in seconds.

Miles to the north of where it chewed this hard-earned
meal, a carpenter was making his way toward Jerusalem
in the blistering heat of midday – his head swimming

through stories of plagues and floods to keep the thirst from driving him mad, his young, very pregnant wife asleep on the donkey behind him. And though the ibex would never know this – though its life, like the lives of all ibexes, would go completely unnoticed and un-appreciated in the annals of history – it was about to become the sole living witness to a truly extraordinary sight.

Something's wrong . . .

Perhaps it was a glint in the corner of its eye, a tiny, almost imperceptible vibration beneath its hooves. Whatever the reason, the ibex was suddenly compelled to lift its head and take in the sight of the vast desert below. There, off in the distance, it spotted a small cloud of dust moving steadily across the twisted beiges and browns. This in and of itself was hardly unusual. Dust clouds sprang up all the time, dancing randomly across the desert like swirling spirits. But two things made this cloud unique: one, it was moving in a perfectly straight line, from right to left. Two, it was being followed by a second, much larger cloud.

At least it looked that way. The ibex had no idea if clouds of dust could, in fact, chase each other. It only knew that they were to be avoided if at all possible, since they were murder on the eyes. Still chewing, it turned back to see if the others had spotted it. They hadn't. They were all grazing away without a care in the world, noses to the ground. The ibex turned back and considered this strange phenomenon a moment longer. Then, convinced there was no danger to itself or the herd, it went back to its meal. The two clouds moved silently, steadily in the distance.

By the time it yanked another blade of grass out of the rock with its teeth, the ibex had forgotten they'd ever existed.

Balthazar couldn't see a damned thing.

He rode his camel across the desert valley, kicking its sides like mad, his eyes the only things visible through the shemagh he wore to fight off the sun and the odor of the beast beneath him. Two overstuffed saddlebags hung off either side of his animal, and a saber hung from his belt, swinging wildly as they galloped along, kicking up the desert behind them. Balthazar turned back to see how close his pursuers were, but all he saw was the Cloud. The same, massive, relentless cloud that had been chasing him since Tel Arad. The cloud that made it impossible to tell how many men were after him. Dozens? Hundreds? There was no way to know. It was, at present, a cloud of undetermined wrath.

From the direction of that cloud there came a faint whistling, almost like the movement of wind through a ravine. At first it was just a single note, its pitch bending steadily lower and growing louder with each second. This note was joined by another and another, until the air behind Balthazar's head was a chorus of faint whistles – each of them starting soprano and tilting tenor as they grew louder, closer. Just as Balthazar realized what they were, the arrows began to strike the earth behind him.

They're shooting from horseback, he thought.

None of the arrows had come close enough to cause concern. Balthazar wasn't surprised. Any experienced archer knew that firing an arrow from a galloping horse was akin to saying a prayer with a bow. Even at twenty yards, you had little chance of hitting your target. From this distance, it was hopeless – a sign of either desperation or anger. Balthazar didn't think the Judeans were desperate. They were furious, and they were going to take that fury out on his skull if they caught up to him. After all, the untold legions in that cloud weren't just chasing the thief who'd made off with a fortune of stolen goods, and they weren't after the murderer who'd killed a handful of their comrades . . .

They were trying to catch 'the Antioch Ghost.'

It was a nickname born of the only two things the Romans knew about him: one, that he was Syrian by birth, in which case it was a good bet that he'd grown up in Antioch; and two, that he had a knack for slipping into the homes of the wealthy and making off with their riches without being seen or heard. Other than those scant facts and a rough physical description, the Romans had nothing – not his age, not even his real name. And while 'the Antioch Ghost' wasn't particularly inspired as nicknames went, it wasn't all that bad, either. Balthazar had to admit, he enjoyed seeing it among the 'known criminals' painted on the side of public buildings – always in red, always in Latin: *Reward! The Antioch Ghost – Enemy of Rome! Thief of the Eastern Empire!* Sure, he hadn't achieved the infamy of a Hannibal or a Spartacus, but he was something of a minor celebrity in his little corner of the world.

There was a second chorus of whistling, followed by a second strike of arrows behind him. Balthazar turned and watched the last of them fall. While still too far away to cause concern, this volley hadn't been quite as hopeless as the last. *They're getting closer*, he thought.

'Faster, stupid!' he yelled at the stubborn beast, kicking its sides with his heels.

If only he could get out of their sight for a minute or two, change direction. Even now, with an indeterminate number of Judean soldiers chasing him through the middle of nowhere, with only a tired, pungent camel and a dull sword to protect him, and even though his pursuers were only two minutes behind him at best, Balthazar still had a chance. He'd spent years memorizing a network of caves to hide out in, shortcuts across barren lands, the best places to scrounge up food and water on the run. He'd trained himself how to survive. How to carry on in times when the whole world seemed hell-bent on snuffing him out. Times like now.

He sensed his camel slowing down and gave it another swift kick in its side.

C'mon . . . just a little longer . . .

The beast had struggled to keep pace with the weight of all that treasure on its back, and Balthazar had been forced to toss some of his heavier spoils overboard as they'd fled Tel Arad. The sight of all that wealth skipping across the sand had nearly made him sick to his stomach. The thought of some lucky shepherd stumbling upon his spoils made his jaw clench and his teeth grind. There was nothing more enraging, more unjust than denying a man the hard-earned fruits of his labor, especially when those fruits were made of solid gold. Balthazar had briefly considered cutting off one of his own limbs to shed an equal amount of weight. But the long-term prospects of a one-armed marauder were limited.

'Faster!' he cried again, as if this would spur on the camel any more than the thousand sharp kicks he'd delivered to its sides. It was still losing steam, and once again, Balthazar was forced to consider the unthinkable: jettisoning more of his hard-earned treasure.

He reached into one of the large saddlebags and fished around until his hands found something that felt heavy. He almost couldn't bear to look as he pulled it out into the sunlight. There, in his hand, was a solid silver drinking cup – nearly the size of a bowl. Intricately carved and adorned with precious stones. It was a stunning piece, made from the finest materials with the finest artistry. It was also incredibly heavy. Balthazar held the chalice out to his side. Then, with his eyes averted and his stomach churning, he let it slip from his fingers. He turned away to spare himself the sight of it rolling across the desert floor and gave the camel another swift kick in retaliation.

C'mon, stupid . . . just a little longer . . .

It *couldn't* be thirsty. A camel could drink forty gallons in one go, and its body could cling to that water for weeks. Its piss came out as a thick syrup of pure waste. Its shit was dry enough to use as firewood, for the love of God. No . . . it wasn't thirsty. Not a chance. Tired? Unlikely.

Camels had been known to live fifty years or more. And while Balthazar had gotten only a brief look at the face of this particular beast in the process of stealing it from a very unhappy Bedouin, he guessed that it was no more than fifteen years old. Twenty, tops. Still in the prime of its wretched life.

Just a little longer, you son of a bitch . . .

No, this camel was just being stubborn. And stubbornness could be corrected with a firm kick or two. Balthazar reckoned the beast could flat-out gallop for another hour. Maybe two. And if that estimate held up – if this camel could be coaxed through its stubbornness – then he had a real shot at making Jerusalem. And if he made Jerusalem, he was home free. There, he'd be able to blend in with the masses that were no doubt choking the streets for the census. He'd be able to disappear. Trade his stolen goods for coins, clothes, food – certainly a new camel.

Balthazar may have been a thief, but he deplored risk. Risk got men killed. Risk was unnecessary. When a man was prepared, when he was in control, things usually went according to plan. But the minute he left something to chance? The minute he trusted in partners, or instinct, or luck? That's when everything went to hell. That's why he was being chased across the desert by a giant cloud atop a stinking, unmotivated beast. Because he'd taken a risk. Because he'd committed the unforgivable sin of trusting his instincts.

As much as it irked him, as much as it went against everything in his nature, Balthazar had to accept that the outcome of his current predicament was beyond his control. He could kick and curse all he wanted . . .

It was up to the camel now.

II

It had all seemed so perfect. All the enticements had been there: a loosely guarded stash of expensive items, a corrupt nobleman, a populace being taken advantage of by the Romans. A more direct route to Balthazar's heart couldn't have been charted by a mapmaker.

Location had been another enticement. The city of Tel Arad was more than fifty miles south of Jerusalem. And the farther you were from Jerusalem, the less likely you were to encounter troops, whether they were King Herod's Judean troops or Rome's elite soldiers. And while Tel Arad still paled in comparison to Judea's great city, it was home to a new, impressive temple of its own. To the noncriminal, that may have seemed like a trivial detail. But to Balthazar, it was everything. Temples meant travelers and money changers. They meant that a man with a strange appearance or accent was less likely to draw attention and that someone looking to trade stolen goods for gold and silver coins could do so with ease. Temples were a thief's best friend.

Tel Arad had been settled thousands of years earlier,

destroyed and rebuilt more times than any of the locals cared to remember. And for thousands of years, it had never grown beyond the rank of 'desolate village.' But times had changed. Empires had sprung up on either side of the once-forgotten settlement and transformed it into a thriving center of trade. Suddenly Ted Arad was the central point between Roman goods heading east and Arabian goods heading west toward Egypt, the Mediterranean, and, ultimately, Rome – and its status had been steadily upgraded to 'small city.'

The strongest sign of its growing importance had come only a year earlier, when Rome had decided to dispatch a governor – Decimus Petronius Verres – to look after the little city. Officially, Decimus was there to make sure Tel Arad adhered to the traditions and upheld the virtues of Roman life. Unofficially, and more importantly, he was there to put troublemakers to death and make sure the locals paid their taxes on time.

Decimus, for his part, had been crushed when he learned of the assignment. It had been presented as an 'honor,' of course. He'd been 'handpicked by Augustus *himself* to represent the empire in the East.' But Decimus knew what it really was: a castration. A punishment for taking sides against the emperor one too many times in the senate.

He'd privately sobbed when he'd heard the news. How could they do this to him? For one thing, the desert was no place for a Roman, especially one of his considerable weight and fair complexion. For another, he had been perfectly happy where he was: safely, quietly ensconced in the suburbs of Rome, surrounded by the trappings of reasonable, if not exorbitant wealth. He was in his fifties – far too old to be picking up his entire life and traipsing around in the heat. Rome was the center of the world. Home to all the entertainment and enticement a man could want. The desert, by contrast, was a death sentence. But the emperor had spoken. And castration or not, Decimus had no choice but to go.

Even the exiled members of Roman nobility weren't expected to travel without the comforts of home. Shortly after his arrival in Tel Arad, Decimus ordered a walled compound built to his exact specifications – a scaled-up, fortified replica of the villa he owned in Rome. The same painter was brought in to re-create his favorite frescos, the same artisans to lay the mosaics on his floors tile by tile. The same formal garden and fountains dominated the courtyard at its center. The same slaves had made the journey to serve Decimus by day and the same concubines to serve him by night.

The finished compound was an impressive sight. A gleaming symbol of Roman superiority hidden from the public behind ten-foot walls. It sat atop a hill overlooking the northwest quarter of the little city, looking down on the temple and the bazaar below, where, as Decimus said, 'the *braying* of animals, *paying* of merchants, and *praying* of men join together in a relentless chorus that deprives me of even a moment's peace.'

But it wasn't all bad in Tel Arad. It had taken some time, but Decimus had warmed to his new city. Not because of its cultural riches or natural beauty – it had neither. Not because of the local women – he'd imported his own. No, he'd taken a shine to his new home because it was, politely speaking, a garbage heap.

In Rome, there was always someone more powerful, someone who had to be placated or paid off. Things like treason and treachery bore very real, very severe consequences. Rome was a city of laws. But the desert was lawless. In Tel Arad, Decimus was the only one who had to be placated. His pocket was the only one that needed to be lined. *He* was the law. It was a role he'd never had the opportunity to play in Rome, and it was one he found himself relishing more by the day.

As the governor of this godforsaken little sandpit, he had the power – indeed, the responsibility – to make sure the Arabian goods on their way to the West were up to 'Roman standards,' a term that had a very loose and ever-changing definition but that could be more or less summed up as: 'things Decimus didn't feel like keeping for himself.'

He deputized a group of local men to serve as his 'inspectors,' then turned them loose on the bazaar, where they conducted so-called quality checks at will. These inspectors targeted everything from jewelry to pottery to fabric to food. And if an item appeared to be of 'lesser quality' or was 'suspected of being a forgery'? It was confiscated and brought back to the governor's compound for further inspection. There, Decimus had the final say on whether the item would be returned or whether it would be held indefinitely, in a room he'd specially built for the purpose. In the six months since the inspections had begun, not a single merchant could recall having an item returned. And if they complained? If they caused even the slightest trouble? Decimus made sure they never set foot in his bazaar again.

Now *he* was the one with the power to exile.

With that many stolen valuables stockpiled in one place, it hadn't been long before Balthazar had caught wind of it. The rumors had reached him through the usual channels, and they'd been conveyed with the usual hyperbolic flair:

'Never has there been such a thieving Roman! He sits atop a pile of riches that would make the gods envious!'

And while these rumors usually amounted to nothing, even the remote possibility of stealing a little stolen treasure, and embarrassing a Roman governor in the process, warranted a firsthand look. And so Balthazar had set out from Damascus, where he'd been chasing another rumor. The one he'd been chasing for years. *The only one that really matters.* He'd ridden south through Bosra, avoiding the roads as much as possible. And on the fifth night of his journey, he'd seen the torches of Tel Arad burning in the distance and the grand white walls of the governor's compound above them.

The next day, he'd asked around the bazaar, hoping to verify some of the stories that had reached him up north. To his surprise, not only did they check out, but also the value of the confiscated goods was far greater than he'd imagined. Gold chalices, silver bracelets, rare perfumes and spices – all of it taken by this 'Decimus.' All of it locked away behind his walls.

It seemed that this was one of those rare instances where the truth was even bigger than the legend.

Balthazar had his motive. Now all he needed was an opportunity. He surveyed the governor's compound from afar, taking note of how many guards there were, when and how they patrolled the grounds, what kind of weapons they carried. Although Tel Arad was a Roman province, and its locals paid Roman taxes, the Roman Army couldn't be bothered to come this far east – not to babysit a governor who'd fallen out of the emperor's favor, anyway. Decimus had been forced to settle for a handful of soldiers from the less-impressive Judean Army, on loan from Herod the Great, to guard his compound. The Judean troops may not have been as professional or well equipped as their Roman counterparts, but they were nothing to take lightly. Storming the compound alone was out of the question.

Balthazar needed a way in. A way through its defenses. Two days after arriving in Tel Arad, he found one.

Her name was Flavia.

At seventeen, she should have been in Rome, enjoying the trappings of wealth and youth in the world's great city, living it up with the other sons and daughters of the ruling class. Instead, her father had dragged her to the desert of the Eastern Empire and left her to wither in the heat. With nothing to do. No one to talk to but concubines and slaves.

Balthazar had watched her for three days. Every morning, she walked down the hill from her father's compound, accompanied by a pair of Judean soldiers. For the next few hours, she wandered up and down the network of crowded streets that made up the bazaar, buying everything from silks to harps to figs, either unaware or undeterred by the fact that *any* of these goods could be had for free back at her father's compound. Then, at midday, she climbed the hill and disappeared behind the compound's walls, not to be seen again until the following day.

When Balthazar finally made his move, he'd done so using the oldest, easiest trick in the book. So easy, that he was almost ashamed of himself.

'Excuse me,' he said.

Flavia turned, as did the soldiers at her side. She was a curly haired blonde – a rarity in this part of the world – with a full figure, a pretty face, and a lightly freckled nose, also a rarity. Not his type, but not bad at all.

'I believe you dropped this.'

He offered his closed hand, which was promptly grabbed by one of the bodyguards. Balthazar smiled and opened his fingers, revealing a beaded bracelet inside. The bracelet Flavia's mother had given to her before she died.

The bracelet that Balthazar had stolen off of her wrist moments before. Flavia studied it in disbelief. *They always do.* She wondered how on earth she could've dropped something so dear to her. Shooing her guards

31

aside, she thanked Balthazar profusely and introduced herself with an extended hand. 'Flavia,' she said.

'Sargon,' Balthazar replied, taking it.

'Sargon . . . would you care to join me for a walk around the bazaar?'

Now I hesitate . . . my face flushed with modesty. Yes, I'll join you for a walk around the bazaar. But I'm going to make you believe it was the furthest thing from my mind . . .

'Come,' she said, sensing his hesitation. 'Let me buy you something. A reward for your good deed.'

'Oh, well . . . I don't know . . .'

Of course I do. But now I hesitate some more. Not too long – not long enough for you to lose interest. Just long enough for you to believe I'd say no. And then, the instant I see that belief in your eyes, I answer—

'I guess I can, but . . . your company is the only reward I need.'

And you silently swoon . . . as I prepare to win you over with a lifetime's worth of lies.

Flavia and 'Sargon' walked for hours, telling each other everything. Two lonely spirits who'd finally – *miraculously* – found kinship in this faraway land. And though her bodyguards eyed this Sargon with suspicion, though they would've liked to rough him up and warn him off, they knew better than to cross the only daughter of Decimus Petronius Verres.

Three nights and three trips around the bazaar later, Flavia snuck Balthazar into the compound and into her bedchamber . . . just as he'd known she would.

The next two weeks had been fun. More importantly, they'd been fruitful.

Each night as Flavia slept, Balthazar rose silently from her bed and went to work – slowly, methodically sneaking his way through the slumbering compound. Mapping it in his mind until he knew its every corner by heart. Until he knew the sleeping habits of every slave and the position of every guard. Until he knew how to walk from one side to the other without setting foot in the glow of the torches. And most of all, until he had examined every confiscated item in the governor's fabled storeroom, which he'd found on the first night, and which, like everything in Tel Arad, had exceeded his expectations.

And on the night that Balthazar felt he could know no more, he'd filled two large saddlebags – the most he could reasonably carry and still move quickly if he had to – with predetermined items chosen for their value-to-weight ratios. Bags stuffed, he'd snuck back along his carefully rehearsed route toward the compound's rear gate. The one that was always unmanned for a ten-minute window at this time of night, thanks to a guard with a *phenomenally* regular constitution.

He crept along in the dark, through the garden – *twenty-seven steps* – past the fountain – *another ten but veering slightly left* – then a sharp right turn at the sundial. After that, it was just thirty steps in a straight line to the gate. *Thirty steps to free—*

'Sargon?'

Balthazar nearly let out a yelp as he spun in the direction of the voice. At first, he thought he'd come face-to-face with a ghost. A translucent white being seemed to float toward him out of the darkness, barely perceivable in the light of the moon. He stood, frozen, as it moved closer . . . until Balthazar saw what it *really* was: a white sleeping gown, fluttering in the warm night air.

'Flavia . . .' he whispered.

'You're . . . you're a thief,' she said.

What gave you that idea? Is it the two huge bags of stolen treasure I'm carrying out here in the middle of the night?

'No—'

'You used me.'

Yes, I used you, and I'd use you again. And who are you to feel used, anyway? You're a Roman. All your kind does is use. All you do is rape, and burn, and steal, and murder.

'No,' said Balthazar. 'Flavia, listen to m—'

'Shut up!'

All she had to do was scream and the guards would come running. And when that happened, the exciting trouble currently making Balthazar's heart pound against the back of his ribs would become real trouble – *blood trouble* – in a hurry.

On the other hand, she could just as easily let him slip away into the night. No one would ever suspect her unwitting part in the robbery. Her chastity would never be called into question, and Balthazar would be halfway to anywhere by morning, with a promise to return and 'take you away, Flavia – when the time is right, take you away from all of this so we can be together.' A promise he would have no intention of keeping.

'Flavia,' he said. 'Listen to me, okay? Yes . . . yes, I was taking these. Taking them from your father's storeroom. But you have to believe me – I have good reason to take them! Your father stole these things from the people of Tel Arad! Poor people! Honest men! I couldn't stand by and watch them suffer. The truth is, I was stealing them, yes. Stealing them from the man who stole them first. Stealing them back so that I could return them to their rightful owners! Aren't you always talking about how cruel and selfish your father is? Well here, Flavia! Here's the proof !'

I'm getting through to her. Now make it personal . . . turn her mind away from the theft.

'And . . . and yes,' he continued, 'I know I should have told you first. But I didn't want to get you involved. What if something had gone wrong? What if you'd gotten in trouble? I wouldn't have been able to live with myself, Flavia. You're too good for this.'

'I . . . I don't know . . .'

Yes, you do.

'Flavia, I swear on our love . . . on my *soul* – everything I say is true.'

She stood there for a moment, conflicted and confused. A victim of youth and inexperience and a deep desire – a *need* – to believe that everything he was saying was, in fact, true.

'Please, Flavia, there isn't much time . . .'

I could always give her a knock on the head. If it came

35

down to it, just a little knock on the head. Not enough to really hurt her, but enough to let me get the hell out of here.

But Balthazar didn't think that would be necessary. His instincts were beginning to tell him this was going to be okay – and he decided to trust them.

She's not going to scream. She hates her father. Yes, she hates her father, hates the fact that he brought her here. Besides . . . we've shared everything. Our deepest secrets. Our deepest love. And yes, that's all bullshit – but not to her. There's no way she'd give me up. She loves me. No . . . I'm a man with a knack for knowing things, and I know she's not going to scream. I've never been more certain of anything in my life.

She screamed.

III

It was clear he wasn't going to make Jerusalem. The camel had been gradually slowing down over the past hour. And as much as Balthazar kicked and cursed, it wouldn't pick up the pace. This wasn't stubbornness . . . he'd stolen a dud.

Balthazar knew of a good-sized village just north of Jerusalem Bethel, if he remembered correctly. Or Beit El. Or whatever the hell they called it. *The one that sounds like 'Bethlehem' but isn't.* It didn't matter. He knew it was there, some eight miles ahead, and it would have to do. With his camel fading fast, he pointed its nose in the village's direction. There was still a chance. He could still get away, as long as the beast held up.

What's that story the Jews tell? The one about the menorah that had enough oil for only one night but burned for eight? That's my camel . . . only enough fuel left for one mile. If it lasts eight, it'll be a miracle.

Miracle or not, the camel made it, and Balthazar galloped into Bethel (he'd been right the first time) only a minute or so ahead of the untold menace behind him.

It was one of the nicer satellites that orbited Jerusalem. A small village of fewer than 2,000 people where many Jewish noblemen chose to escape the noise and bustle of the city with their families. There were no inns to accommodate travelers, no massive temple spewing sacrificial smoke or bazaar spewing noise and fragrances. And while the census was currently packing the streets of Jerusalem only eight miles away, you'd hardly know there *was* a census looking at Bethel. Fewer than ten people took note of him as he galloped into the village's small central square.

Balthazar brought the camel to a stop, which it was all too happy to do, and leapt to the ground. He pulled the half-empty saddlebags off its back, threw both of them over his left shoulder, and gave the camel a firm smack on its hindquarters. He couldn't have it standing around. God knows how many soldiers were about to come riding into the village with orders to find and kill him at all costs. If they saw the camel, they'd have a pretty good idea where to start looking.

'Go! Get outta here!'

It didn't budge. He smacked it again.

'GO!'

It groaned deeply, knelt forward on its spindly legs, then fell over on its side with a ground-shaking thud – all 1,200 pounds of it.

Dead.

Balthazar took a moment to consider this. In retrospect, maybe he *had* ridden it a bit too hard. And now that he got a better look, it wasn't nearly as young as he'd thought. Not even close to fifteen or twenty. In fact, it was one of the oldest camels he'd ever seen. Come to think of it . . . it *was* a miracle they'd made it this far.

Balthazar didn't know what to say. Partly because he was pressed for time, but mostly because sincerity wasn't his strong suit, he settled on, 'Sorry.'

Then, the grieving period over, he ran like hell.

He knew the villagers would keep him safe. They hated the Romans just as much as he did. *Okay, so these aren't actual Roman troops chasing me – they're Judeans. But really, when you get right down to it, is there a difference? They all take their orders from Rome, just like Herod the Great, that lying, festering, murderous puppet.* If there was one thing the Jews hated more than Augustus Caesar, it was the client king who ruled Judea for him. And while Balthazar wasn't a Jew per se, he was certainly no friend of Herod. That had to count for something, right? The enemy of my enemy?

He was the Antioch Ghost, and people loved a celebrity. Even a minor one.

No, the villagers would take pity on him. They would keep him safe and hidden when the army came kicking down their doors any minute now. And if pity wasn't enough, then bribing them with a share of his remaining treasure would make up the difference.

Balthazar ran across the square, his bags half full of twice-stolen gold and silver, frankincense and silk, his face still covered by the shemagh. He was headed for the largest building in sight – the only one with a second story and one of the few made from brick. The building had an arched roof and small, glass-paned windows along its eastern and western faces, an extravagance rarely seen outside of Rome. And though Balthazar couldn't see the source, a column of white smoke rose from behind the building. There wasn't much strategy behind his choosing it. A bigger building offered more hiding places. And more hiding places meant a greater chance of survival.

But as soon as he crossed the threshold, Balthazar knew he was a dead man.

He *had* to be dead . . . for this was surely heaven. There were wet, naked women everywhere. Beautiful. Bare. Steam rising off of their glistening bodies, the vapors glowing in the rays of sunlight that streamed through the glass above.

A bathhouse.

An arched ceiling peaked twenty feet overhead, its smooth surface painted to resemble olive trees reaching toward a cloudy sky. The bath itself, which took up most of the room, was lined with mosaic tiles. Mosaic tiles and the naked bodies of fifteen women. Women who were currently staring at the dusty man with a covered face and large bags over his shoulder. The man who had no business being in the women's bath.

This was no Flavia situation. There was no question in Balthazar's mind that *these* women were about to start screaming unless he acted quickly. Shaking himself back into focus, he brought a finger to his lips – *shhhh* – and in as nonthreatening a voice as he could manage, said, 'A thousand pardons . . .'

He pulled the shemagh down, revealing his face – a handsome mix of sunburn and stubble, a prominent scar on his right cheek in the shape of an *X.* He gave them a smile. Charming, reassuring. Even a bit dashing, he suspected. It was a smile he'd spent hours practicing in the reflective waters of the Orontes River, and it was, if he didn't mind saying so, one of his stronger assets.

'I,' he continued, 'am the Antioch Ghost.'

Was that the twinkle of recognition in some of their eyes?

'I'm just looking for a place to hide from Herod's men. Once they're gone, I'll be on my way without another word. You have nothing to fear, my sisters – I promise you.'

They didn't scream.

People love a celebrity.

Short of his remaining treasure, Balthazar would've given anything in the world to stay and soak in this sight a little longer, but he could hear the rumble of horses' hooves growing near outside. *Time to disappear.* Certain that he and the women had reached an understanding, he proceeded as rapidly and respectfully as possible across the room, toward a row of women's robes hanging on the opposite wall. Enough of them to hide a man and a pair of saddlebags behind, no problem.

It was perfect. The soldiers wouldn't dare intrude on the privacy of bathing women. Nor would the women likely run into the streets and tattle without their clothes. Balthazar could hear the muffled sounds of orders being shouted outside, the clanging of swords and armor as men fanned out. Seconds later, three Judean soldiers entered. Balthazar watched as the men had the same sequence of reactions he'd had: shock, followed immediately by embarrassment, followed immediately by excitement.

One of the soldiers regained his composure enough to speak: 'Pardon us . . .'

Go ahead, you dog. Go ahead and ask them if they've seen a man come through here. My sisters won't say a word. If anything, they'll tell you to go to hell.

'Have you seen—'

Balthazar's heart sank as every last woman pointed toward his hiding place in unison.

They didn't even let him finish the question . . .

So here it was. After a day in the desert, a dead camel, and a fortune in abandoned spoils, it would come to this.

Balthazar was an exceptional thief. An excellent aggravator and proven survivor. But what he excelled at, what he was truly gifted at, was taking human lives with his sword. This wasn't a point of pride. *Well, maybe just a little.* But in general, he measured success in treasure, not blood. 'Success,' he was fond of saying, 'is stealing a fortune without drawing your sword. Failure is a pile of bodies and no profit.'

The three soldiers drew their swords and started across the room, toward the row of hanging robes the women had pointed to.

None of them had more than a few seconds to live.

Peter could almost taste his victory. As a captain in Herod's army, there were few priorities higher than catching the Antioch Ghost. And now it seemed he was within moments of doing just that. Such an honor would mean a promotion, of course. Money. Land. Maybe even a slave to farm it for him. Best of all, it would mean a ticket out of Tel Arad and an end to dealing with that fat, corrupt Roman, Decimus Petronius Verres.

His men were kicking in every door, searching every house in the area. The Ghost couldn't have gone far. They'd reached the square less than a minute after he'd reached it, and he'd stupidly left a dead camel as a starting point for their search. The fact that he'd taken the time to kill it for no reason showed just how vile their fugitive really was.

Of course, some of his men doubted that their target really was the Antioch Ghost. But Peter knew. He'd been around long enough to recognize his methods. His choice of prey. Even before Flavia had described the man she'd seen robbing her father's compound – *tall and olive-skinned, with a strong build, dark hair to his shoulders, and an X-shaped scar across his right cheek* – he'd known. He also knew enough to suspect that she'd left out the part about inviting him into her bed, but that wasn't important. So when reports of a similar-looking man stealing a Bedouin's camel came in, Peter had gathered as many soldiers as he could and given chase across the Judean Desert – choking on dust and praying that the

Ghost didn't beat him to Jerusalem, where he would've disappeared in seconds.

Captain Peter had asked God for a miracle, and God had answered. Here he was in Bethel. The last place he'd expected to be when he'd woken up this morning. The place he would always remember as the home of his great victory . . . assuming God would help him just a little more. Once again, Peter appealed to the Lord . . .

Give me a sign, Heavenly Father. Help me bring this murderous thief to justice. Help me to protect the children of Israel and uphold your law, O God.

Of course, he left out the part about being rewarded with money and land and slaves, but that wasn't important. Once again, God delivered. For no sooner had Peter finished his prayer than a sound reached his ears. A beautiful sound that meant glory was at hand:

Muffled screams coming from the bathhouse.

The head landed in the water, its eyes still blinking as it sank to the bottom, and the women finally released their pent-up screams. They climbed over each other, trying to get out of the bath as a dark red cloud spread through it.

Balthazar had waited until the advancing soldiers were within arm's length before jumping out from behind the robes and swinging at the closest man. It'd been one of those lucky swings – one in a hundred, really – where the blade had hit the neck *just* right, between the vertebrae, and gone clean through. Before the first soldier's head had even splashed down, Balthazar had kicked the second in the chest, knocking him onto his back. Then, just as the first screams began to echo through the room, he'd run the third soldier through the belly and out the back. He'd held the soldier – who wasn't much more than a boy – up with his blade, watching his face drain from pink to ash white, then yanked it out, spilling his blood and entrails onto the tiled floor.

By this point, the second soldier had managed to get back to his feet. But it was only a brief stay. Balthazar swung again and cut his throat. The soldier dropped his sword and clutched at the wound – the blood pouring through his fingers in sheets. His face turned that same shade of white, wore that same mask of fear as he came to that same old, dreadful realization. The one Balthazar had seen so many other men come to: *This can't be happening. This can't be the day I die.* And then it was done. The soldier fell face-first into the bath, his blood mixing with the other's. Naturally, this only served to elicit more screams from the already-screaming women.

Those screams will bring more soldiers any second now. Time to go.

He stood for a moment, mourning the days and weeks he'd spent working to fill those saddlebags. Mourning the lost fruits of his labor. Then, another brief grieving period over, he ran like hell again.

Failure is a pile of bodies and no profit . . . and this is shaping up to be a dismal failure.

Balthazar ran out the rear of the building and into the small, dirt-lined courtyard, enclosed by a six-foot wall and a wooden gate that led into the street. It was empty, save for a massive brick furnace that abutted the bath-house. This furnace, Balthazar knew at once, was the source of the white smoke he'd seen earlier. A male slave stood beside its open iron door, stoking the raging fire inside. Its hot air channeled into a system of ducts under the bathhouse floor, keeping the water nice and warm for the nude elite. Even where Balthazar stood, ten feet away from the flames, the heat was almost too much to bear, and the noise of crackling wood and rushing air was almost deafening. As such, the slave had been oblivious to the screams coming from the bathhouse and the shouts of Judean soldiers swarming outside. But now, as he looked up from his work and found himself face-to-face with a blood-spattered, sword-wielding Syrian, he abandoned his post and ran for his life – out the open wooden gates and into the streets. Balthazar was about to do the same thing when a disembodied voice cried, 'Stop where you are!'

He turned and saw a lone, boyish Judean soldier standing in the bathhouse's rear doorway, his sword trembling in his hands.

'OVER HERE!' he shouted to his comrades. 'OVER HERE! I'VE FOUND HIM!'

Balthazar wasn't about to be held prisoner by a lone soldier with a trembling sword. And he certainly wasn't going to wait around for others to arrive. He started toward the wooden gate.

'Stop!'

The soldier lifted his sword and held it out in front of his body, exactly as he'd been trained to hold it.

He charged at Balthazar, exactly as he'd been trained to charge. But as he prepared to run his enemy through, just as he'd been trained to do, the soldier experienced something he was entirely unequipped and unprepared to handle: Balthazar rolled onto his back and used his legs to launch him into the air –

– and into the open furnace.

The soldier heard the clang of the iron door slam behind him. He heard the latch close. He tried to stand, but there wasn't enough room to do more than crouch. Instinct grabbed hold of him, and he tried to push the flames away with his hands, but they were already burning. He could see his flesh blistering and blackening, sliding off of his bones like wax down the side of a candle. He could feel his clothes burning against his body, becoming one with his skin, his hair melting against his scalp.

Balthazar could hear his screams through the iron door. He closed his eyes and turned away as the pounding of fists rattled it from the other side. When he opened them, there were ten soldiers standing in front of him.

'Drop your sword!' one of them yelled.

Faced with the idea of taking them all on, Balthazar placed the sword in his mouth – its blade still dripping with blood – turned back, and climbed the brick wall of the bathhouse. He could always fight his way across the rooftops, jumping from building to building until he found a horse, or a camel, or anything better than fighting ten men at once.

But when he pulled himself onto the arched roof and

got to his feet, he felt the hope run out of his body like blood from a severed head. There were nearly a hundred men in the square below, plus the corpse of his miraculous camel. The Cloud of Undetermined Wrath had become a crowd of *very* determined soldiers, and Balthazar had to face the fact that he was completely, hopelessly surrounded.

His options were thus: He could fight to the death and take as many of these emperor-worshipping bastards as possible with him. Result? One hundred percent chance of death. Or, he could surrender and be all but certainly executed. Result? Ninety-nine percent chance of death.

It was a no-brainer.

Balthazar's wrists had been bound firmly behind his back, his clothes meticulously searched for contraband. With a soldier holding his arms on either side, he was marched across the square to where Peter waited with a deeply satisfied smirk on his face. The victorious captain hesitated a moment, taking it all in. Relishing it. He was face-to-face with the end to all his troubles.

'The Antioch Ghost,' he said at last. 'Scourge of Rome.'

'You forgot "plunderer of the Eastern Empire,"' said Balthazar.

Here it comes . . .

Sure enough, Balthazar was rewarded with a jaw-rattling punch for daring to speak. But snide remarks were just about all he had left in his arsenal. For the first time he could remember, he couldn't see a way out. There was no hidden weapon to pull at the last second. No well-timed distraction on the way. His fate was completely out of his hands now. He'd risked everything on a 1 percent chance of survival.

'On your knees,' said Peter, drawing his sword.

Oh well . . . it was worth a try.

Balthazar didn't budge, so the soldiers helped him, pushing down on his shoulders and making him kneel in the dirt. He braced himself, wondering if he would feel his spine break or feel the blade tear through his neck and throat. He wondered if he would still be able to see as his head fell to the ground and rolled across the sand. *What a strange sight that would be . . . rolling along with no breath or body, fading to nothing as the blood ran out of me . . .*

Balthazar examined the faces of the Judean soldiers closest to him, felt the binds on his wrists with the tips of his fingers, smelled the desert air. He looked at the sand beneath his feet and the sky above his head, taking it all in. Relishing it. Here it was, the sum of his twenty-six years. He would die on his knees in Bethel – or 'Beit El.' Or whatever the hell they called it. His blood would run into the dirt. The soldiers would spit on his corpse, hack it to pieces, and leave it to the dogs. And that would be that.

Lesser men would've prayed at a moment like this. Would've begged God's forgiveness as they were confronted by his imminent judgment. Balthazar took comfort in the fact that even now, he felt no such compulsion. Even now, in the final seconds of his life, he stood firm. And while he couldn't help the fact that his heart was pounding harder than it ever had – *which will make the blood shoot higher from my headless neck and hopefully right into this captain's face* – he refused to give his executioners the satisfaction of seeing him squirm.

What's this?

Balthazar was suddenly confronted by a vision. A sea of stars dancing before him.

It had already happened.

Here he'd been, wondering about what it would be like when his head was cut off, and he'd missed the actual moment. The world narrowing, darkening into a single, distant point. Somewhere, far away – where the winds blew cool and the naked women bathed – he felt a sharp pain wash over him. And he could see something in that distant light, something moving. It was hard to make out, but yes, there was definitely something there. A man. A man leading an animal through the desert . . . a woman on its back . . .

So . . . this is what it's like to die. Funny . . . men spend so much effort, so much anxiety trying to avoid this moment. But really, when it's all said and done, dying isn't so bad. In fact, it's kind of . . .

The soldiers watched Balthazar slump forward, then fall to the ground, his blood running into the dirt. Peter examined the blunt handle of the sword he'd bludgeoned him with, making sure it hadn't been soiled by flecks of blood or tufts of hair, then returned it to its sheath. He'd given the Antioch Ghost a ferocious whack on the skull, and it'd done the trick.

Balthazar was out cold.

Decimus had ordered the thief executed on the spot, his head brought back to Tel Arad to be displayed as a warning. And as much as Peter would've enjoyed that – as much as he would've liked to behead this piece of filth for slaughtering his men and making him spend an entire day in the desert – he had orders to take the Antioch Ghost alive.

And those orders came from a power higher than a Roman governor.

Twin Palace of the Puppet King

'When Herod heard this, he was frightened; and calling together all the chief priests and scribes of the people, he inquired of them where the Messiah was to be born. They told him, "In Bethlehem of Judea; for so it has been written by the prophet."'

—*Matthew 2:3–5*

I

The spirit that had once called itself 'Balthazar' was swimming.

Swimming through an ocean without end, an ocean of space and time, where all that had ever been and all that ever would be converged into one. As Balthazar looked up at its infinite, shimmering surface, he could see the whole of creation reflected back, every detail of the universe – from the stars in the heavens to the smallest insects of the earth. He could see every moment of his past and future. But as he swam, his movement created ripples in these images, warping them into ever-changing suggestions of the truth: Here was the man again, leading an animal through the desert . . . the woman on its back. Here was the distant star in the heavens and the trees with a secret. Here was the face from his past . . .

And the faster Balthazar swam, the farther into the future he went. The stronger the ripples became, the harder those reflections were to see: Here was an army of strange soldiers and a wooden beam, splitting in two. Here was a great city in flames and his brother,

Abdi, as a grown man. At least that's what it looked like.

Balthazar was suddenly aware that he was no longer swimming. He was flying – floating above the earth, as if carried by a pair of outstretched wings. The shimmering surface he'd been looking up at was now miles below him, and the whole Judean Desert – no, *all of Judea* – stretched out as far as his eyes could see. Deep ravines were suddenly nothing more than jagged little lines in the sand. Soaring mountains were suddenly scaled with the tip of a finger. He could see flocks of birds beneath him, flying in formation above the waters of the Jordan River. He could see the tops of clouds and the shadows they cast on the desert floor.

Balthazar had never felt such peace. Such freedom.

I'm descending . . .

The tops of the clouds were growing closer. Almost close enough to skim with his outstretched feet. Closer . . . until the birds were above him, and Balthazar was immersed in the dense fog of the clouds themselves. And when he broke through the bottom, the desert was much closer than it had been. Close enough to make out the scattered bits of green that had managed to push their way through the rocks . . . and close enough to see the tiny procession of Judean soldiers and cavalry below.

No . . .

The victorious captain and his hundred men, trekking from Bethel to Jerusalem with their unconscious prisoner in tow.

No, not there!

Balthazar could feel himself being pulled out of this

56

glorious world, could feel the memory of his former self come flooding back. And he could see the prisoner beginning to come around . . .

No . . . no, I don't want to trade places with him! I want to stay up here! I want to st—

Balthazar woke up retching. He felt the muscles of his stomach contracting against his will and its contents climbing up his throat. Instinct told him to cup his hands, but his hands told him they were still tied behind his back. He thought about fighting the urge – thought about bearing down and commanding his muscles to obey. But it was too late. His body had taken the reins. He was just a passenger now. And so the paltry contents of his stomach were ejected over his chin, down his front, and onto the tail of the horse below. The horse he was riding *backward*.

This was immediately followed by a chorus of cackling and harassment on all sides. And though Balthazar couldn't see the men who were laughing and hurling insults at him, as his eyes were still only half open and flooded with the involuntary tears of his involuntary purge, he had a pretty good idea who they were. Just like he had a pretty good idea *where* he was, and how he'd gotten here.

He'd been knocked out with a blow to the head. That much was obvious, thanks to the blurred vision and the skull that throbbed in a way he'd never thought skulls could throb – the pain broadcasting all the way to the tips of his fingers. And while he wasn't able to check at the moment, on account of his hands being tied, Balthazar also suspected that the hair he felt clinging to his scalp was glued there with dried blood. He was dizzy and nauseated from the force of the blow and from dehydration – judging by his maddening thirst and cracked lips. His neck was too stiff to turn more than a few degrees in either direction.

No, they'd cracked him on the skull, no doubt about it. And while he'd been off swimming through the infinite, Balthazar's unconscious body had been lifted onto a soldier's horse, their waists tied together so he wouldn't slip off. Why they'd put him on backward was a bit of a mystery. He could only assume it was some kind of insult. Something the Judean cavalry had dreamt up for its prisoners maybe. But whether it was tradition or an insult improvised at the last minute, it was effective. Besides being generally disorienting, it gave the soldiers behind him a clear shot at his face, which they used to mock him with words and gestures.

Also, having one's nose directly above a horse's ass wasn't pleasant either.

But obscene gestures and the persistent smell of manure aside, Balthazar was alive. For the moment, anyway. He was almost certain they were headed toward Herod's Palace in Jerusalem, where he'd be presented like the prize that he was and then killed in any number of terrible ways before the day was out.

If he could only turn around, Balthazar was sure he'd find Captain Peter riding at the front of the pack, grinning ear to ear, silently rehearsing his grand presentation to his king and counting the reward money in his head. Herod would do a little gloating, and then order Balthazar executed on the spot – that was, assuming the festering wound on his scalp didn't kill him first.

As the sun baked the last drops of moisture out of his body, Balthazar replayed the day's events in his aching head – a forensic accounting of every action and reaction. A study of what had gone wrong. Had it been the attempt to calm the bathing women instead of running away and finding another place to hide? Should he have taken on the ten soldiers behind the bathhouse instead of climbing up the side of the building? Stolen a horse instead of a camel? Should he have given Flavia that knock on the head when he'd had the chance?

I never should've gone to Damascus.

That had been the real error in judgment, hadn't it. That was the decision that had ultimately led his nose to a horse's ass. If he'd never gone to Damascus, he never would've heard about Tel Arad and its corrupt governor. But he *had* gone, chasing down his one weakness. That one elusive piece of treasure . . . the same piece he'd been chasing for years.

The pendant . . .

Balthazar had followed rumors of its existence all over the empire, and those rumors had always – *always* – proved to be a waste of time. He should've known Damascus would be the same. He should've stayed put in Crete, which had been good to him in so many ways. But whenever that old rumor found him, no matter how

59

unsubstantiated or far away it was, Balthazar dropped everything and chased after his little flittering gold purpose in life.

That was the real tragedy here. Not that Balthazar would die. But that he'd die before he found it. Before he finished what he'd set out to do. What he'd *sworn* to do.

II

The eastern approach to Jerusalem was the real jaw-dropper. The one that led you over the Mount of Olives and into the Kidron Valley, the whole city revealing itself at once, rising from the desert, with the Great Temple in the foreground. But even here, from the north, Jerusalem struck an impressive sight.

Herod the Great may have been famous for his excessive cruelty and lavish lifestyle. He may have been decried for being a puppet of Rome and hated for his heavy taxation. But even his fiercest enemies had to admit – the man was one hell of a builder.

As a young king, Herod had learned that there was no scandal, no discontent that a few shiny new buildings couldn't hush away. And over his thirty-year reign, he'd used this philosophy to transform much of Judea – building temples and coliseums, improving roads, and building aqueducts to carry fresh water to his subjects. But while Judea was his kingdom, Jerusalem was his showroom. The place he'd transformed from the little city of Solomon into one of the Marvels of the East.

Since he'd taken power, there'd seldom been a time when the city had fewer than three massive building projects under way. Many wouldn't even be completed in his lifetime. It didn't matter. Placating his Jewish subjects wasn't Herod's only priority. It wasn't even his top priority. What Herod really wanted was Rome's attention. He wanted to create a city so grand, so indispensable, that even the mighty Augustus would be proud to call it home. A city worthy of being called 'the Rome of the East.' And he wanted his sons, his grandsons, and *their* grandsons to rule over it for all time, each generation praising the name of the visionary king who'd started it all.

And who was to say? In time, maybe his descendants would build a whole empire of their own. Maybe the children of Augustus would find themselves kneeling before the children of Herod, instead of the other way around.

Jerusalem was home to some 150,000 people. Still little more than a suburb when compared to Rome's million-plus inhabitants, but it was on its way to becoming one of the grandest cities in the empire – right up there with Alexandria and Antioch. And with the census in full swing, its population had swelled to nearly twice its usual size.

The hordes barely noticed as Balthazar was paraded through the packed streets – streets that had changed so drastically, even in his lifetime. Where Balthazar remembered nothing but dirt, Herod's amphitheater now rose more than a hundred feet off the ground, its stage home to the newest works from Rome and Greece. There was the Antonia Fortress, which Herod had named in honor of his friend and patron Marc Antony; the monument to King David, who'd ruled from this very city a thousand years before Herod's birth; and, of course, there was Herod's Temple – the city's biggest, most stunning feature.

A city unto itself, the temple took up nearly half of Jerusalem's eastern border. The outer walls measured 1,600 feet by 950 feet and rose 100 feet above the ground. Those walls supported a collection of inner courtyards and buildings, all of which surrounded the gleaming, white marble temple in the center. The biggest of these was the Court of the Gentiles, with its money changers and barbers; its priests scurrying about in their white robes; and merchants selling sacrificial animals, food, and souvenirs to the throngs of pilgrims.

At the center of it all was the temple itself – a white marble tower, from which the smoke of burning sheep and doves never ceased to rise. Unlike the noise and activity of the complex around it, the temple and its walled-in courtyards were strictly for worship and sacrifice, and strictly for the faithful. Non-Jews were expressly forbidden, on punishment of death, from setting foot inside. Even Herod would've risked a riot if he'd insisted on entering. For though he'd officially converted to Judaism when he took power, he was still considered an Arab by most of the local population.

The temple was the grandest flourish of Herod's grand flourishes. But while he publicly boasted of the house he'd built to honor God, he was privately fondest of the house he'd built to honor *himself*: his palace in the Upper City.

Herod had palaces throughout Judea. In Caesarea near the Mediterranean coast and in Tiberias on the Sea of Galilee. In Masada and Jericho. Each one beautiful and grand. But even though some of these palaces were bigger than his home in Jerusalem, none of them approached its magnificence. Like the Great Temple, it was built on a raised platform, a rectangle measuring nearly 1,000 feet long and 200 feet wide, and surrounded by high walls and guard towers. Officially, it was built as a fortress to protect the Upper City, on Jerusalem's west side, from invading forces. In reality, it was an offering from a mighty king unto himself. The towers were spaced evenly along the four walls. Each had a name. One for the king's brother, one for a friend, and one for his beloved second wife, Mariamne.

Mariamne . . . oh, what a beauty she'd been. Oh, how Herod had loved her. And oh, what a shame that he'd been forced to have her executed. *And* the man he'd suspected her of having an affair with. *And* her brother. *And* the two sons she'd borne him, lest they grow up to resent their father for having their mother executed. Mind you, it hadn't given Herod pleasure to do this. Ordering one's own children put to death was one of the more unsavory of a king's duties. But, as Herod was fond of telling his remaining sons, 'Emotion is emotion, and politics is politics, and one has nothing to do with the other.'

Now all that remained of Herod's favorite wife was a guard tower bearing her name above the north gate. The gate through which Balthazar was unceremoniously led into Herod's Palace for the first and last time in his life. Backward. Covered in his own blood and vomit.

Thirty-three years later, another man would be paraded through the same gate to face another Herod – also covered in his own blood, and also on the way to his death.

Once Captain Peter and his men were inside the palace walls, Balthazar was finally untethered from his chaperone and lowered to the ground, still slightly dizzy and *very* thirsty. It took a moment to steady himself, especially since his hands were still tied behind his back.

After gaining his balance, Balthazar turned away from the north gate . . . and found himself transported to another world. A world almost as surreal and infinite as the one he'd flown through in his dreams. It was a world of lush green and cool marble. A world of polished bronze fountains and meticulously groomed dogs. It was, simply, paradise on earth. *The Garden of Eden, rediscovered at last.*

Inside the rectangular outer walls, the interior grounds were divided down the middle into two smaller, perfectly symmetrical rectangles – each half mirroring the other down to the smallest detail. And while outsiders probably imagined Herod's Palace as a single structure behind those walls, just as Balthazar had, there were actually *two* identical, sprawling palaces inside – both facing each other across a vast rectangular courtyard.

Running down both sides of the courtyard, covered walkways and rows of neatly planted trees offered shade in the hottest months. And when those weren't enough, a pair of circular pools – each fed by identical bronze fountains – stood ready to provide relief from the heat.

Balthazar knew at once why Herod had built two identical palaces. One of them undoubtedly contained his throne room, where he held court, threw official banquets, and greeted foreign dignitaries. *And where he dreams up new atrocities to commit against his people and lives in fear of a man 1,000 miles away.* This palace was distinguished by the courtiers, military officers, and wise men – a title that covered a broad range of functions, from advisor to physician, but that usually referred to priests – milling about in front of it.

Across the courtyard, some 300 feet away, the other palace served as Herod's private residence, with apartments for his wives, his sons and *their* wives, heated baths, and a personal harem of some forty women – all of whom he'd 'recruited' from the local population and not one of whom was older than sixteen. This palace was distinguished by the hordes of children playing and young women sunning themselves in front. Two palaces. *One business and one pleasure.*

You had to give the man credit. He was one hell of a builder.

Predictably, Balthazar was led toward the business

palace by his soldier escorts. But business aside, there was scarcely a doubt in his mind that Herod was going to take plenty of pleasure in killing him.

III

Balthazar had assumed he would be led straight into the throne room. Paraded before Herod for a minute or two, mocked, perhaps tortured, depending on the king's mood, and executed for the amusement of all. Quick and easy.

But the king was a busy man, and even a prisoner of Balthazar's stature had to wait for an appointment. Here he was in an antechamber, almost an hour after arriving at the palace, sitting on a stone bench just outside the closed doors of the throne room. Judean soldiers sat on either side of him, their captain pacing nervously nearby, silently rehearsing his presentational speech. *And designing the new house you're going to build with all that money, you self-righteous—*

'This again!' someone screamed.

The gravelly, muffled voice had come from the other side of the throne room doors.

Herod.

It had to be. Who else would scream like that in a throne room?

It was funny – the two of them shared so much history, caused each other so much grief. Yet they'd never seen each other in person. Balthazar had no idea what his nemesis looked like. Sure, there was the familiar profile stamped on all those coins – and the mosaics and the carvings and the statues. But in Balthazar's experience, those likenesses tended to be a bit flattering when compared to the real things.

Even through the closed doors, Balthazar and the Judean soldiers – who did their best not to look like they were listening – could make out every word:

'Thirty years!' the gravelly voice continued. 'For thirty years I've built this city into what it is! I've shepherded Judea into a new age! But no matter what I do – no matter how many glorious monuments I build to honor their God – I'm still forced to listen to *this*! This nonsense! This treason!'

'And when the Great Temple has been rebuilt,' said a calmer voice, quoting the prophecies, 'when the city of David has been overrun and the ruins of Judea born anew, the Messiah shall appear – born of a virgin in the town of Bethlehem.'

'Yes . . . I've heard it all before.'

'And with him the dead shall rise, and the plagues of old retur—'

'You're wasting your breath.'

'The plagues of old return to smite the nonbelievers. The kings of the earth shall be rendered powerless, and a voice shall be heard, the voice of mothers weeping for their children, because they are no more.'

'I said ENOUGH!'

A short silence followed the outburst. Then, in a more conversational tone, the gravelly voice continued. 'If I heeded the warnings of every screaming prophet in this city, I would drive myself mad in an hour's time. I will not cower before old superstitions.'

'All the same, Your Highness, never have there been so many signs from so many prophecies: the temple rebuilt, the cities of Judea born anew, the crowds in Jerusalem for the census. All that remains to be seen is a light in the east.'

'And what would you have me do? Would you have me go and tell Augustus that he should fear a child who may or may not exist? That Rome should recall its mighty armies from Gaul and Germania and lay siege to the town of Bethlehem? Do you have any idea what a fool he would think me?'

'The prophecy is clear, Your Highness. The Messiah shall topple *all* the kingdoms of the world. Even yours.'

There was a loud crash. The sound of something being knocked (or more likely *kicked*) over. Something metal. From the sound of the impact and the resulting smaller clangs, Balthazar guessed it was a table, from which several chalices and serving platters had fallen.

A considerably longer silence followed. Balthazar caught a few of the Judean soldiers trading nervous glances.

When Herod finally spoke again, it was to issue an order: 'There will be no more talk of Messiahs.'

IV

A cry went up through the town of Bethlehem, reverberating through the torch-lit houses in the village and the caves that had been carved into the hills above it many thousands of years earlier. It was brief and sharp, and it came from a small stable on the north side of the little town. A stable that was unremarkable in every way – except for the star that shone directly over it in the high heavens, brighter than any in the eastern sky. A star that hadn't been there an hour before.

Joseph and Mary felt like every innkeeper in the Upper City had turned them away. Every house had been full to bursting, every room taken, every patch of bare earth spoken for. With Mary's contractions growing more frequent and Joseph's fuse growing shorter, they'd given up on Jerusalem and taken the road south to Bethlehem – where, rumor had it, there were still a few spaces for smaller families.

But Bethlehem had proven every bit as full, and they'd been turned away from the first two places they inquired. With the sky growing dark, Mary no longer able to ride or walk, and Joseph ready to throw up his hands and curse every man in Judea, an old shepherd and his sons had taken pity on them. And though the shepherd's home – like all the homes in the area – was packed with boarders and relatives for the census, he'd offered them the cramped stables behind it. After laying out some fresh straw and water and hanging a small oil lamp, he'd left them alone. The birth of a child was a sacred, private affair. No place for men or strangers.

And there they were. Surrounded by the stench of animals. The glow of a single flame. *A fitting place for the birth of a king*, thought Joseph.

If they'd been in Nazareth, Mary would have been attended by the women of the village. She would've been comforted by familiar faces and voices and surrounded by those with years of childbearing experience. But here she was utterly alone. A fifteen-year-old girl, lying on hard straw and the few blankets they'd carried across the desert, sweating and pushing her way through the worst pain she'd ever known.

There had been times – *many* times – throughout the night when Mary had been convinced something was wrong. It's not supposed to be this hard, this painful. *It's not supposed to take this long. I must be doing something wrong.* And there had been times – *many* times – throughout the night when Joseph had been close to rushing in. But he couldn't. It was forbidden. He couldn't lay eyes on her in such an indecent state. He couldn't touch her when she was unclean. And so he'd done the only thing he could – he'd shouted words of encouragement to her through the stable walls, and prayed.

The infant had cried at first, an announcement of health. A cry that had echoed across Bethlehem. *A voice that shall be heard the world over*, Mary thought as she held the baby to her chest. And then it had been silent. Calm. It had looked into Mary's eyes for a moment. Not the all-knowing look of an all-knowing God, but merely the quizzical look of an exhausted infant. Then it had slept.

Mary and Joseph lay beside each other, watching the baby sleep as the sun peeked through the slats in the stable walls, and the animals around them began to stir.

It was tradition that a male child's name not be spoken aloud until its eighth day. The day of its circumcision. But there was no need to speak.

The angel had told both of them what to name the child.

V

The doors to Herod's throne room were finally opened, and Balthazar was ushered in to meet his punishment, with Captain Peter proudly leading the way.

The throne room was every bit as symmetrical and rectangular as the rest of the palace grounds, with the doors on one end and the throne on the other, so as to make guests walk the maximum distance for added dramatic effect. But unlike the lush paradise he'd seen outside, Balthazar found the interior cold and drab by comparison. Stone columns lined both sides of the narrow passage. Daylight filtered in through the windows behind those columns and from the large, square opening in the center of the ceiling, some forty feet above. At night, the torches and lamps mounted along the length of the room would provide ample light and heat, although Balthazar guessed that Herod didn't spend much time in here after dark. *Why would he, with a whole pleasure palace waiting across the courtyard?*

As they neared the throne, Balthazar saw slaves hurriedly cleaning an overturned table to its right and the chalices and platters that had been knocked off of it. And as he silently congratulated himself for correctly guessing that it had, in fact, been a table overturned, his eyes turned back to the throne itself, and the figure slumped in it.

Balthazar had seen a lot of gruesome things in his twenty-six years. But *nothing* he'd seen had prepared him for his first glimpse of Herod the Great.

There had been whispers that the king had been sick for years. He didn't venture out among the people anymore. He no longer came to supervise and bask in the glory of his construction projects. Even the lavish private box at his beloved theater had been empty for years. Some speculated that he was dead. That his sons were secretly sharing power and using their father's feared name to their advantage. But Herod was alive . . . if you could call it that.

He was hunched forward, his spine twisted. His eyes were yellowed, his teeth blackened, his pale flesh covered with open sores. His sunken eyes and cheeks barely looked strong enough to support the weight of his wispy, graying beard, and his robes hung off of him like sheets from a clothesline.

This was the mighty Herod? This shriveled little man? This wisp? This was the King of Judea? He looked less like the man who had rebuilt Jerusalem and more like one of the lepers begging blindly on its streets. In contrast, his throne was grand, its white marble seat embellished with gold accents. But while it had been designed to inspire awe, it only served to make the tiny man sitting in it look that much smaller.

Peter stepped forward, his captain's helmet under one arm. He snapped his heels together and – just like he'd rehearsed on the way from Bethel – addressed his king. 'Mighty Herod! It is my honor to present to you the Ant—'

'Yes, yes,' said Herod with a wave of his hand. 'Leave us.'

Balthazar saw Peter's face sink at the realization that he was being brushed aside. He could see the visions of promotions and slaves and reward money burning away before the captain's eyes. It almost made his current predicament worth it.

As Peter sulked away, Herod considered Balthazar from his throne. Studied him with those yellow eyes.

In Balthazar's experience, men of power were either cats or dogs. Dogs were simple. Direct. If you wronged a dog, it barked, sank its teeth into you, and shook you until you were dead. But cats . . . cats were devious. Cats liked to toy with their prey before eating it.

'The Antioch Ghost,' Herod shouted, opening his arms wide and walking down the steps from his throne. 'You do me a great honor by gracing my humble palace.'

Cat.

Herod continued down the steps until he was close enough to put a hand on Balthazar's shoulder. So close that Balthazar could smell the decay coming off of him. The rot of fungus and boils. The smell of death. Balthazar suddenly had a vision of Herod traipsing through his harem at night, pressing his naked, diseased flesh against that of his concubines. Forcing his decaying self on girls a quarter his age. He nearly retched again.

'Here we are at last. The two most famous men in all of Judea.'

Balthazar looked straight ahead. Not at Herod, not past him, but through him. Just as he'd refused to give the Judean troops the satisfaction of seeing him squirm, he wasn't about to give their king the satisfaction of an answer – even if he was a little flattered at having his fame compared to Herod's.

'Although, how famous can a man be if he doesn't even have a name?' Herod stepped back and admired his prize for a moment. 'Please,' he said. 'I must know. I must know the true name of the man who's taken up so much of my time these many years. Whose name I have – I admit – often cursed from this very chamber.'

Not a word from Balthazar. Not so much as a quiver of his cracked lips.

'Yes,' said Herod after a few silent moments. 'Well . . . I suppose a man has to take something to his grave.'

Herod backed away and began to pace, much to the relief of Balthazar's nostrils.

'You know,' he continued, 'some of my advisors say that I should have you put to death immediately. Right now, in this very room. They tell me that a public execution is too risky. That you have too many admirers among the people.'

Balthazar couldn't help but feel a little rush of pride. *People love a celebrity.*

'But I told them no! "You overestimate the public!" I

said. For the one thing the people love more than an outlaw is seeing him punished!'

Sadly, Balthazar suspected he was right. But he said nothing. 'Tomorrow, I'm going to give you the execution you deserve. The horrid, excruciating death you've been begging me to give you for years. And despite what my advisors think, I can tell you with absolute certainty that your suffering will please the people of Judea almost as much as it will please me.'

No . . . t's too perfect. I have to say it.

'You mean it'll please your Roman masters.'

A hush blanketed the room. Balthazar saw Herod's priests trading nervous looks.

Here it comes . . . here comes the punch in my insolent face. Though I doubt this one will have as much behind it as the captain's did.

But Herod simply broke into laugher. His rotting teeth exposed. His foul breath attacking Balthazar's senses once again.

'You see?' said Herod. 'That's exactly what I hoped you'd say. That's a response worthy of the Antioch Ghost.'

And before the conversation had even really begun, it was over. Herod turned away and slowly, frailly climbed the steps to his throne. His advisors stepped forward with the next items of business, and Balthazar was ushered out the same way he came.

The king was a busy man.

VI

B althazar had to admit, Herod's dungeons were among the nicest he'd seen. The sand-colored walls and floors were smooth and dry, and at ten feet by ten feet, the cells were on the larger side. But the real attention-getting amenities were the small, iron-barred windows on the east-facing walls of each cell. *Windows . . . in a dungeon. What a world this is.*

He was led down a corridor by no less than six torch-wielding palace guards and pushed into a cell at the far end, where he was slightly disappointed to see two other prisoners sitting on the floor against the opposite wall. He'd assumed that a guest of his stature would be afforded private quarters. One was an African, lean and muscular, with a per-manent scowl and a bald head. The other looked Greek, though it was hard to tell through his thick brown beard. Whatever his nationality, he was round and short. From the looks of them, they'd been through ordeals of their own.

'The Mighty Herod will hear your last request,' said the chief guard.

Balthazar thought about it for a moment. In truth, there was nothing on earth he wanted more than food – any food – and water. But a plan was a plan.

'I'd like a priest,' he said. The guard made no effort to hide his surprise, and the other prisoners exchanged bewildered looks behind him. 'I'd like a priest to come and offer me comfort before they take us. One for me' – Balthazar turned and examined his cellmates – 'and one for each of them.'

'Save your priests the trouble,' said the African, in an accent Balthazar was almost positive was Ethiopian. 'My friend and I are comfortable enough.'

'Please . . . I insist,' said Balthazar. Then, turning back to the guards, 'Three priests. One to comfort each of us.'

The chief guard considered this request for a moment. 'Suit yourself,' he said, and removed the binds from Balthazar's wrists, which felt *almost* as good as a drink of water would have. And with that, the guards were gone, taking the light of their torches with them. The door was shut and locked, and Balthazar was suddenly alone in the dark with a pair of strangers. Nothing but a few feet of cell and a few slivers of moonlight between them. He swung his arms in circles, trying to loosen his aching shoulders, trying to get the blood back in his wrists.

'Congratulations,' said the African. 'You are, perhaps, the dumbest man I have ever met.'

'You're probably right. But it'll save time if you call me Balthazar.'

'Gaspar,' he said. 'And this is my partner, Melchyor of Samos – the finest swordsman in the empire.'

Balthazar had listened to his share of dungeon boasts. Criminals were a bragging breed, especially around other criminals. But that was among the more ridiculous he'd heard. Gaspar's round little companion didn't look like he could *lift* a sword, let alone kill something with it. But as he was too weak for the usual verbal jousting that went on in these cells, Balthazar chose to ignore it.

'And you?' he asked Gaspar. 'I suppose you have some extraordinary talent, too?'

'My only talent is being smart enough to partner with the best swordsman in the empire.'

'He must not be *that* good,' said Balthazar, 'if the two of you ended up in here.'

'We were captured trying to steal a golden censer from the Soreg,' said Gaspar. 'Turns out I don't make a very convincing Jew.'

'We're to be put to death in the morning,' said Melchyor, in a way that suggested he didn't fully understand the implications of what that meant.

'What a coincidence. I'm to be put to death in the morning, too.'

'And you?' said Gaspar. 'What did you do to end up as a guest of Herod the Great?'

Here we go.

'If I tell you,' said Balthazar, slumping against the opposite wall, 'you'll think I'm a liar.'

'I already think you're a fool. Any man who turns down food and water in favor of a priest is a fool.'

What difference does it make? I'm a dead man. Let these two spend their last night on earth thinking I'm a liar.

'I'm the Antioch Ghost.'

This was followed by a considerable silence, as it always was.

'Nice to meet you,' said Gaspar. 'I'm Augustus Caesar.'

Melchyor guffawed.

'Believe me or don't believe me,' said Balthazar. 'It doesn't change the fact that we'll all be dying together in the morning.'

'If you're the Antioch Ghost,' said Gaspar, 'how was it you were captured? I thought he had the strength of ten men.'

'I heard he was eight feet tall,' said Melchyor.

'Eight feet tall,' said Gaspar, 'and faster than a horse. And yet here you are with us, a man who needs the comfort of a priest in his final hours.'

'Look, if you don't mind, I'd like to just . . . think for a while.'

'By all means. You're going to need your strength to knock down the dungeon walls and free us.'

As Melchyor guffawed again, Balthazar stared through the iron bars on the eastern wall and at the unusually bright star that hung in the sky. A plan was a plan.

Even when it was a stupid plan with virtually *no chance* of succeeding

3

THE UNSPEAKABLE
IDEA

'People do not despise a thief if he steals to
satisfy his hunger when he is starving.'

—*Proverbs 6:30*

I

There were plenty of ways to pick a pocket.

There was the Bump, wherein your accomplice 'accidentally' collided with your target on a crowded street. And while he apologized profusely, you made the lift. The Beggar, wherein your accomplice – or even better, *accomplices* – mobbed the target with requests for money in the front, while you took his coin purse from behind. The Fight, wherein two or more accomplices pretended to brawl in the street, and you picked the pockets of the men who stopped to watch. The False Arm, the Switch, the Victim, the Prophet. But no matter the method, the steps were always the same: distract, act, and disappear.

The first part was easy. A few pigeons taking flight, a faraway yell, a beautiful woman passing by – any one of them could distract a man long enough to part with his money. And disappearing was easy, too, since most victims didn't know they'd been victimized until minutes – even *hours* – later. But the *lift*. The lift was the thing. *That* was the element that required skill and practice.

That was the art, and Balthazar was an artist. There were plenty of ways to pick a pocket, sure. But no one in Antioch could pick them quite as well as he could.

And he was only twelve years old.

Already a man by any standard of the day, and already a seasoned criminal – the best pickpocket in the Eastern Empire, by his own reckoning. He'd helped make his first lift at the age of four, acting as an accomplice for the older boys. By six, he could pick the pockets of easier targets – namely drunks and the elderly – by himself. By eight, he had accomplices of his own, most of them older than he was.

Over the next four years, Balthazar had honed his craft. Developed his own methods for setting up lifts and tricking targets into revealing the location of their coin purses. One of his favorites was also the easiest:

'Be careful, sir,' he would warn an intended victim. 'There are pickpockets all over this forum.'

And lo and behold, nine times out of ten, the target would instinctively reach for his money to make sure it was still there. Later, Balthazar learned that he could simply put up a sign that said *Beware of Pickpockets* in any public place and get the same result.

An aspiring pickpocket couldn't have asked for a better place to hone his craft. Antioch was a mere 300 years old, still in its infancy compared to the other great cities of the world. But in that relatively short time, it had experienced explosive growth and become what many called 'the Jewel of the East.' A city to rival the greatness of Alexandria, with some 300,000 free men and 200,000 slaves.

The vast majority of the population was Greek, but it was also a melting pot of Macedonians, Jews, Chinese, Indians, native Syrians, and Romans – who, as usual, were the all-powerful minority. With the Romans had come all the attendant innovations: an amphitheater; an aqueduct to deliver abundant fresh water; and a circus for horse races, one of the largest in the empire, with seating for up to 80,000.

But of all the Roman upgrades, the feature that really defined Antioch was its Colonnaded Street. Its scale was almost unimaginable: a cobblestone road, thirty feet wide and four miles long, with covered walkways (or 'colonnades') running on both sides for the entire length It cut a straight line, north to south, through the center of Antioch, parallel to the Orontes River, which ran along the city's western border. Beneath these covered walkways, merchants sold food and wares of every variety, some from permanent shops, others from movable stalls. At night, the entire four-mile stretch was illuminated by torches, and the crowds would continue shopping, eating, and socializing into the early hours of the morning. The north and south halves of the Colonnaded Street met in a huge, round marketplace, which would, centuries later, be rebuilt into a forum by the Eastern Emperor Valens.

Though he had four miles of busy colonnades to choose from, Balthazar liked to work the forum. It was the heart of Antioch. A place where meetings could be arranged, where merchants could be heard haggling, political debates could be heard raging, and caravans of camels could be seen arriving with exotic goods from the East at all hours. The forum also happened to offer the most pockets to pick and the greatest number of escape routes. But the privilege didn't come cheap. There were kickbacks to be paid. Tips to be rewarded. Accomplices to be cut in. As with any business, it took money to make money. And as in real estate, prime locations came at a premium.

Balthazar liked to hang out on the perimeter of the forum, near the money changers. He would spend hours watching the men line up in front of their tables, waiting for the right target. Patience was the all-important virtue of the pickpocket. Balthazar had seen too many of his colleagues undone by hastiness, too many boys his age walking around with stubs where their hands had been. You needed patience. You needed a plan.

Sometimes the money changers would give him a tip – in exchange for a hefty kickback, of course. But Balthazar hadn't needed a tip today. He'd spotted the target himself: a tall Greek businessman who looked to be in his forties, with hair to the middle of his back and a chinstrap for a beard.

A good target was a combination of three things: distracted, alone, and carrying a lot of money. Today's scored two out of three. He was carrying quite a bit of money, and he was certainly distracted – his eyes darting around, his sandals tapping impatiently as he yelled at the money changer to hurry up. He was a man who clearly needed to be somewhere, and that was always a plus. The problem was, he wasn't alone. There was another Greek with him. Slightly younger, and slightly less distracted.

Pairs were bad. Mathematically, they doubled your chances of getting caught. But there were ways to make them work in your favor. Balthazar gave a signal to his two accomplices – a pair of younger boys waiting on the other side of the money changers. When he was sure they'd seen the target, he gave them another, using his right hand to mimic the carrying of a handle.

He'd decided on the Spill. It was his go-to move for pairs. Balthazar would follow closely behind the two Greeks as they made their way across the crowded forum, waiting for his accomplices to strike. If everything went as designed, the boys would emerge from nowhere, hurrying along with a jug of wine. They would clumsily run into the two Greeks, spilling its contents all over their robes. And as the men examined themselves – as they cursed and yelled and threatened to beat the boys for their clumsiness – Balthazar would make the lift: passing behind the target, slipping a small knife imperceptibly toward the Greek's coin purse, cutting the small leather strap that held it to his belt, and snatching it away without breaking his stride in the slightest. The target would never know what hit him, other than a jug of wine. When it worked, it was a thing of beauty.

When it didn't? You ran.

Balthazar went as fast as his spindly legs would carry him – which was, it seemed, only a fraction faster than the Greeks chasing him. It had been a bad lift from the start.

The Spill had been clumsily delivered, spilling onto their feet instead of their robes. Worse, the Greek's companion had clearly been a victim of pickpockets before. Once the initial shock of the spill had worn off, the younger Greek immediately checked his own coin purse and began looking around. Balthazar had made the lift despite the botched spill. Unfortunately, he'd gotten only a few feet away before he heard the dreaded, 'Hey! You!'

So here he was, pushing his twelve-year-old legs well beyond their intended use, with two much bigger Greeks chasing him – their feet stained red with wine, yelling, 'Stop that boy! He's a thief!'

If they caught him, it would mean the loss of both hands, at a mininum. More likely, he'd be put to death, either by stoning or by beheading. Pickpocketing had become an epidemic all along the Colonnaded Street and in the forum, and the Romans were cracking down. There was no place for rampant crime in a Roman city. Just as there seemed to be no place for its native Syrians.

He ran east along one of the canals that carried fresh water into the center of the city – part of the network of channels, tunnels, and pipes that made up the aqueducts built by the Romans. This particular canal was dry at the moment, littered with dirt and sticks and garbage. And that was *exactly* why Balthazar was following it.

The neighborhood – if I can make it to the neighborhood, I'll be safe . . . I'll be able to disappear.

There were dozens of small villages packed together on the outskirts of Antioch, so dense that they formed a sort of second wall around the already walled city. There were incredibly rich sections, marginally rich sections, middle-class sections, and poor sections. And then there were the Syrian slums. The slums toward which Balthazar now ran with death nipping at his heels.

'Syrian filth!' he heard one of the Greeks yell behind him. 'I'll tear your arms out of their sockets myself!'

Balthazar knew every inch of the four square blocks that made up the section called Platanôn – a maze of tiny, tightly packed houses and narrow, unpaved streets where most of the city's native Syrians lived. He knew every face on those streets, every name of every resident of every house. And he knew that he could rely on any one of them to keep him safely hidden from the Greeks. But first he had to get there – and that was going to take a minor miracle.

Actually, three minor miracles.

As Balthazar ran along the dry canal, the wide cobblestone streets and gleaming colonnades of the city dissolved away, becoming the narrower streets and houses of a poor suburb. Ahead, the houses abruptly stopped at the edge of a hundred-foot ravine, but the canal kept going, continuing across a narrow, unfinished bridge.

The old bridge had collapsed during a recent earthquake, one of the unpleasant realities of living in Syria. Roman engineers had shut off the water while they built a new one. One team had started on the near side of the ravine, another team on the far side. The plan was to have the two halves of the bridge meet in the middle, and they were almost there, only twenty feet to go. A wooden crane sat on the edge of both sides, each of their

91

outstretched arms supporting the ropes used to hoist stone blocks to the top – the ropes Balthazar hoped would carry him to freedom in a few seconds.

The first of Balthazar's three minor miracles occurred: the bridge wasn't under construction today, though this barely qualified as a 'miracle,' given the notoriously relaxed pace of Roman construction. The second miracle occurred immediately after: the rope hanging from the crane on the near side was within his reach. Now all he needed was a third miracle: to grab on to the hanging rope and swing safely across.

When he neared the edge of the ravine, Balthazar diverted off the road, down into the canal, and out onto the unfinished bridge, the men nearly close enough to touch the back of his clothes.

You can make it.

He ran with every bit of speed he could squeeze out of those spindly legs as he closed in on the edge of the bridge and the hanging rope. *You can make it, Balthazar.* And with a last leap, he grabbed on to the rope and swung off the end. *You can make it. Just don't look down and you'll —*

There was no way he was going to make it. As soon as Balthazar swung out over the ravine, he knew he was in trouble. The distance between the two sides was *twice* what it'd looked like from the bridge, and the drop twice as far. Worse yet, the top of the crane he was swinging from wasn't centered between the two bridge sections – it was *much* closer to the side he'd started on. As he approached the bottom of his arc, Balthazar suddenly found himself with two unsavory options: He could either hold on to the rope and return to the side he'd swung from – the side where two big men were waiting for him – or he could let go and jump. Either way, there would be no more miracles today.

He let go.

Once again, it was a decision met with instant regret. He wasn't going to make it across. Not on his feet, anyway. There was a chance – a *sliver* of a chance – that he could reach the edge of the other bridge with his fingertips. Balthazar pumped his exhausted legs as he flew, as if running on air would propel him farther.

I'm descending.

He reached his arms out in front of him as the uneven, unfinished stones of the other bridge rushed at him. But it was his *chest* that hit first, smacking against the bottom of the other canal and knocking the air from his lungs.

The impact startled a rat that had been picking through litter on the other side of the canal. It looked up, a half-chewed maggot in its mouth, and saw a human boy clinging to the edge of the waterway, struggling to pull himself up. It was a brief struggle, for the boy began sliding back toward the drop almost immediately. The rat watched as the boy's fingers grabbed at the bottom of the stone channel, trying to hold on. After a brief but valiant effort, the boy disappeared over the side. The rat, who assumed the human had fallen to his death, went back to its rummaging.

Balthazar had absolutely no idea how he'd caught himself. He hung by little more than the grit beneath his fingernails, pumping his feet. Trying to push against a surface that wasn't there. *Don't look down. It's very important that you resist the urge to*

He looked down. It was a hundred feet to the hard gravel road below, but it might as well have been a mile. He could see a pile of carved stone blocks beneath him, waiting for their turn to be hoisted up. He could feel himself falling, *smashing* against those blocks. Feel his brains squeezing through the cracks in his sku—

Look up, you idiot!

Balthazar brought his left hand up to the bridge and grabbed on. His skinny arms shook as he pulled, trying to claw his way back to the top, trying to ignore the searing pain he felt in his empty lungs. He swung his legs back and forth, using the force to help propel his body upward. And it did. With each swing, he was able to grab a little more of the canal above with his hands, until at last he managed to get his elbows over the lip and squirm up the rest of the way.

The third miracle . . .

He rested on his belly for a moment, his face against the stone, catching his breath, unaware of the rat that he'd frightened off. Balthazar got to his feet – chest heaving and fingers bleeding – remembering that his pursuers might be thinking about performing the same rope trick and following him across. But the Greeks were thinking no such thing. They just stood and stared at him from the other side of the unfinished bridge, dumbfounded by what they'd seen.

Balthazar wasn't sure *why* he did what he did next. Maybe it was the bewildered look on their faces; maybe it was a by-product of fear – but he flashed them a smile. The same confident smile that would infuriate many of his future pursuers, the way it infuriated the Greeks now as he turned and disappeared into the impenetrable fortress of the slums.

II

There were five of them altogether: Balthazar; his mother, Asherah; his younger sisters, Melita and Tanis, twins, both nine; and his baby brother, Abdi, two.

Balthazar was fond of his mother, and on some level – although he had yet to discover where it was – he loved his sisters. But Abdi was his shadow. His audience. His worshipper. The boy who wanted to play with him every waking moment, who laughed at every funny face he made, and who – despite being small for his age – was every bit as brave as his brother. When Balthazar left for the forum each morning, Abdi often ran after him, tugging at his leg and crying, 'Bal-faza! Bal-faza! You stay right here!'

On those rare occasions when Balthazar didn't work, they would spend the day together. Balthazar would carry his brother up and down the Colonnaded Street, stopping to watch musicians perform or petting the strange animals that came from beyond the Himalayas. Once in a while, he would even splurge on a handful of cinnamon dates to share between them, their secret. In the afternoon, Balthazar would take Abdi to the banks of the Orontes and to the shade of their favorite palm tree. The one with the deep gash down the side of its trunk. *The one that looks like a scar.* And there, in the shade of their scarred little tree, Balthazar would sit and watch the men fish as Abdi napped in his arms, running his fingers through his brother's brown hair. Sometimes he dozed off himself.

At night, with the five of them crowded in a single room, Balthazar would tell Abdi some of the stories he'd loved as a child: the conquests of Alexander the Great and Leonidas, the Battles of Carthage and Salamis. And then the five of them would sleep, each on his own straw mat on the dirt floor.

Until two years ago, there had been six mats.

Balthazar's father had made his living the same way most of the neighborhood men had: by spending hot, backbreaking days hammering away at stones in a quarry north of the city. It was one of the few jobs deemed acceptable for the Syrian locals. In the old days, they'd been farmers and merchants. But then Rome had descended on Antioch, and they'd been pushed out of the fields and forums and into the slums.

Conditions in the quarry were dangerous. Ropes broke. Hoists toppled. Men were routinely hit by heavy pieces of debris, sliced in half by slivers of rock that broke loose from the walls. Sometimes, like Balthazar's father, they were simply crushed to death beneath twelve-ton blocks when a wooden hoist failed.

Balthazar had never seen his father's body, and he was

thankful for this. But he'd heard descriptions of men who'd suffered similar fates – their bodies all but liquefied by the force, and he hadn't been able to keep himself from imagining what his father had looked like when they finally hoisted that stone off of him: every drop of blood and bile and piss squeezed out of his organs, the contents of his stomach and bowels exploding outward in a grotesque sunburst pattern, his brains forced through his eye sockets, and his skull rendered a mosaic of tiny, shattered tiles. One second, he'd been a hardworking man with a wicked sense of humor, a meticulously trimmed beard, and a love of cinnamon dates. The next, he was a blood-soaked bag of broken tiles. Erased from existence in the blink of an eye. The snap of a rope.

Tragedy had made Balthazar the Man of the House. The sole provider for his mother and three siblings. And while his mother didn't approve of Balthazar's methods, she didn't forbid them, either.

'Stealing is a sin,' she'd told him with a sigh on learning of his pickpocketing, 'but starving is an even greater one.'

She *had* drawn the line, however, when she'd learned about one of Balthazar's self-taught methods: donning a prayer shawl, going into the Jewish temple, and picking men's pockets while they were deep in prayer.

'It's an abomination,' his mother had said, 'whether you worship the God of the Hebrews or not.'

After paying off his accomplices, rewarding tippers, and doling out the necessary kickbacks, the coins Balthazar nicked from the forum were barely enough to keep them all fed and housed. There was no extra money for extravagances like new clothing, or lamp oil, or sweetmeats. No rugs to sit on or chalices to drink from.

And it was getting harder to provide as time went on. The forum was becoming too dangerous. Balthazar was being recognized, questioned by the Roman soldiers who patrolled the Colonnaded Street. Money changers were getting nervous about offering tips, since capture could mean crucifixion.

But what could he do? Picking pockets was all that Balthazar was good at – today's fiasco notwithstanding. He knew of some boys, just a few years older than he was, who'd been arrested for murdering a money changer and stealing his inventory. He'd known these boys since he was born. He knew all of their parents and siblings. Like him, they'd started out picking pockets in the forum. Like him, they'd reached a point where they became too recognizable. A point where they'd needed more than a few coins to get by. And so they'd turned to another method. And for that, they'd all been put to death. Strung up by the Romans and thrown in a ditch on the other side of the Orontes.

And *that's* what had first given him the idea.

Every day, men were rounded up by the Romans for any number of reasons – including no reason at all – and put to death. Every day, their bodies were carried to an unmarked field on the other side of the Orontes and buried. And with their bodies went their rings and bracelets and necklaces. Yet it never occurred to the Romans to take that jewelry for themselves. And why

99

not? Because of the one thing the Greeks, Macedonians, Romans, Indians, Chinese, and even his fellow Syrians had in common: *religion*. They were all superstitious. Frightened of the unknown. Sufferers of a mass delusion, a hysteria of genuflection, ritual sacrifice, and old words. Not even the Romans, for all their Imperial brutality, would dare defile a dead body. But religion wasn't a hysteria Balthazar suffered from.

He never had. Not for lack of instruction. His father, like most Syrians, had worshipped the old pagan gods. And his mother, while not overtly religious, was one of the world's most superstitious women. Balthazar had simply never found a use for it. He was more concerned with feeding his family than throwing himself at the feet of some statue, more concerned with tomorrow than the rants of a prophet who'd lived a thousand years before his birth. A prophet who never heard of Rome or Herod. He found nothing abominable about eating certain foods on certain days or wearing this kind of hat versus that kind of hat, or even – *God forbid* – no hat at all. Beliefs like that put you in a cage.

And Balthazar was going to set himself free.

III

He waited on his belly, wet and alone in the dark. To the east, the lights of the city danced off the waters of the Orontes. To the west, nothing but desert. Balthazar had decided to avoid the bridge and swim across. You never knew when you were going to run into a Roman patrol. And he was paying for that caution by shivering in the cold desert air.

He'd seldom been on this side of the river. There wasn't much to see other than a few hermits and fields of shallow graves, one of which he now observed from afar. He watched as four slaves worked together to bury the day's victims, supervised by a single Roman soldier. Two of them used shovels to dig a knee-deep trench, another transferred bodies from a wheeled cart and placed them in, and the fourth filled in the dirt on top of them.

He hadn't told a soul about his plan. No one could know – not his oldest, most trusted friends from the slums. Not his accomplices from the forum. *No one.* Picking pockets was one thing. Even murders could be forgiven. But *this* . . .

He was tampering with the unspeakable.

Balthazar dug with his bare hands. It had taken another miserable, shivering hour, but the slaves and their cart had finally gone, and the soldier with them. Now it was just him, alone in a field of bodies, kneeling over a fresh grave in the dark of night. As he dug, Balthazar told himself to breathe. *Relax.* Superstition was for the weak-minded, right? Of course it was. He told himself to think of the spoils. All the gold and silver waiting under this loose dir—

Was that something moving?

He could've sworn something had brushed against his finger beneath the dirt . . .

No, it wasn't 'something moving.' There's nothing 'moving' out here because dead things don't m—

A hand burst through the dirt and grabbed Balthazar by the throat. Then another – unnaturally strong, squeezing his windpipe. It pulled him toward the loose dirt. Pulled him down into the gra—

No, it didn't. Stop being a baby . . .

But he *had* felt something.

It was the familiar shape of a hand, a hand unlike any he'd ever touched. A hand no warmer than the dirt it was buried in, its skin rigid and leathery. Balthazar suddenly realized something. Something he *really* wished he'd considered earlier: he'd never touched a dead body.

He'd seen them, sure. You couldn't get to be twelve

years old in the slums of Antioch without seeing a dead body. But when it came to dead bodies, seeing and touching were oceans apart. Still, he took a breath and brushed the last of the dirt aside . . .

Here was a man – barely twenty, from the looks of him. Judging by the dark red line around his neck and the unnatural angle of his head, he'd been hung. For what, Balthazar would never know. It didn't matter. What mattered was the pendant around that neck. A gold pendant on a leather string.

All I have to do is reach out and take it.

No matter what tricks his young imagination played on him – no matter how real it seemed when the man's bloodshot eyes snapped open and his hands reached for Balthazar's throat, it wouldn't be. People didn't come back to life. There was no God to fear, no sins to commit. There were nothing but superstitions and the rants of long-ago prophets.

All he had to do was reach out and take it . . .

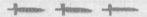

Balthazar returned home that night filthy beyond comprehension, and rich beyond his wildest imagination. He promptly informed his mother that they were moving to a better neighborhood.

It had been a bigger haul than he'd ever dreamed. In one night, he'd raided nine bodies. And from those nine bodies, he'd netted a total of six rings (four gold, two silver) and four pendants (three gold, one silver). All told, it had taken less than three hours. *Three hours!* Balthazar would have been lucky to pick one pocket in the same amount of time. And with pickpocketing there were the risks, the payoffs, the kickbacks. No, this was the answer. This was the way. He had the whole west bank of the Orontes to himself. And the best part was, there was no end in sight. As long as the Romans kept putting men to death, Balthazar would keep finding uses for their unused valuables.

The next morning, he took Abdi into the city, and the two of them ate cinnamon dates until they were nearly sick. And when they rested beneath their favorite tree on the Orontes – the one with the scar down its side, not far from where Balthazar had entered the water the night before – he presented his brother a little present from his first plunder of the dead. A keepsake. It was a gold pendant on a leather string, a thin, coin-shaped wafer bearing the likeness of the god Plutus on one side.

'The god of wealth,' said Balthazar as he hung it around Abdi's neck.

The only god worth worshipping.

The pendant flittered in the afternoon sun, spinning round and round as Abdi jumped and laughed along the riverbank, proud of his gift – but more proud of the fact that his big brother had given it to him. Balthazar watched from the shade of the scarred tree, smiling from ear to ear, a gold disk of reflected light sweeping across his face every so often. The light from his brother's pendant. The pendant he would spend much of his life searching for.

4

A Strange Eastern Light

'During the time of King Herod, Wise Men from the east came and asked, "Where is the one who has been born king of the jews? We saw his star when it rose and have come to worship him."'

—*Matthew 2:1*

I

Herod smiled, the tips of his blackened teeth showing through thin lips. He'd been right, of course. The one thing people loved more than an outlaw was seeing him punished.

Thousands had turned out to witness the death of the Antioch Ghost. Contrary to the fears of his advisors, there were no protests or demands for his release, no weeping in the streets of Jerusalem over his imminent demise. There was only a sea of people waiting anxiously in the square outside the palace's north gate, all of them crowded around a small wooden platform that had been erected in its center. A sea of people waiting anxiously for their glimpse of a minor legend. More specifically, for a glimpse of his blood.

Herod stood high above them in the Tower of Mariamne, watching it all through a small widow but taking care to keep his diseased face hidden from view. His soldiers had spent the day canvassing every square inch of Jerusalem, from the poorest suburbs to the porticos of the Great Temple, spreading the word that the famed murderer – the demon known as 'the Antioch Ghost' – was going to be executed outside the palace at sundown. Across the city, merchants had closed their shops early. Prophets had canceled their afternoon street sermons. Weary travelers had even given up their places in long census lines and diverted to the square. Herod had expected big crowds, and his expectations had been exceeded.

There'd been some deliberation in the throne room regarding the method of execution. There were so many to choose from, each with their unique advantages and disadvantages. Crucifixion was degrading, but too prolonged. It risked a sympathetic response. Burning alive was dramatic, but too dangerous in the middle of a large, overcrowded city. Hanging was simply beneath the dignity of the occasion.

In the end, it'd been decided that beheading was the best way to go. Quick and easy, yet sufficiently savage and humiliating. In accordance with tradition, the prisoners would be gagged and covered with black hoods, depriving them of any last words or glimpses of the living world. The hoods also hid the fear on the victims' faces, dehumanized them, therefore lessening the chances that the onlookers would sympathize with their plight.

After being paraded onto the platform, the condemned would be made to kneel over a stone block, and their heads would be promptly hacked off with an iron ax. Although, depending on a number of factors – the size of the neck, the sharpness of the blade, the skill of the executioner – it could take several whacks before the top parted company with the bottom.

As soon as the blades were clean through, the hoods would be removed and the heads lifted for all to see: the jaws hanging slack, the blood draining out of the neck and the color out of the face. If you were lucky, the eyes would still be open. If you were *really* lucky, they'd be darting around, looking fearfully at the cheering faces of the crowd.

The beating of drums suddenly filled the square as the doors of the north gate were opened, and Herod's grown son, Antipas, paraded through it accompanied by royal guards. Antipas was everything his father had once been: muscular and tall, his spine straight, his olive skin perfectly healthy, and his face lightly bearded with dark hair. Herod often imagined what he would give to trade places with his son, what atrocities he would commit if it meant having that many years again, that much health and beauty. Would he kill his own beloved Antipas if it meant gaining his own health? There wasn't the slightest shred of doubt in his mind: *Of course I would.*

Antipas climbed the four steps to the platform and quieted the crowd with a wave of his hand.

'People of Jerusalem,' he shouted, 'children of Israel! Today we come to see three criminals meet justice!'

A cheer went up, not so much for the concept of justice, but for the bloody method in which it was about to be delivered.

'We come to honor the laws of God! And we come to honor my father, the mighty Herod!'

Antipas indicated the tower above the north gate with his arm, and another cheer went up, no less than was required to seem convincing but not so loud that it was patronizing. A cheer of appropriate reverence. Thousands of eyes were treated to a rare glimpse of mighty Herod himself – his beard thick and brown, his cheeks full and his skin unblemished. Herod had never looked better, and he waved a hearty hand to his subjects below.

Away from the window, the *real* Herod looked on as his double completed the illusion.

He couldn't go out among his people anymore. Not in his current state. Not until a cure was found. But he didn't want the Jews getting any ideas, either. Spreading rumors. Perceiving him as anything but the ferocious, robust king he'd been until a few years ago.

Herod's double waved a few seconds more, then disappeared out of sight as he'd been instructed to do. No need to have them looking up at the 'king' the whole time, scrutinizing the illusion and distracting from the main event.

'We come,' Antipas continued, 'to witness the death of three thieves – the first two caught trying to steal sacred objects from the Great Temple!'

A chorus of angry shouts went up as the drums began to beat again, and the doors of the north gate swung open. Gaspar and Melchyor were marched out under heavy guard – black hoods over their heads, their wrists bound behind them.

Rather than meet their deaths with the quiet dignity

that had become a hallmark of men in their position, both of them struggled against their bonds, trying to free themselves from the grasp of the guards. Naturally, the more they struggled, the more the crowd cheered, working itself into a frenzy. It was all music to Herod's ears, and it made him wish all the more that he could trade places with Antipas. He wanted to be down there on that platform, to personally lift the head of the so-called Antioch Ghost and present it to the heavens. Grab it by the hair and shake it until the last of the blood ran down his arm. Look into its eyes as they looked helplessly around for a few seconds, then faded into a thousand-yard stare. As he had countless times over the past three years, Herod silently cursed the whore who'd made him this way. The whore whose charms had been his undoing.

She'd been so young ... so new and naïve. He'd enjoyed her so many times, in so many ways. And though she'd resisted at first, Herod was sure she'd grown to enjoy him, too. But then he'd found the mark. The lesion on her breast. Within a day, there'd been another on her neck. Within a week, she'd been covered in them. Covered in sores that oozed a foul-smelling milk. Her eyes had gone yellow, her skin a deathly gray.

And then he'd seen it. The first lesion on his own flesh. Herod had ordered his physicians to carve it out, but two more had appeared in its place. Then ten more – each one oozing and foul, each one sucking the pigment from the surrounding skin until his entire body was gray and withered. Until his teeth rotted in his mouth and his appetite vanished. His physicians diagnosed it as leprosy, though they had to admit they'd never seen a form quite like this one.

A king. A builder of great cities . . . undone by the wretched disease of beggars.

No, Herod couldn't go out among the people anymore, but he could still lead them. It took a bit of trickery, a bit of illusion. But he could still rule from the shadows, as he did now – standing in the tower named for his dearly departed wife, watching as the hooded Gaspar and Melchyor were led onto the platform, fighting every step of the way. Trying to pull free, as if they'd be able to escape. As if they'd be able to run past dozens of guards and thousands of onlookers with hoods over their heads.

Amazing, thought Herod, *the things a man will do to preserve himself.*

The shorter of the two prisoners was dragged over to the block and forced to kneel in front of it. The stone had metal rings protruding from either side, through which a rope had been threaded. As soon as Melchyor's hooded face hit the stone, the rope was laid across his shoulders. Guards on either side of the block then took the ends of the rope in their hands and pulled it taut, holding the prisoner's body down despite his struggles.

'And now,' said Antipas, 'the Greek known as "Melchyor" goes to his death!'

The crowd went absolutely cold quiet. They wanted to hear this. Hear the familiar crack of a breaking neck and metal hitting stone. The executioner lifted his ax and held it aloft for several seconds, making the most of the

112

moment. Then down it came. The crack of shattered vertebrae could be heard clear across the square, but not the clanging of the blade against the block.

It hadn't gone clean through.

Quickly, as Melchyor's body began to twitch and dark blood began to pour down the sides of the stone block, the ax was raised again and the job finished. The instant it was, Antipas pulled off Melchyor's hood and lifted his head for the crowd to see – blood pouring down his forearm and onto the wooden planks.

Herod had never seen this little Greek before. He was just a common criminal, and as such, he'd been taken straight to the dungeon. No audience with the king. Just a death sentence and a cell. Still, there was something vaguely familiar about him, although from this distance it was hard to tell. *Besides*, Herod had to admit, *all Greeks look the same to me.*

It didn't matter. Here he was, his mouth gagged and slack jawed, his eyes moving, taking in the exuberant faces with their fists raised in the air. Taking in the last few seconds they would ever see. Here he was, a reminder of Herod's absolute authority. And the crowd couldn't have been happier.

When he sensed they'd had their fill, Antipas handed Melchyor's head to a guard, who carried it off to be stuck on the end of a pike, where it would shrivel in the sun for the next month or more. It was Gaspar's turn, and like his smaller companion, he wasn't going to go quietly. It took four guards to force him to his knees and all the strength of the rope men to hold him down. The executioner was

determined to strike a clean blow this time, and he did –
straight through to the stone block, with enough force to
split the wooden handle of his ax. Once again, Antipas
removed the hood and lifted the head for all to see. Once
again, the crowd cheered wildly.

And when he felt they'd cheered long enough, Antipas
handed the second head off and raised a hand in the air.
The crowd fell silent. It was time.

'And now,' said Antipas, 'we come to the criminal
known as "the Antioch Ghost." A criminal who's long
stolen from the innocent people of Judea, who's
murdered so many of her brave soldiers in cold blood. A
criminal who's deceived many of you into believing that
he's a giant! Tricked you into thinking he could never be
captured! And yet, my father – our mighty king – has
done just that!'

A cheer went up, just as Antipas had intended it to.

'Now we shall see that this "Ghost" is nothing more
than a man! Now we shall see what happens to the
enemies of Judea and her people!'

The cheering reached a fever pitch as the drums
resumed, and the north gate swung open. Balthazar was
marched out – a black hood over his head, his wrists bound
behind him. As the guards led him into the center of the
square, men and women stood on their toes and pushed
each other aside, all trying to get a look at the legend. Those
who did were almost universally disappointed by what they
saw. This was no giant. This was just a man. A man who –
like the late Gaspar and Melchyor – was struggling against
his bonds. Trying to free himself, even now.

Watching from his little window above, Herod could see Balthazar struggling, too, fighting the guards as he was led up the steps of the wooden platform. Nothing could've made him happier. Not only was the Antioch Ghost going to die, but also he was going to meet his death like a coward for all of Jerusalem to see!

As if answering Herod's thoughts, Balthazar did something completely unexpected and undignified as he took the platform. Something completely incongruous with the legend he'd cultivated, and far more embarrassing than struggling against his bonds.

He pissed himself.

Herod wouldn't have known this had Antipas not noticed the dark circle on the front of the prisoner's tan robes. Expanding. Working its way down his legs.

'Look at him!' cried Antipas, pointing to the evidence. 'Here is your mighty Antioch Ghost! The Scourge of Rome soils himself in the face of death!'

Laughter and cheers erupted throughout the square. Insults came from every corner of the crowd. Herod couldn't believe it. *No . . . it's too good to be true.* His blackened teeth showed themselves once again. The legend of the Antioch Ghost would soon be as dead as the headless, piss-soaked body of the man himself.

Like Gaspar and Melchyor, Balthazar had to be forced to kneel in front of the stone block. Unlike them, he was kneeling in his own urine. His face was forced down onto the cool stone block and the rope pulled taut across his back. It took all the strength of the men holding it to keep him in place.

'And now,' cried Antipas, 'we rid the earth of a demon!'

The crowd fell silent again as the executioner raised his spare ax. After pausing a little longer than usual for dramatic effect, he let out a grunt of effort and brought it down on the squirming prisoner. But as the ax fell, Balthazar gave a final pull against the rope with all of his considerable might, lifting his hooded skull halfway up off the block, making the blade miss his neck.

But there would be no dramatic escape for Balthazar today. For while the blade didn't hit his neck, it *did* chop a sizable wedge into his brain.

He was dead.

So was the crowd. The cheering stopped. Exuberant faces turned quizzical – silently watching the spurts of blood that shot through the black hood. Watching the embarrassed executioner pull his ax out of Balthazar's skull. This wasn't the beheading they'd come for, the beheading they'd dropped everything to attend. This wasn't the event they'd waited hours in the heat to witness. Their silence quickly gave way to boos.

Herod was more disappointed than any of them. Even in his last moment, the Antioch Ghost had refused to cooperate. Even in death, he'd managed to embarrass the King of Judea. Managed to mock his power. But . . . at least he was dead. True, it hadn't been the execution he'd hoped for, but it had been an execution nonetheless. The goal of ridding the earth of a demon had been achieved. And that, in the end, was all that really mattered.

Antipas hurried onto the platform. Eager to win back some of the momentum, he ordered the executioner to finish the job – chopping the partially collapsed prisoner's head off anyway. Hell-bent on redeeming himself, the executioner did the job in one blow, and the crowd cheered anew. Even Herod's spirits were lifted by the sight of the Antioch Ghost's head being finally and irrevocably separated from his body.

Just as he had with Melchyor and Gaspar, Antipas pulled off the hood and held the head aloft for all to see.

Only it wasn't the Antioch Ghost's head.

Just as it hadn't been Melchyor's or Gaspar's.

The crowd kept cheering, and Antipas kept smiling – neither aware of what the Antioch Ghost *actually* looked like . . . or that this wasn't, in fact, him.

But Herod knew.

From high up in his perch, he knew. He knew that the Antioch Ghost had beaten – *no, humiliated* – him. Humiliated him in front of his people. He felt such a rage crawling up his back, such an urge to scream. But he couldn't find the voice. He was powerless. A powerless king, trapped in a tower named for the wife who'd humiliated him. Trapped in a body that humiliated him. He could only watch as his stupid, grinning son held the wrong head in the air.

II

—————

Three wise men walked east across Jerusalem as the sun went down. Each with his head wrapped and his face covered. Each wearing the robes of a dead man.

Once again, Balthazar had relied on religion to set him free. It had never occurred to the dungeon guards that anyone, even notorious murderers, would harm a priest. It hadn't occurred to the guards to remain in the cell, to protect their king's religious advisors while they offered comfort to the condemned. Nor had it occurred to the guards to get a good look at the three wise men when they knocked on the cell door and announced they were ready to come out – their head coverings reconfigured to hide their faces.

The guards weren't alone in their assumptions. It hadn't occurred to Balthazar that three innocent men would pay for his freedom with their lives – struggling, screaming through their hoods and gags, and pissing themselves. His plan had merely called for overpowering the wise men, stealing their robes, binding and gagging them up with strips of fabric ripped from their own garments, and slipping out of the palace before anyone noticed the switch. He'd been sure that an alarm would go up when the guards reentered the cell and found the wise men bound, gagged, and half naked inside. Only it hadn't occurred to Balthazar that they might not be the *same* guards.

In fact, the men who returned to the cell, the men who fit the bound and gagged prisoners with their execution hoods and led them to the chopping block, had no idea what Balthazar, Gaspar, and Melchyor looked like, because they'd been on duty for less than an hour. In the end, the real wise men had been doomed by a shift change.

In the excitement of the execution, no one had noticed that the little round Greek was no longer quite as little or round or that the tied hands of the Ethiopian called 'Gaspar' were no longer the same color. Just as no one had questioned the three wise men as they'd made their way out of the dungeon in their nobleman's robes, through the palace, and across the courtyard. The guards had dutifully opened the north gate without a second glance, and the prisoners had simply slipped into the square, where the masses were beginning to gather for the execution of the year.

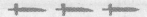

They walked as slowly as they could, given the fear and excitement beating through their bodies. There was only a street and the desire to keep following it. The desire to get as far away from Herod's Palace as they could. They continued clear across the city, until they reached the Pool of Bethesda, where the people of the surrounding suburbs bathed, and Balthazar stopped to have the biggest drink of water any human being had ever had.

The pool was adjacent to a market that ran along the north wall of the Great Temple – a collection of merchants and vendors that stretched several blocks. His thirst mercifully quenched, Balthazar finally had the wits to form another plan.

First, he put his old sleight of hand skills to use, walking from one end of the market to the other, stealing coins from the pockets of passersby and trinkets from the merchants who hadn't yet closed up shop for the execution. He took small pieces of gold jewelry, frankincense. Things they'd be able to trade for food and favors in the coming days.

Next, he'd used some of the stolen coins to buy as much food and water as he and the others could carry. Balthazar also bought a little myrrh to dress his wounds with – a trick he'd learned from the Asian traders in the forum as a boy. A little of that stolen jewelry was used to buy a camel for each of them. Camels they rode south past the temple walls. The men had no idea where they were headed, and they didn't care, just as long as it was far away from Jerusalem.

If Gaspar and Melchyor had harbored any doubts that their companion was, in fact, the Antioch Ghost, the chatter on the streets of Jerusalem put them to rest. The whole city seemed to be talking about the execution. *The Antioch Ghost* was on every tongue. Balthazar had saved these thieves' lives, and they were in his debt. In accordance with tradition, they were his servants until that debt was repaid in kind. It was a code as old as the desert, and it applied to career criminals just as much as any other man. Even Balthazar, who never met a tradition he didn't despise, had honored this one in the past. It wasn't a tradition in the religious sense, like eating this animal versus that, or wearing this hat or that hat or no hat at all. It was simply common sense.

Every service had a price. Every object a value. If some-one made you a sword, you paid him the appropriate amount or traded something of equal value with him. If a man saved your life, you either paid him the amount you considered that life worth, or you saved his in return. Until either of those things was transacted, you were in his debt. It was business. And if Balthazar believed in any-thing with religious fervor, it was that.

Everything had a price. And though he didn't yet know that his freedom had cost the wise men their heads, Balthazar knew he'd just upped the price on his.

III

Screaming echoed through Herod's throne room. The servants had made themselves scarce, fearful that they'd be condemned to death for some unperceivable transgression. Advisors kept to the corners of the room – away from the warm, flickering glow of the torches, away from the cooler moonlight that streamed in through the windows with unusual intensity. They cowered in the shadows, even hid behind the rows of columns that ran along either wall.

The king paced in front of the steps of his throne, his body hunched forward. Three Judean generals stood before him, their helmets tucked beneath their arms and their tails between their legs.

'I don't care if you have to burn this entire city to the ground to find him! I won't be made a fool of by a common thief!'

His already raspy voice had been strained to its limits. He'd spent the last hour cursing anyone who dared to come into his field of view. Demanding the heads of everyone who'd played even the slightest role in his humiliation: the dungeon guards, the north gate guards, even the executioner. All dead.

'I want every legion, every last man, every horse, and every sword hunting him down, and I want him brought to me alive!'

Even his beloved son, Antipas, had disappeared in the wake of this disaster. He knew better than to put himself in the path of his father's rage.

'And if a word – if one WORD – of this is spoken outside these walls, I'll have all of you and your families put to death! None of your men are to know who they seek! As far as they and all of Judea are concerned, the Antioch Ghost is dead! Do you understand?'

The three generals all nodded. Even a simple 'yes, Your Highness' could be misinterpreted in this situation.

'Good . . . now go find him.'

The generals bowed to their king, turned on their heels, and marched away as quickly as they could without betraying their fear. As they did, a timid face emerged from the shadows beside Herod's throne. It belonged to an advisor – a beardless man with short graying hair and a tall, wiry build. He'd been waiting for a lull in the tirade, waiting for the right moment to deliver the news. The worst possible news. The advisor knew there was a very real chance he would be put to death just for being the bearer of what he had to say. But someone had to do it. The king had to know. *Tonight, of all nights . . .*

'Mighty Herod,' he said.

The king spun around and found him already in a deep, apologetic bow.

'What?'

'Mighty Herod, I . . . I must inform you of—'

The advisor had come out of his bow and met Herod's eyes. Those horrible, yellowed eyes cutting through him. The advisor suddenly realized that he'd lost all power of speech.

'Of WHAT?'

'I . . . it is my sad duty to . . .'

'Use your tongue or I'll have it cut out of your mouth!'

The advisor gave up all hope of getting the words out and simply pointed to the east wall. Herod's yellowed eyes traced the path of his arm.

'What?' he asked. 'What would you have me look at? All I see are my columns and the spineless nobles hiding behind them.'

'Perhaps . . . if Your Highness would condescend to look out one of the windows . . .'

Herod was tired. He was tired, and he wanted this wretched day to be over. Whatever this idiot was trying to tell him, it couldn't be any worse than the humiliation he'd suffered earlier. He dragged his tired feet across the stone floor, toward the eastern wall.

Realizing that the king would see them if they stayed put, the advisors, wise men, and courtiers who'd been hiding behind the columns shuffled toward the rear of the throne room. They retreated as quietly as they could as the king neared – but not quietly enough to escape his attention. Did they think he was deaf? Blind? Did they think a great king held on to his throne for thirty years by being a fool?

Herod was struck by a wonderful vision as he passed the columns and neared the east wall. A vision of a world in which he was the sole inhabitant. A world with no outlaws to chase. No duplicitous courtiers or inept generals, no diseased whores or beautiful, covetous sons. A world with no fools to suffer. Perhaps that's what heaven would be like when he arrived. A whole world for himself. A world to build in his own image. It was a nice thought.

On reaching one of the windows behind the columns and looking out, Herod understood why it had been so hard for the advisor to tell him. He also knew his long night was only beginning. His breath was taken away by what he saw, even in the instant before he'd fully comprehended what it meant. For there, in the eastern sky beyond the silhouette of the Great Temple, was a star brighter than any star he'd ever seen.

'The prophecies, Your Highness.'

The advisor was cowering behind him. Waiting for the outburst he knew would come. But Herod felt no scream crawling up his throat. No rage climbing up his crooked spine. He was almost . . . amused by it all. Earlier in the day, he'd had the Antioch Ghost in his dungeon. Now, only a few hours later, the Ghost was a free man, and – if one believed in ancient prophecies – the heavens had just signaled the arrival of the man who would topple all the kingdoms of the world, including Herod's.

Perhaps it was the soreness in his throat. Perhaps it was just the fact that he was exhausted. But when Herod next spoke, he did so with a soft, almost affectionate voice.

'Call the generals back in, please.'

The Antioch Ghost would have to wait. He had bigger problems.

IV

They'd been arguing about what it was. A comet? A fire burning on a clouded hillside? Was it, as Melchyor feared, the all-seeing eye of Herod himself, looking down on them? Whatever it was, it was bright. A small sun, hanging low in the sky to their left, washing out all the other fires in the heavens as they rode south.

The wise men needed a place to stop and rest for a couple of hours. None of them had slept more than a minute or two the night before, and they had a journey of untold length and hardship ahead. It couldn't be Jerusalem. Not with Herod's men kicking down every door in the city looking for them. And it couldn't be the desert, either. Not with that thing up there – that night-time sun, taking away the biggest advantage the desert had to offer: vast expanses of total darkness in which to disappear.

Unless they were willing to ride for another two or three hours, that left them with very few options. Namely, one of the villages on the outskirts of the city. Balthazar wasn't about to go north to Bethel – not after the lack of hospitality they'd shown him during his last visit. Herodium was too far. And it had *Herod* in its name, which, even to a man of few superstitions, seemed like a bad idea.

That left Bethlehem.

It was a shepherd's village. That meant there'd be stables to hide in. More importantly, stables to hide their camels in. They couldn't have them tied up in plain sight – not in a village where the only animals were goats. Three camels would seem out of place to all but the most dim-witted soldier. Especially one looking for three escaped criminals.

On the northernmost edge of Bethlehem, before the village organized itself into a series of cobblestoned streets and evenly divided lots, the wise men came upon a cluster of small, brick homes on their right, each with a wooden stable beside it. The largest of these stables looked just about big enough for three men and their camels to squeeze into for a couple of hours. It was also the farthest from the main road, making it that much more appealing.

'Don't you think we should keep going awhile?' asked Gaspar. 'See if there's something better in the center of the village?'

Balthazar looked down the road into Bethlehem. Other than a few small fires, the village was sound asleep. The streets all but empty. Every rooftop, every cobblestone was clearly visible in the light of that strange star. It wouldn't be hard to spot three men on camelback. They could spend another hour looking around for something better with that thing shining down on them, or they could grab a couple of hours of sleep now.

Balthazar regretted his choice almost immediately.

It had begun the moment the wise men had poked their heads into the stable and surprised the breastfeeding girl. With her scream still ringing in their ears, the carpenter had come out of nowhere and tried to stab them with a pitchfork. Balthazar had, naturally, responded by grabbing the carpenter's throat and punching him in the face – blackening his right eye and bloodying his nose. Seeing this, the girl had screamed some more, the baby had started crying, the camels had reared up, and Balthazar's head had begun to throb all over again.

Now the carpenter was struggling to stay on his feet, clutching the pitchfork with his right hand and pinching his gushing nose shut with his left. The girl was trying to steady him while keeping her eyes fixed on the intruders and holding on to her crying baby at the same time. Balthazar took a step toward them with his palms held out in a nonthreatening posture, the way one might try to calm a spooked animal, but the carpenter responded by thrusting his pitchfork again, nearly connecting with Balthazar's face. Under normal circumstances, this would have cost the carpenter his life. But Balthazar didn't have a sword, and he couldn't risk extending this racket and drawing unwanted attention. He needed peace, and he needed it now.

'Easy,' said Balthazar. 'Everybody just . . . calm down.'

He backed away, his palms still held out, and motioned to his fellow wise men to do the same. The girl stopped shouting. The baby stopped screaming. Balthazar would've thought the latter strange, but he was too tired to notice.

'Good,' he said. 'Now, what's your name?'

The carpenter glared back at him for what seemed an eternity – his chest heaving, blood already beginning to dry on his lips and chin. Just when Balthazar was beginning to think he would never answer, the carpenter said, 'Joseph.'

'Joseph, good. Nice to meet you, Joseph. And her?'

'My wife,' he said after another pause. 'Mary.'

'Good. Joseph? Mary? My name is Balthazar. This is Gaspar . . . this is Melchyor. We don't want to hurt you . . . we're just looking for a place to rest. But, Joseph? If you don't put that pitchfork down, I'm going to take it from you and stab you to death in front of your wife and child. Do you understand?'

Balthazar watched the carpenter think it over for what seemed an eternity. *Hard, isn't it? If you give up the pitchfork, you'll be defenseless. If you don't, you might have to kill all three of us. So . . . what'll it be?* As if answering Balthazar's thoughts, the carpenter threw the pitchfork to the ground. Gaspar was quick to make a move for it, but Balthazar held his hand out and stopped him. He needed peace.

'Good,' said Balthazar. 'Now, let's all sit and talk for a minute.'

The wise men tied their camels up, sat in the hay, and leaned their weary bodies against the stalls. Joseph and Mary sat, too, keeping to the opposite side of the stable, which was a scant ten feet away. Mary held the baby close to her body, still reeling from the shock of seeing her husband beaten and the embarrassment of being seen in such a private, indecent state. Joseph sat beside her, still pinching his nose shut.

'What business,' asked Mary after an extended silence, 'do three men have barging into someone else's stable in the middle of the night?'

'*Your* stable?' asked Gaspar.

'Our stable. We were here first,' said Mary.

'We just need a place to rest our heads for a little while,' said Balthazar.

'Well you can rest them somewhere else,' she said.

'Afraid we can't.'

Mary looked them over. Their robes were among the more expensive she'd seen. They were adorned with gold jewelry, and she could smell the frankincense they were carrying.

'You're obviously noblemen,' she said. 'Go and force one of the shepherds from their homes. Better yet, go to Jerusalem and force one of the other nobles out of theirs.'

'Our situation is . . . complicated,' said Balthazar.

'He's the Antioch Ghost,' said Melchyor.

Balthazar had to suppress the urge to break the little Greek's jaw. How could anyone be so stupid? Here they were, in disguise and running for their lives, and he casually offers up the one piece of information that could

131

get them all killed faster than any other. Now, the moment they fell asleep, the Jews sitting across from them would go running to the nearest soldier and give them up. Sell them out for whatever reward Herod was offering. Now he'd have to tie their wrists. Gag them.

There was no going back now. It was out in the open. Balthazar waited for the familiar wide-eyed reverence to wash over their faces . . . and waited, until it became clear that Joseph and Mary had no idea who or what the Antioch Ghost was.

This aggravated him even more. Everything aggravated him: his aching head, his weary body, the bleating of goats in the stalls behind them – everything.

'I go here and there,' he said at last, 'taking what I can from the Romans and those who serve them, then disappearing. Some people have taken to calling me "the Antioch Ghost."'

'So . . . you're a thief,' said Mary.

'Not just a thief,' said Gaspar. 'The best thief who ever lived.'

Balthazar allowed himself a private swell of pride. Obviously there was no way to know if he was 'the best thief who ever lived.' But at the same time, there was no way to prove he wasn't. Either way, it was nice to be recognized.

'Whether he's the best or not doesn't matter,' said Joseph through a pinched nose. 'Stealing is a sin.'

'Really?' asked Balthazar. 'And trying to kill three unarmed men with a pitchfork – is that a sin?'

Joseph looked at the weapon in Gaspar's hand. Before tonight, he'd never so much as raised a fist in anger. It

132

wasn't in his nature. He looked away, suddenly frightened by how close he'd come to committing the sin of murder.

'I thought you were Herod's men.'

Balthazar and Gaspar exchanged a look. They could've almost laughed at the irony of anyone thinking *they* were Herod's men were it not for the chill they both felt down their backs. What did they know?

'Why, would Herod's men be looking for you?' Gaspar asked.

'Not looking for us,' said Joseph. 'Looking for the child born in the city of David . . . the one the prophets call *Messiah*.'

Balthazar was suddenly back on the stone bench outside Herod's throne room, surrounded by the soldiers who'd chased him through the desert. Listening to the raspy king rant through the doors. Something about 'prophecies.' Something about the 'dead rising,' and 'plagues' and a 'Messiah.' But as recent as the memory was, it was vague. His mind had been on other things at the time. Namely his impending death and how to avoid it.

'That's very interesting,' he said at last, 'but what's it have to do with you?'

Now it was Mary's and Joseph's turn to exchange a look. Should they tell him? They didn't know these men. They were criminals by their own admission. Then again . . . the fact that they were criminals made them unlikely to go running to Herod.

'It began before we were married,' said Joseph.

He explained it all as earnestly and clearly as he could.

He told them about the archangel Gabriel visiting Mary in a dream. About Mary getting pregnant, though they hadn't lain together, and the message that the son of God was growing in her womb. He told them about his own visions, including the most recent one – the one he'd had only last night. The one in which the angel Gabriel warned Joseph that Herod was going to slay all the newborn males of Bethlehem. He and Mary had been preparing to flee on their own when Balthazar and the others barged in.

When Joseph was finished telling the story, the six of them sat in silence. The wise men with their mouths closed, processing what they'd heard. The baby was asleep, its chest rising and falling in Mary's arms. Only the occasional bleating of goats around them.

'And you believe all that?' asked Balthazar. 'You believe that your son is . . .'

'The son of God,' said Joseph.

'And that the king of Judea is sending soldiers to kill . . . a baby?'

'Of course I believe it,' said Joseph.

'You don't think it's a little suspicious?'

'Suspicious?'

It was the obvious question. The *only* question. Balthazar suddenly felt a little tinge of sympathy for the carpenter. Did he really have to point it out?

'She gets pregnant before your wedding, and you think it's some kind of . . . miracle?'

Joseph glared at Balthazar, the yellow bruise beneath his eye already turning blue.

'I know what I saw,' he said.

'I think the only "miracle" is that you believed her,' said Gaspar.

Balthazar couldn't help but laugh. Melchyor joined in, though he didn't quite understand the joke. But he did understand the way Joseph got to his feet and came at them – and he didn't like it. He and the other wise men got to their feet and stood chest to chest with Joseph in the middle of the stable. Balthazar saw that look in the carpenter's eye. The look of a man who'd just had his honor insulted and was thinking about doing something about it. *Go on, little carpenter. I'll give you more than a bloody nose this time* . . .

Mary rose behind Joseph, still cradling the baby. She took him by the arm. 'It's pointless,' she said.

'I know what I saw,' he said again, looking Balthazar dead in the eye, 'I wouldn't expect a man like you to believe me.'

'Good,' said Gaspar. 'Because only a fool could be expected to believe a story that absurd.'

Now it was Mary coming at them, and Joseph holding her back.

'You can insult me,' she cried, 'but I won't hear you insult my husband!'

She kept coming, pointing her free hand in their faces and screaming at them. Joseph did all he could to hold her back without hurting the baby – who, despite the noise and movement, remained quiet.

'I won't hear you insult what we saw!' she cried. 'And I won't hear you insult the name of God!'

'Fine,' said Balthazar. 'Just calm dow—'

'I won't calm down! You come in here and attack us! Insult us!'

'Silence your woman!' cried Gaspar to Joseph. 'She'll wake the whole town!'

'I won't be quiet!' yelled Mary.

'Don't tell me what to do!' yelled Joseph to Gaspar, holding her back.

'Hey, hey, hey, HEY!' cried Balthazar.

The force of the last syllable was enough to shut their collective mouths. Silence hung over the stables again. Even the animals seemed to get the message.

'Enough . . .'

He ran his fingers through his hair, massaging the scalp beneath. His head was still killing him, and this wasn't helping. All he wanted to do was close his eyes for a minute.

'Look, I'm sure everything you're saying is true. I'm sure the angels came down from heaven and told you whatever it was they told you. Whatever you say, we believe it, okay? But the three of us? We have better things to do than listen to a couple of zealots tell stories. Namely, sleep for a few hours.'

There was that look in the carpenter's eyes again. But in the interest of resolving this thing and getting some rest, Balthazar chose to ignore it.

'Now . . . I'm afraid we can't let you leave,' said Balthazar.

Joseph spoke up. 'But Herod's men are—'

'I don't care. I can't risk having you go off and tell some

136

soldier where to find three sleeping escaped criminals.'

'Why would we go to the same soldiers who are looking for our baby?' asked Mary.

'As soon we're gone, you're free to go. But if I open my eyes and find you trying to sneak out of here, or if I see him reaching for that pitchfork again, some very bad things are going to happen in here. And that's how it's going to be.'

Balthazar didn't wait for a response. He didn't care. All he cared about was closing his eyes. He sat down. Gaspar and Melchyor followed suit. Joseph led his wife back to their side of the stable and helped her to the ground.

'You should be ashamed of yourselves,' she said.

'I'm sure you're right,' said Balthazar, rolling onto his side. 'Now stop talking.'

'All of you should be ashamed of yourselves. Any man who would turn his back on—'

'I said ENOUGH!' Balthazar lifted his head and stared her down, this time with a look that couldn't be mistaken for anything other than a warning.

Satisfied she understood, Balthazar rolled over again and shut his eyes.

There was nothing to do now but grab a few hours of sleep and hope they didn't wake up to the pounding of hooves.

For the next three hours, three wise men slept in a cramped stable beside their gold and frankincense, their wounds dressed with myrrh. Joseph, Mary, and the infant across from them. Silent.

All of them beneath the star of Bethlehem.

The Black Creature

'When Herod realized that he had been out-
witted . . . he was furious, and he gave orders
to kill all the boys in Bethlehem and its vicin-
ity who were two years old and under.'

—*Matthew 2:16*

I

The thieving wise men rose before dawn, unhitched their camels, and led them into the bitter cold. The sky was just waking up to the first hints of deepest blue, but the sun was still a good half hour from revealing itself behind the eastern hills. Stars could still be seen shining clearly between the dark outlines of clouds. But not the star of Bethlehem. Sometime during the past few hours, it had simply vanished. Snuffed out by the desert wind. Balthazar wasn't surprised. Nothing that bright burned for very long.

Joseph and Mary hadn't said a word when the men woke, hadn't so much as looked at them as they left, not even when Melchyor had wished them well in his affably stupid way. Balthazar didn't blame them for the lack of civility. In the space of a few cramped hours, they'd managed to beat the carpenter bloody, insult his wife's honor, hold them both hostage, and denounce everything they believed in as a joke. All the same, he was happy to be rid of them. Let them babble about their paranoid fantasies to someone else.

The wise men mounted their camels and looked south into Bethlehem. The village was already alive, smoke rising from cooking fires and clay ovens, young girls shaking the dust off sleeping mats in the streets. The shepherds had risen before the first hint of blue and taken their flocks out to pasture, their sons in tow. The women had risen to cook for them. And now, with the men gone for the day, they and their daughters busied themselves with housework and tended to the younger children. The ones who were too small to help.

It was a village almost entirely devoted to goats, but not all the men of Bethlehem were shepherds. A few of them could be seen leading their small herds north along the road that passed by the wise men's stable. They were almost certainly headed to Jerusalem to sell their animals for meat or as sacrifices at the Great Temple. Dragging their goats up and down the road in bare feet, five miles each way. Day after miserable day. Up before sunrise, home after dark. All in the hopes of selling a single, stinking animal. All in the hopes of making enough to put a crust of bread in their children's bellies. When life was that hard, anyone who didn't steal for a living was crazy.

The sight of three noblemen riding at this early hour was unusual but not strange enough to warrant a second look from the goat draggers they passed on the road to Jerusalem. It was best to avoid staring at noblemen too long, anyway. There was always the chance they'd take offense and have you lashed, or worse.

Though the wise men wanted to get as far away from Herod as possible, they were headed back in the direction of his palace. Their plan was to take the road north toward Jerusalem, then, a mile or so before the South Gate, make a hard right and cut fifteen miles east through the desert to Qumran – a tiny settlement on the shores of the Dead Sea.

Qumran was home to a small sect of Jewish monks who called themselves the Essenes. But while the word *monk* evoked an image of clean, quiet reverence, the Essenes were more like mad hermits – men who shunned material wealth, carnal pleasure, and regular bathing in order to devote themselves to their beliefs. From what Balthazar could tell, those beliefs amounted to scribbling ancient nonsense on scrolls and then hiding those scrolls in the caves that dotted the surrounding mountains of the northern Dead Sea. Why they hid them, or who they hid them from, were mysteries.

Balthazar had taken refuge in those caves on several occasions, and he'd made some handsome donations to the monks in return for their hospitality. While they didn't particularly care about material wealth, they loved the things it bought: rugs for their floors, clothes for their bodies, parchment and ink for their mysterious musings. Balthazar knew many of the Essenes by name. He also knew they could be trusted to keep his whereabouts a secret. Most important of all, he knew that Herod's men wouldn't dare disturb such a sacred Jewish settlement. That was one of the great things about the Judean Army. It was made up almost entirely of Jews.

After the trail was sufficiently cold, Balthazar would cut his loyal servants loose, and disappear with the seven winds. He didn't like traveling companions. It was one of the reasons he never worked with partners. Partners couldn't be trusted to do the right thing a hundred percent of the time. They slowed you down. They had differing opinions. When you enlisted them to help you pick pockets, they screwed up spilling wine on your targets and got you chased across aqueducts. Partners were bad news, even when they were in your debt.

The wise men were less than a mile from Bethlehem when the first whispers of trouble reached their ears. A faint rumble from the half-darkness ahead. A growing rumble, like the beating of hooves against earth. With it, the clanging of armor growing sharper against the air.

'What is that?' asked Gaspar.

Balthazar knew at once. Even before he saw the first shapes crest the hill on the road ahead, before he saw the outlines of swords and spears against the faint desert sky, he knew. They were finished.

Herod's troops were galloping south toward Bethlehem. Dozens of them, from the sound of it. Without discussion, Balthazar, Gaspar, and Melchyor veered their camels off of the road and into the desert on their right, making way for the approaching horsemen. They lifted the fronts of their shemaghs to cover their faces. This, Balthazar realized, was a useless piece of instinct.

As if the sight of three wise men riding beside the road isn't suspicious enough. As if anyone can even make our faces out in this light.

'What do we do?' asked Gaspar. 'There must be a hundred of them. We have no weapons.'

Balthazar was suddenly struck by how stupid they'd been to stick together. The soldiers would be looking for three men, and here they were, three of them. They'd been stupid to stop in Bethlehem. It was too close to the city. They should've gone into the desert. Yes, that star had made the night almost as bright as the day, but there was a lot more desert to cover than villages to search. Why hadn't he thought of that? Why hadn't they kept riding? Because they'd been tired? Was being tired worse than being dead?

'Balthazar, what do we do?'

If they took off now, they were sure to draw the army's attention. Running was an admission of guilt, an invitation to be chased. The only shot they had – and it was an absurdly long shot – was that the soldiers hadn't spotted them yet. That they'd be missed in the relative darkness of dawn.

'Keep riding.'

'But—'

'If they see us, we take off in different directions. Understand? Split them up, try and lose them in the desert. Melchyor? Do you understand?'

'Lose them in the desert . . .'

He wasn't listening. He was focused on the armored men riding south, kicking up a cloud of dark dust. The men who would reach them in a few seconds and tear them to pieces.

'Not yet,' said Balthazar. 'Nobody take off yet. Not unless they see us . . .'

Of course they were going to see them. They were barely fifty feet from the road, and silhouetted against the eastern sky, which was growing brighter by the minute.

Don't mind us, thought Balthazar. *Just three wise men riding along a dark road for no reason whatsoever . . .*

The army galloped by to their left. There was no question they were close enough to make out the shapes of the wise men, no question that some of the soldier's helmets were turning toward them – their eyes focusing in like arrows on a stretched bow. Balthazar gripped his camel's reins tightly, readied his right leg to deliver a swift kick to its side as soon as the first horse turned in his direction.

But none of them turned. They just kept on riding south toward Bethlehem. Balthazar couldn't believe it. They'd seen them; he was sure of it. They'd seen three wise men riding along the road at a strange hour, yet they hadn't even stopped to question them.

As the rumble of hooves passed by and grew weaker behind them, the wise men stopped and pointed their camels south. They watched in silent disbelief as that dark, dusty mass of horses and men, that creature, crawled along the road, toward the smoke of cooking fires and clay ovens in the distance.

'I don't understand,' said Balthazar.

'What is there to understand?' asked Gaspar. 'The Fates are with us!'

'But . . . they saw us.'

'We can discuss it on the way to Qumran! Let us go, now!'

Balthazar watched the creature slither along the road toward the north of Bethlehem, the dark blue of the heavens growing lighter by the second. For some reason, he could hear the faint, raspy voice of Herod in his skull. Raging at his advisors, shaking the walls of his throne room.

'Balthazar – to Qumran, quickly!'

Gaspar was right. What was there to understand? They'd been lucky, that's all. They could sit here and wonder why, or they could take advantage of that luck. The wise men pointed their camels north and rode toward their freedom, even as that faint voice echoed in Balthazar's brain. Deep down in the smooth-walled, iron-barred dungeons, where all the bad things belonged. He knew they'd been spotted. He'd felt those eyes on him. Those arrows . . .

They'd gone only a few feet when they heard something on the air. Something distant and shrill. Something that could almost be mistaken for the howl of a wild dog. But it was a scream. A woman's scream. Then another.

The wise men turned back and found the road empty, all traces of the creature gone. It had been absorbed into the village. Absorbed like blood into cloth. And somewhere beneath the smoke of cooking fires and clay ovens, it was making a woman scream.

'Balthazar . . . you don't think . . .'

Do I think the carpenter and his wife were right?

Herod was many things, but a murderer of infants? No. No man was capable of that. Not even the twisted, decayed wisp of a man he'd come face-to-face with at the

147

palace. And even if he was capable, he was too smart. There would be riots in the streets if word got out. A civil war. Herod was many things, but he was a politician first. He knew better.

But the voice . . . that voice faintly raging in the depths of Balthazar's brain told him otherwise.

'We're going back,' he said.

'Are you mad?'

'I just want to have a look, that's all.'

'The Judean Army is out there looking for us, and you want to go look for—'

'They saw us, Gaspar. They saw us and they weren't interested.'

'So?'

'They should've been. Three men on camels? Three men with their faces covered? They should've—'

He was cut off by another scream. Gaspar and Balthazar turned away from each other and looked back toward the village. This had been a different scream. The same woman, maybe – but a different scream altogether.

'Just a look,' said Balthazar. 'That's all.'

Balthazar kicked the side of his camel and took off down the road to Bethlehem. Gaspar and Melchyor shared a look behind his back, then followed. They were in his debt, after all.

The sun had finally pushed its head above the crest of the eastern hills – beginning a journey that would see it reach the pinnacle of the heavens before growing old and dying peacefully in the west. Its orange light spilled onto the wise men's backs as they looked down from a ridge on the east side of Bethlehem. From here, they could see down some of the wider cobblestoned streets in the village's center. But where those streets had been full and awake with the activities of daily life, they were now suddenly, eerily empty.

Empty except for a woman in dark robes, running barefoot toward them down one of the cobblestoned streets. Running faster than she'd ever run in her life, because nothing in her life had ever been as important. From their perch, Balthazar and the others could see why:

There was a baby in her arms.

Naked. Tiny. Held to its mother's breast as she ran from the horse. The black horse galloped after them with a soldier on its back, his armor clanging around him, his sword drawn.

Balthazar could hear that faint voice in the dungeon growing louder with each fall of the horse's hooves. He could hear the diseased rants of a king obsessed with power. A king who had once ordered his own wife and children put to death. Who'd turned on his own blood. *Why wouldn't he? If a man could murder his own children . . .*

The soldier swung his blade and struck the woman in the back. She fell forward, and though she tried with all of herself to hold on, the baby flew out of her grasp. It landed on the cobblestones and rolled for a few feet, too fragile, too new to brace itself against the impact. It came to a stop on its back, lay silent for a moment, then let out a terrible shriek, its lungs doing their work brilliantly. Its eyes shut. The woman responded with a shriek of her own, crawling toward it as the soldier dismounted and walked over to where the infant lay crying. Crying out for its mother's comforting touch.

The soldier stood over the baby a moment, then ran his sword through its belly.

The soldier ran his sword through its . . . the soldier ran his—

Stop.

It didn't happen that way at all. Balthazar's eyes had betrayed him. He was back in the world of infinite oceans and distant visions. No, it wasn't real. It couldn't be. Only . . . the cold, sick water in his blood told him that it was. That familiar feeling. The one that had sent him chasing after the flittering gold pendant.

The baby's cries sharpened, then stopped. Its arms and legs flailed weakly for a moment . . . then it was still. The soldier withdrew his blade. Wiped it on the bottom of his sandal.

He's dead, he's dead, he's dead . . .

The mother was still crawling across the cobblestones toward her son – screaming her throat raw. The soldier walked back to her casually – *you coward, you dog . . . you won't do it, I'll kill* – and ran the blade through her back. But she kept crawling. Crawling toward her son, so the soldier ran her through again. Her body tensed briefly and was still.

Gaspar and Melchyor couldn't believe their eyes. They were criminals. All of them, criminals. They'd seen their share of murder and cruelty. God knew they had.

But neither of them had ever seen anything like this. Neither of them had ever imagined it possible. They'd been rendered mute by the sight.

Balthazar's teeth clenched so tightly around his lower lip that blood had begun to pool in his mouth.

This simply wouldn't do.

The hell with Qumran. The hell with all of it. He decided to kill them. All of them. He was going to snuff out every one of their worthless lives, stand over every one of their dismembered bodies. He didn't know how he was going to do this, seeing as he didn't have any weapons and was outnumbered at least twenty to one, but he *knew*. His being was overflowing with something. Not rage. Something stronger than rage. Something more powerful and just.

The woman lifted her head as she lay dying in the street. The black horse was leaving with the man on its back. Riding away. Leaving them both to bleed in the street. She held her head up as high as she could, determined to look at her son one more time before she left this life.

The sun was rising. Its hard orange light had caught some of the infant's fine hair. Hair whose color would never change. His eyes closed, his chest no longer rising or falling. His hands. Tiny, delicate, cold. But there was something else. Something above him. Above all of Bethlehem in the early light. The woman thought she saw the shapes of three men on camelback, but it was hard to tell. The sun was directly behind them, creating a blinding halo around their heads. With her last thought, she wondered if they'd come to welcome her into the next world.

When Balthazar spoke at last, he had to will every syllable into existence.

'The two of you are in my debt?'

'Yes,' said Gaspar, 'but you can't be think—'

'The two of you are in my debt?'

Gaspar hesitated. He knew what was coming next.

'Yes . . .'

'With me.'

Balthazar kicked the side of his camel and rode down into the village. In accordance with the law of the desert, but against every one of their instincts, Gaspar and Melchyor followed him.

Joseph and Mary could hear the screams too. And though they didn't dare leave the stables to see, they knew. They knew it was happening. Right now. Right here in Bethlehem. They could hear the hooves beating against the road, the clanging of armor as it entered the village. It was too late to run. There were too many of them out there.

Joseph hurried Mary and the baby into one of the stable's tiny stalls. A black-and-white spotted goat protested as Joseph shoved it aside to make room for his wife, who lay beside it in the fetal position, the baby beside her. Joseph covered them with as much hay as he could – much of it matted together with dry manure. There was barely enough of it to cover them both, but it would have to do.

Having hidden them as best he could, Joseph slammed the stall shut and tried to look like he belonged, grabbing his old friend the pitchfork and pretending to clean up the stable. If the soldiers barged in, they'd see a man going about his work, nothing more. They'd leave him alone and look elsewhere. But if they didn't – if for some reason they decided to look around, God forbid, he could use the pitchfork to buy Mary a little time.

Joseph waited and prayed. Prayed that the soldiers wouldn't bother with the stable at all. *Why would they? It doesn't make sense. Stables are for animals, not infants.* He prayed that the shepherd who'd taken pity on them – who'd given them their lodging in the first place – wouldn't give them up now. Mostly, Joseph prayed that the baby wouldn't start crying. So far, remarkably, it had stayed happy and calm as it had been covered with hay and manure.

A lone soldier chased a twelve-year-old boy over the cobblestones near the village center. Not to slaughter him, but the baby brother he held in his arms. The baby he'd snatched away from his mother, certain that he could ran faster than she could. And he'd been right to do it. He was faster than she could have ever hoped to be. But he wasn't faster than the black horse with the clanging man on its back.

The soldier drew his sword as he closed in on the boy's

back, unaware that three men on camels were currently chasing him down the same street. Unaware that the Antioch Ghost was almost on him, kicking the side of his camel harder than he'd ever kicked anything in his life. Harder than he'd kicked his ill-fated camel in the Judean Desert. *Faster you piece of shit.* Gaspar and Melchyor riding close behind him . . .

The camel responded, galloping across the cobblestones and pulling up just behind the black horse. Close enough to strike with a sword, if he'd only had one. Balthazar settled for the next best thing: He grabbed the back of the soldier's collar and yanked him off his saddle and onto the cobblestones, where he was promptly trampled by Gaspar's and Melchyor's camels. They hadn't meant to run him over – they simply couldn't stop in time. But now they did, pulling up on their reins and circling back to inspect the damage.

Balthazar stopped his own camel and watched the soldier's horse gallop on for a hundred more feet, stop, then trot in a circle, unsure what to do with itself. He watched as the boy kept on running with the infant in his arms, unaware that the menace behind him was gone.

Run, boy, and don't stop running until you drop from exhaustion.

The soldier was lying motionless on his back, a deep dent in his breastplate where a camel's foot had struck his chest. He was older than most men of his lowly rank, a tinge of gray at his temples. He was coughing up blood, the result of a splintered rib cage and torn organs, Balthazar guessed. *Good.* His left arm had been mangled beneath another camel foot, flattened below the elbow and rendered useless. He writhed, moaned.

Good . . . I hope it's the worst pain you've ever known.

Balthazar jumped down off his camel and walked toward him. He walked calmly, like the dead man he was. He stepped on the soldier's wrist, leaned over, and took his sword away. It wasn't much to look at. Standard issue for a low-ranking Judean soldier. But it would do.

Balthazar held the tip of the sword over the soldier's throat.

'P-please,' said the soldier, struggling for breath. 'D-don't—'

'Don't what?' asked Balthazar, cupping a hand to his ear.

'Don't k-kill . . .'

'Don't kill you? Is that what you're trying to say?'

'Don't k-kill me . . .'

The soldier was sobbing. Balthazar was almost embarrassed for him.

'And if you'd caught up with that boy and baby, would you have shown it the same mercy?'

'Ple—'

Balthazar pushed down until he felt the 'pop' of the blade going through the soldier's Adam's apple. The man clutched at it with his right hand – the blood bubbling up on either side of it. He tried frantically to pull it out of his throat, but Balthazar only pushed harder and twisted the blade, tearing an even bigger hole open. There was that same shade of white . . . that same mask of fear . . . that same dreadful realization that he was going to die.

Good, thought Balthazar. *I hope you're afraid . . .*

Gaspar and Melchyor had dismounted behind him, watching the soldier die on his back. His limbs moved weakly, then not at all. Balthazar lifted his eyes from the dying soldier's face, drawn by a renewed clanging of armor in the distance. Looking up, he saw five Judean soldiers emerge from a house at the far end of the street, their swords stained with blood, a mother's and father's screams coming from inside. The soldiers were halfway to their waiting horses when one of them caught sight of Balthazar standing over the body of their dying comrade. Upon bearing witness to this tragedy, the soldier and his four companions reached the same conclusion that Balthazar had only minutes earlier:

This simply wouldn't do.

Balthazar watched them charge – so incensed, so focused on righting this injustice, that they'd forgotten to bring their horses with them. If the wise men mounted their camels now, they could escape, no question. But Balthazar hadn't ridden into Bethlehem to run. He'd come to kill every last one of them, or die trying.

He pulled the sword out of the dying soldier's throat and walked to the middle of the street to meet them. The Judeans had every advantage. Numbers. Armor. But Balthazar didn't care. He would stand his ground. He would take them all on.

'Give me the sword,' said Melchyor.

Balthazar didn't flinch. His kept his eyes fixed on the approaching men.

'I'll do it.'

'Give . . . me . . . the . . . sword.'

There was something about Melchyor's voice. A different quality. Those words hadn't come from the quiet simpleton he'd met in the dungeon, or the harmless cherub who cooed and made stupid faces at the infant when they'd left the stable.

Balthazar looked to Gaspar. *Is he serious?* Gaspar nodded.

'Give him the sword,' he said.

Balthazar didn't exactly know why he handed their only sword to the shortest, fattest member of their group. But he did. Somehow, it just felt like the right thing to do. Melchyor gripped it in his fingers. Swung it from side to side, getting a sense of its weight. He ran his fingers along its blade, getting a sense of its power. Speaking to it. It wasn't much of a sword, but it would do.

After all, there were only five of them.

When the soldiers were almost upon them, Melchyor held the sword out in front of his body and charged. The Judeans were taken aback – even amused by the sight of the little Greek coming at them all alone. The soldier who was farthest out in front of the pack planted his feet and readied his blade, turning his body to the side in a classic fencing stance. He was ready for anything. Especially the mad charge of a little man.

A second later, his left leg was gone, and he was crying out from the ground.

The little Greek had rolled forward at the last second and swung his blade across the soldier's firmly planted lead leg. He'd never even gotten a chance to fight back.

And as the soldier lay there on his side, feeling for a leg that was no longer there, his four comrades weren't getting their chances, either.

One by one, Melchyor spun and struck his way through the soldiers – cutting them down as if they were following his instructions: striking him when he wanted them to strike, leaving themselves defenseless at exactly the moment he was ready to attack.

The second soldier twisted his torso, winding up for a ferocious swing. But with his side momentarily exposed, Melchyor shoved the blade through the space between his front and back armor plates, upward through his intestines.

His sword was still in the second soldier's gut when the third came at him, swinging for his head. Using his short stature to his advantage, Melchyor ducked beneath the blade, yanked his sword free, and struck back at the off-balance opponent, cutting the soldier's throat with such force that only his spine stopped the blade from going all the way through.

The fourth and fifth soldiers attacked together, bringing their swords down on Melchyor's head in unison. Melchyor used his own sword to shield himself, then did something incredibly stupid. Something that ran counter to everything anyone had ever been taught about sword fighting:

He dropped to his knees, as if in prayer.

The soldiers kept striking. But their blows were different. Weaker, clumsier. And now Balthazar saw the brilliance of what Melchyor had done. The Judeans wore large steel breastplates to protect their organs. Plates that ran from their necks to their belts. And while these were great for protecting their innards during an upright assault, they made it difficult for them to bend forward and robbed any strike below the waist of its power. All Melchyor had to do was keep blocking their awkward blows and wait for one of them to make a mistake.

The fourth soldier made just such a mistake, leaning too far forward and falling on his face to Melchyor's left. A second later, he paid for that mistake with his life, as Melchyor drove the sword into the back of his neck, severing his brain stem.

Now it was just one-on-one. The last soldier wasn't quite as hopeless a swordsman as his companions, but he wasn't particularly good, either. After becoming the only man to make contact with Melchyor's body – landing a graze across his shoulder – he went for the kill, thrusting forward. But his sword was too far out in front of his body, his feet too far apart. Melchyor knocked the soldier's weapon out of his hands and thrust his own forward. The fifth soldier held his hands up in an attempt to block it, but Melchyor's sword simply went through his left hand, pinning it to the soldier's face an instant before the tip of the blade lodged in his brain. Melchyor held it there until he felt the soldier's full weight hanging dead in the air, then pulled it out, letting his useless body fall to the ground.

Now it was Balthazar who'd been rendered mute.

The little Greek was the best swordsman he'd ever seen. Quicker, more powerful than any man had a right to be.

There couldn't be a doubt about it. Criminals were a bragging breed, but this had been no boast. This was *fact*.

'I told you,' said Gaspar. 'Best in the empire.'

A second ago, there'd been five soldiers bearing down on them. Now there were five men lying in the street – two of them dying, the other three dead. There were so many questions. So many tricks to learn. But they'd have to wait. The screams of women and children were still coming from every corner of the village.

Balthazar and Gaspar each grabbed a sword from one of the dead soldiers, then mounted their camels and rode as fast as they could.

Joseph's prayers weren't answered. There were soldiers outside. Dismounting. Any second, they'd cross the threshold.

Had the shepherd been forced to give them up? Had the criminals sold them out for a reward? It didn't matter. Nothing mattered now. Nothing but the plan. Joseph was a simple shepherd, cleaning up his stable. No, everything would be fine. They'd question him; they'd leave. What use was there in looking around unless you enjoyed the smell of goats and their filth? All he had to do was stay calm. Not come off as nervous or jittery. All the baby had to do was stay quiet.

There were three of them. Two younger, one older, the latter with a more intricate helmet and breastplate. An officer of some kind, if Joseph had to guess. They entered and took in what little there was to take.

'Who are you?' asked the officer.

'A simple shepherd, sir. This is my stable. These are my goats.'

The officer examined Joseph's face for a moment, then looked around again. It wasn't much of a stable. Hardly worth his time. There were a thousand places to hide in Bethlehem. Almost any of them would've been more appealing than this one. What would a baby be doing in a stable, anyway?

Satisfied that only the lowliest forms of life would stoop to sleeping in such a place, the officer motioned to the other soldiers to follow him out.

Joseph felt a wave of relief wash over him. He'd done well. He hadn't come across as nervous or jittery. The baby hadn't—

'What was that?'

The officer spun around. He'd nearly been out the door when a squeal had filled the little stable. Not the bleating of a goat. Something different.

'Just a goat, sir.'

The officer was on the verge of convincing himself that it was nothing, when another squeal came from one of the stalls on the right. This one almost a laugh.

No, Lord . . . please . . .

Under a thin covering of hay and manure, Mary had her hand pressed to the baby's mouth, trying desperately to stifle her son's cooing.

'It's just the animals, I assure you.' Joseph had lost his calm. He could feel himself beginning to sweat, feel himself getting nervous and jittery.

'Hold him.'

The other two grabbed Joseph and forced the pitch-fork from his hand. They held him against the wall while the officer drew his sword and began opening stall doors.

'I'm telling you, it's just the anim—'

'Quiet!' The officer turned to his men. 'If he talks again, kill him.'

One of the soldiers drew his sword and held it against Joseph's throat. The officer turned back to the stall door. The last one on the right side of the stable. He opened it . . .

There, beneath a black and white spotted goat and a thin layer of hay and manure, was a girl covering a baby's mouth with her hand. Mary screamed as the officer pulled the back of her robes, trying to yank her away.

Joseph pulled free of the soldier's grasp, ran at the officer, and jumped on his back. He got an arm around his throat and pulled as hard as he could, knowing that he'd be run through with a sword from behind any second. It didn't matter. Let them run him through. Until they did, he planned to keep squeezing – keep choking this man until his last breath, in the hopes that Mary might free herself and run.

The officer dropped his sword and grabbed at Joseph's arm with both hands. He managed to pry one under Joseph's arm and pull it loose. His breath restored, he found the strength to throw Joseph over his back and into the stall with his wife and baby. Quickly, the officer looked down for the sword he'd dropped . . .

But it was gone.

He turned and found himself face-to-face with two men he'd never seen before. Two men who were standing on either side of the Antioch Ghost. The same Antioch Ghost he'd captured and dragged into Herod's Palace from Bethel. The same one who was supposed to have been his ticket to a better life. He also saw the bodies of his men on the stable floor, their throats cut.

'But you're . . . you're supposed to be dead,' said the captain.

But I am, thought Balthazar. *Don't you understand? I am dead.*

Balthazar cut the captain's throat.

Joseph climbed onto the back of Melchyor's camel. Gaspar made his animal kneel and helped Mary onto its back, the infant in her arms. Balthazar rode alone, with a sword in each hand.

They could make it if they went now. If they crossed the road and kept going, straight into the desert. But those screams continued to echo through Bethlehem. There were still dozens of soldiers out there, searching from house to house. Slaughtering children who'd barely known the earth. Mothers and fathers who were giving the last of themselves to save them. Now, at this very moment.

That screaming wouldn't stop. Not until time itself stopped. You couldn't get sounds like that out of your ears. Not completely. Never completely. They would always be there, faint whispers in that underground dungeon, where all the bad things belonged. Balthazar knew this. Just as he knew that they could make it if they went now. Just as he knew that saving all of them was impossible. And still, he couldn't bring himself to move.

Gaspar could see it on his face. In the way he clenched the reins until his knuckles turned white, staring south into the village. 'Balthazar . . . we can either die trying to save them all, or we can save this one while there is still time.'

Gaspar was right, of course. Balthazar had faced this choice before. The choice between dying a noble death and living to fight another cowardly day. The temptation to die could be overwhelming. The temptation to let the anger wash over you, to baptize you into a new, glorious existence. Burning briefly and brightly. But it was just an illusion. For no matter how many you killed in those final moments, it was never as many as you would have killed over time. That was the trick of it. The longer you lived, the more of them you could eventually kill. It was easy to forget a truth like that with the anger burning a hole in you.

There was still time. He would save this one. He would fight another cowardly day. And he would find a way, someday, to burn their whole world to the ground. Maybe even find a way to get those screams out of his ears. Balthazar swore this to himself and kicked the side of his camel.

They would ride straight into the desert this time. They would push their camels as fast as they would go, and they wouldn't let up until they reached Qumran. The Essenes would keep them safe for at least a night or—

'You! Stop!'

Balthazar turned back. A pair of horsemen had spotted them from the south, one of average height and build, the other simply gigantic. Both were chasing them, side by side, up the road from Bethlehem with their swords drawn.

'Keep going!' said Balthazar to the others. 'Stay with them!'

He turned his camel around and charged at the two horsemen – his left hand on the reins, his right behind his back. He would save this one. Gaspar and Melchyor would keep it safe, and he'd catch up with them in the desert as soon as this was done.

Balthazar rode straight at them, his camel's nose pointed directly between their horses. He'd ride straight into them if he had to, but he wasn't going to flinch. The soldiers were less than twenty feet from impact when they realized this and turned their horses to either side to go around him. As they did, Balthazar took his left hand off the reins, reached behind his back, and grabbed the two swords – holding them out to his sides like wings. *Like a man with wings.* Knocking both soldiers off their horses and into the dirt.

He circled back and dismounted, a sword in either hand. The smaller one was still trying to stand up, still trying to shake the impact off. But the bigger one was on his feet and on him in a hurry. With a low grunt, he ran at Balthazar and thrust the point of his sword toward his chest. But Balthazar was able to move out of its path and make him miss, tripping him in the process.

The smaller was up on his feet again, swinging wildly at Balthazar while his partner recovered. But the fall had taken a lot out of him, and Balthazar cut him to shreds, avoiding his armor and slicing deep gashes in his bare arms. When the bigger came at him again, he took a cue from Melchyor – dropping to his knees and hacking away at both of their legs, until the smaller fell onto his back and the bigger retreated out of reach.

'You tell Herod,' said Balthazar to the bigger man, 'that the Antioch Ghost is laughing at him.'

The soldier's already fearful eyes grew even wider.

'You tell him I'm laughing. . . . You tell him I'll stand over his grave.'

The soldier considered this, then ran back toward the village, determined to fight another cowardly day. Balthazar watched him go a moment – a giant running on shredded legs – then turned his attention to the soldier squirming below him. The soldier pulling himself along the ground despite the deep gashes in his limbs. He was trying to get away, and yet he knew there was no chance of that happening.

'We . . . we were ordered . . .'

'You were WHAT?'

'We were ord-ordered to do it, by Herod himself.'

'Ordered to do what?'

'To . . . k-kill all the male infants of Bethlehem.'

Balthazar raised the sword above his head and held it

there. He gripped the handle's leather straps so tightly that his entire arm shook.

'Any man who follows an order like that doesn't deserve to walk the earth.'

Balthazar brought it down and struck the soldier's face with the broad side of the blade. The first blow broke the soldier's nose, cracking a dam behind his nostrils and sending a flood of red over his chin. The second broke his left eye socket and all but liquefied the eye inside it. Before Balthazar could land a third blow, the soldier's instinct finally caught up with his shock, and he held his hands out to protect himself. Balthazar pulled the sword back and swung across his body, striking the soldier's left wrist. The hand attached to it fell toward the road but was caught by a few strands of sinew and skin before it landed. Balthazar resumed striking him in the face, again and again and—

His jaw's broken you should probably stop hitting him he's unconscious Balthazar you can stop hitting him now his teeth are shattered stop Balthazar he's dead he has to be dead by now what are you doing Balthazar why are you still hitting him there go the brains out the top of his skull stop Balthazar he's not the one who did it I know but he's the same he's just like the one who killed—

A hand grabbed Balthazar's wrist from behind as he raised the sword for another strike. He spun around, ready to kill whoever dared touch him. Ready to bash their brains right out of their ears.

But it wasn't a Judean soldier. It was the carpenter, looking down at him from the back of Melchyor's camel.

'He's dead.'

They were all looking down at him. All but Mary, who'd turned away from the gruesome sight with the baby held tightly to her chest. Balthazar yanked his wrist out of Joseph's grasp.

'Others will be coming,' said Joseph. 'We have to go.'

Once again, he knew. He knew they had to go . . . but he couldn't get his feet to move. In fact, he couldn't get anything to move. Balthazar was having trouble catching his breath. He felt faint. Weak. They were all looking at him with strange expressions . . .

'Balthazar . . . you're bleeding.'

Who'd said that? The carpenter? Gaspar?

He looked down at his robes. There was a growing patch of blood on the right side of his chest. He pulled them apart and saw the wound. A puncture from a sword between his ribs. With his every breath, minuscule air bubbles formed in the bright, rich blood running from the wound.

The soldier hadn't missed.

The sun had barely crested the eastern hills, but Balthazar could feel it setting already. Night was coming, and with it, some much-needed rest. For a moment, he thought that the strange, brilliant star in the east had returned.

This time, he was the only one who saw it.

The Dream

'Get up,' he said. 'Take the child and his mother and escape to Egypt. Stay there until I tell you, for Herod is going to search for the child to kill him.'

—*Matthew 2:13*

I

Six fugitives rode east, into the rising desert sun. Only four of them were conscious.

They rode over a lifeless planet of rocky hills and jagged ravines, of beiges and browns tangled together in a senseless embrace, blending into one as they approached a horizon they would never reach. It was a place devoid of vibrancy. A place where joy had been banished. Even the cloudless blue sky seemed drained of its color.

Balthazar was draped facedown over the back of Gaspar's camel. He was pale, drenched in sweat. Blood continued to seep from the hole in his chest and pool on the animal's fur. Gaspar kept one hand on his reins and one hand on Balthazar's back, trying to keep him from bouncing off as he led the party over uneven terrain. Melchyor rode behind them, a sword hanging at his side, the blood of five men still wet on his robes. Joseph was last, with Mary behind him, cradling the sleeping baby in her left arm and clinging to her husband's robes with her right.

Gaspar didn't know the way to Qumran. He didn't

know the Judean Desert very well at all, just the roads that had been beaten through it by time and desire. The roads that connected Jerusalem to Jericho, Jericho to Antioch, Antioch to the rest of the known world. But the desert was a different story.

Out here, spinning columns of dust could rise without warning, dancing across the earth and blinding all they touched. Out here, scorpions and snakes waited to poison the unfortunate souls who crossed their path, and the nearest water was often days away. Heat, exhaustion, and thirst had a way of burrowing under a man's skin. Of eating away at his will, until the urge to lie down and sleep in the blinding sun seemed rational. The urge to remove those stifling robes and walk naked seemed wise. There were countless stories of men drinking mouthfuls of sand, tearing at their own flesh and cupping mouthfuls of blood to their cracked lips to quench the thirst that had driven them mad. There was a saying in Judea: 'The desert is filled with the bones of strong men.'

The hills became steeper as the fugitives continued west. The desert slowly rose up on either side, enveloping them in rock. Swallowing them. Like drops of water being squeezed out of an ocean and into a narrow channel, the fugitives were funneled into a ravine – a giant fracture in the bones of the earth, twisting its way through the twisted beiges and browns.

They'd followed the ravine for just over a mile, steering their camels through its jagged walls, when the baby started crying, and Mary realized that it had been hours since he'd been fed.

They stopped and sat in the shade offered by the rock walls around them – Mary with the infant hidden beneath her robes, Joseph beside her, taking small sips from a stitched leather canteen. Gaspar had lowered Balthazar to the ground, washed his wound out with water. But no sooner had he wiped away the clot than blood began to run out of the puncture again. It was hopeless.

None of them spoke a word. Melchyor sat cross-legged, drawing pictures in the sand with his sword. If he felt any lingering effects of what he'd just seen, any remorse over the lives he'd taken, his face didn't betray it. He seemed completely divorced from the world around him, completely at peace with his situation.

Gaspar, however, was clearly distressed. Not by the visions of slaughtered infants. He'd stored those away in a place where they could never be found, down in the tombs where he kept all the wretched things he'd seen and done. Rather, he was distressed by facts.

The fact that no road in Judea was safe to travel. The fact that he didn't know the desert well enough to disappear into it or survive off of it. The fact that his best chance of escape was currently lying on the ground, dying. The fact that they would run out of water in a matter of hours.

And then what? The carpenter and his wife would only slow them down. The baby would die from exposure or dehydration within a day or two, followed by the girl, until all that was left were three madmen cupping mouthfuls of blood to their cracked lips – that was, assuming Herod's men didn't find and slaughter them first, which was more likely than any other scenario. It was hopeless. All of it.

It was Balthazar who finally broke the silence with a series of wheezing, unconscious coughs. When the fit was over, Joseph could see blood running from his mouth. His color was getting worse. He was beginning to shiver.

'Is he going to die?' asked Joseph.

'Yes,' said Gaspar.

Joseph was struck by his matter-of-factness. It was as if he'd asked about the color of Balthazar's robes, and not his life.

'"Yes"? That's it?'

'Yes.'

'Isn't there something we can do?'

'I have seen men with this wound before. There is nothing that can be done. He will not live to see nightfall.'

'But he saved our lives. All of our lives. We're in his debt.'

'And that is why I carry him with me, instead of leaving him to die alone.'

'Carrying him on the back of a camel isn't going to help him. There has to be something we can—'

'I told you he is DEAD!'

The word bounced off the walls of the ravine and into the unknown twists ahead. It was followed by another considerable silence. Only the sounds of the camels shifting their weight on their feet, of Melchyor scraping his sword through the dirt.

'After what we have done,' said Gaspar, 'Herod will send all of Judea after us. He is dead, and we are alive. We still have a chance. He does not.'

'No,' said Mary.

Gaspar had almost forgotten the girl was there. He considered her with his deep-set eyes. She was so slight, so weak. He could break her arms and legs like pieces of charred firewood if he wanted to.

'He came back for us,' she said. 'I won't just sit here and watch him die.'

'I told you . . . there is nothing we can do for him.'

'Yes,' said Mary, 'there is.'

Gaspar had no idea what she meant. Joseph wasn't sure either, until she turned to him and said, 'Zachariah.'

When Mary was very young, her uncle Zachariah had been a physician – sewing up wounds and treating coughs in the little village of Emmaus, ten miles northwest of Jerusalem. He was in his seventies now, enjoying a quiet life with his wife, Elizabeth, and their young son. To Mary's knowledge, he hadn't so much as wrapped a bandage in over ten years. And his own health had been in decline. But they had to try.

Mary turned back to Gaspar. 'I know someone who might be able to help him. A physician. A relative who can be trusted.'

'Where is he?'

'In Emmaus.'

Gaspar shook his head.

'It is too far.'

'We can be there in two hours if we take the roads.'

'The roads? Have you not listened? Every soldier in the Judean Army will be on the roads looking for us.'

'The roads leading in and out of Bethlehem, yes. And when they don't find us there, they'll start looking on the other roads and in the desert. But not in a little village like Emmaus. Not yet.'

I could break your bones like charred firewood . . .

'We can stay out here until we're dead, or we can try to reach Emmaus – where there's food and water. Where there's a place to hide and a chance to save him.'

'If we do not get killed first.'

'Just get us that far. Get us to Emmaus. We can take care of ourselves from there.'

Gaspar tried to think of a better option. But he knew she was right. If they hid in the desert, they'd all be dead in a matter of days. If they tried to reach the village, there was a very good chance they'd run into soldiers on the roads. But at least they'd have a fighting chance.

'You said it yourself,' said Mary. 'You're in his debt. We all are.'

Balthazar broke the silence with another fit of coughing. Gaspar looked at him. The mighty Antioch Ghost. The man who'd saved his neck.

II

Balthazar was suddenly aware of being carried. Held aloft by a pair of arms wrapped around his chest, held by a man with broad white wings that beat in a gentle rhythm above. A man whose face he couldn't see but somehow *knew*. There was no fear of this stranger, no fear of being dropped. There was only the wind in his ears and the beating of wings.

There was a city below them in the desert. A city of tents, gathered at the base of a great mountain. Tens of thousands – maybe hundreds of thousands of people – moving around in a circle, dancing. They danced around something large, something shining and gold. Balthazar wanted nothing more than to be one of them. To have a closer look at the large, shiny golden thing and see if there were pieces to be pulled off and hidden in his robes. But this wasn't where the Man With Wings was taking him.

They flew past the great mountain and its dancing masses, descending closer to the desert's surface, until sand became sea in the blink of an eye. Not the strange, endless sea of time and space that Balthazar had seen the universe reflected in, but an actual, earthly body of water. They moved over the face of this water, faster than Balthazar thought it possible for men to move without having their bodies ripped apart by the force of the wind.

They flew until the water became shore, and shore became desert, and desert became a gleaming city of the sun. A city of hieroglyphs and temples, of obelisks and pyramids. He'd seen this place with his living eyes, too. He'd looked up at these three sisters – these pyramids that made fools of empires with their splendor. But he never imagined he'd be looking at them from above as he did now.

The Man With Wings set Balthazar gently down on the top of one of these pyramids, the largest of the three. The tallest structure in the world, as it had been for more than 2,500 years. But the pyramid was falling apart, the white stones of its four sides having crumbled away over the centuries. Some sections were still perfectly smooth. Others had broken loose and tumbled into the sands below, exposing the darker stone blocks beneath.

When those white wings settled and tucked behind his back, Balthazar saw the man's face for the first time. The strength in his legs left him at the sight. He wept, his body shuddering with his sobs. Balthazar couldn't remember the last time he'd cried this hard. He couldn't remember the last time he'd seen anything so beautiful.

'How?' he asked through his tears.

The Man With Wings extended his arms and held his hands out for Balthazar to see. The hands he'd been holding Balthazar with. They were stained red.

Balthazar looked down through his tears and found the robes above his chest drenched in dark blood. He pulled them apart, panicked, sure he'd find a grotesque wound beneath. But there was nothing. Nothing but a small scratch in the center of his chest. He looked up to see if the Man With Wings had any explanation. But he was gone. Not a trace of him in the sky. Balthazar was alone on top of the world.

Something hit his foot. A droplet.

He looked at his chest again. The scratch was beginning to bleed. Just a few drops, like the remnants of the tears on his cheeks. But it was growing. Growing into a slow trickle, then a steady stream – the blood running down his chest onto his stomach, pooling in his navel and spilling over. A red river.

The scratch was slowly ripping itself open. Skin tearing itself apart like a leather hide, exposing muscle and ribs and lungs. Tearing away until his heart could be seen beneath, beating faster . . . faster. Balthazar grabbed the two halves of his chest, trying to pull them back together. Trying to keep everything where it belonged.

'No!'

His ribs began to splay open, each one awakening and extending outward like the legs of a white spider. Balthazar let go of his skin and tried to hold them down. If the ribs went, then the organs would follow. Everything would come spilling out of him, and he would be left here for all time – a pile of bones and organs and loose skin on top of the world. He pushed down as hard as he could, but the spider wouldn't be denied its freedom. As he pushed, Balthazar saw his fingernails begin to lift themselves out of their beds and the skin on his fingers peel away, leaving the arteries beneath naked and pulsing with each beat of his heart.

He could feel the same thing happening to his toes . . . his feet. He could feel his eyelids peeling back and could see the blood begin to run over his corneas.

Balthazar was falling down the side of the great pyramid. Tumbling down, just as so many smooth pieces of stone had over the centuries, leaving a trail of muscle and sinew and blood and bone as he broke apart. Every vein unraveling as he went, pulling free of his body like the roots of a great tree torn out of the earth.

By the time he reached the sand, there was nothing left but his clothes.

Zachariah was far too old to be cutting into people. Too old to perform the kind of surgery this man required. His vision wasn't what it used to be. His hands shook. But what choice was there? What other surgeon could see him in time or be trusted to harbor the fugitives who brought him in?

Joseph held the lamp over the man's chest. The Ethiopian and the Greek sat near the door, ready to help if Zachariah needed them. His niece, Mary, waited in the next room with the baby. She wasn't one for the sight of blood, and there was a lot of it here. The man had been stabbed, and the blade had gone into his right lung.

'Is he suffocating?' asked Joseph.

'Drowning,' said Zachariah as he worked.

'Drowning? But how can he be—'

'Air seeps in through the wound, air presses down on the lung, blood gets trapped in the lung and drowns him from the inside. We drain the air? The lung inflates, the blood drains and maybe, maybe, maybe he lives. Now be quiet and let me work.'

His wife, Elizabeth, assisted her husband as he worked, just as she had twenty years ago, when he'd been a spritely fifty-seven and she'd been a thirty-six-year-old widow. Brown eyed with hair to match. Childless and beautiful. Meeting her had been the wonder of Zachariah's life. A miracle. And though the years had proven her barren, he'd treasured every moment of their marriage – happy to have a companion in his dwindling years.

But then, seven years ago, when he was seventy and she forty-nine, Elizabeth had become pregnant. Zachariah had been doubtful at first. Slow to receive the gift that God had given him. But her belly had continued to grow, and she'd given birth to a healthy baby boy, despite the fact that she was beyond the childbearing age. Another miracle. A miracle they'd named John.

Zachariah slowly, carefully inserted a small metal tube into the wound – every ounce of his concentration devoted to keeping his hands steady. These were the dangerous seconds. The ones that would determine whether the patient lived or died. Do it right, and a hiss of air would escape through the tube, followed immediately by a good deal of blood. With the lung reinflated, the patient could be sewn up and – God willing –

returned to health. Do it wrong, and you only made him drown faster.

Elizabeth kept a cloth pressed firmly around the tube, soaking up what little blood trickled out. She'd seen her husband try this only once before, on a local man who'd been stabbed by a Judean officer for spitting in the street. That had been fifteen years ago, before Zachariah's hands shook. Before his eyes had become clouded over. And that patient had died right here in this room. On this table.

She'd been happy when he'd decided to give up medicine, to live these last years for himself. For his family. She was happy that John still had a father who could impart wisdom. Teach him how to be a man. Especially since she alone knew that her son was different. That he was destined to do something extraordinary.

Shortly before John was born, a man with glorious white wings had come to her in a dream. He'd told her that her conception was indeed a miracle and that her child's birth would herald the coming of the Messiah. 'The son of God shall walk the earth,' he'd said, 'born of another in your house. And your son shall be his prophet.'

John waited outside with Mary. She sat on a small bench near the closed door. John stood beside her, staring at the swaddled infant in her arms. The infant was staring back, looking up with his new, blue eyes. Eyes that couldn't make out anything beyond the length of his arms. Yet he stared intently at the face over him now. Fascinated by it. Drawn to it. John stared back with equal fascination. He'd seen other babies before. He had other cousins. But there was something different about this one. He felt a strange, powerful kinship with it. A vague sadness too.

'May I hold him?'

Mary wasn't sure. He was too young to be trusted with something so fragile. But there was something about him. Something that seemed older than his six years.

'Very carefully, and only for a minute.'

She handed him over, gently, and John took him with equal care. He cradled the infant. Held him up to his shoulder and rubbed his hand on his back. He rocked the baby gently back and forth, just as his mother had taught him to do. And when the infant rested his head against his shoulder, John tilted his own to meet it.

It was the same head that Herod's son, Antipas, would order cut off decades later, when he was known as John the Baptist. But there was none of that now. None of the toil and death that would follow both of them in days both near and distant. None of the same and famine. There was only the quiet of their breath and the sound of the unconscious man gasping for his in the next room.

Balthazar opened his eyes and screamed, but the sound was choked back by water; the air in his lungs carried in bubbles. He was drowning. Struggling to reach the sunlight that filtered down through the silt. With a last kick of his legs, he broke the surface and sucked in a mix of water and air, which brought sharp, painful coughs but gave him the strength to swim to the nearest bank. He dragged himself onto the sand with his fingertips, still coughing up the water in his lungs.

Fingertips.

Balthazar examined his hands, expecting to see the skin peeled away and the veins unraveled. But they were whole. Every part of him was. With his breath coming steadily again, he lifted his head and took in his surroundings through strands of wet, black hair. Above him, only feet from the river's edge, were rows of towering columns and stone pharaohs – each one intricately carved, each telling a different story about the triumphs of a different pharaoh.

To his left, Balthazar could see a wooden barge sailing down the Nile in the midday sun, loaded with goods. On the opposite bank, he could see fishermen casting their lines, some of them resting in the shade of palm trees, just as he and Abdi had years ago.

'Hey!' he shouted across the river. 'Hey, over here!'

Though they were well within range of his voice, the fishermen ignored the soaked man standing on the opposite bank, just as they'd ignored him when he was drowning.

But they didn't ignore the fish.

One by one, fish began to float to the surface – some thrashing and panicked, others simply belly-up. Before Balthazar could process what this was, one of the fishermen, who'd been wading in the river up to his knees, suddenly let out a scream and hurried back to the shore. Balthazar could see blisters on his legs when he emerged, just as he could see steam rising from the water's surface. The river was beginning to boil. Tigerfish, catfish, and perch floating to the surface by the hundreds. Cooked alive by the river itself.

Night was falling unnaturally fast, the sun retreating toward the west, frightened off by what it saw below. The world was growing dark before Balthazar's eyes, and the Nile with it. But not for lack of light. The river was turning dark because it was bleeding.

A red river.

Only the moon loomed above now, casting its full gray glow over Egypt. But there was something different about it tonight. Something wrong. There were strange lines in its surface, and they were growing wider.

The moon was breaking apart.

Like a gray plate slowly shattering against a black marble floor, pieces began to break off and fall from the heavens, each shard the size of a mountain. The pieces began to rain down on the opposite bank – whole cities falling from the sky, making the earth tremble with each impossible impact. Terrified fishermen ran for their lives as one of the pieces crashed down, less than a mile from where they stood. But Balthazar didn't move. He *knew*. He knew this was all just an illusion. There was no need to run, not even as another sliver grew bigger in the night sky above his head.

Trust yourself, Balthazar.

And he did. But when the sliver was close enough for

Balthazar to see the outlines of craters in its surface, his feet overruled his brain and began to move on their own. Slowly at first, then into a full sprint, up the riverbank and into the desert beyond.

He felt the earth shake as the sliver collided with the desert behind him, just like the earthquakes he remembered in Antioch, only a thousand times more powerful. Behind him, a wave of debris lifted off the desert floor, carried by the shock wave of the impact. There were many things a man could outrun, especially a man of Balthazar's speed. But a shock wave of the moon and earth colliding wasn't on the list. The only thing Balthazar could do was hit the ground and try to ride it out. He dove onto his belly and lay as flat as he could against the sand, covering the top of his head with his arms.

The first flecks of debris pelted his legs from behind. The stinging grains of the sandstorms he'd weathered before. And then the wave. Slamming into him like a giant fist. The noise deafening. The debris tearing away at his clothes and skin.

The pressure sucking the air out of his lungs. If there was a God, this would be the sound of his voice.

Then it was gone. And the desert with it.

Balthazar lifted his head and found himself in a vast room of brightly colored walls, their surfaces smoother than he thought possible. Smoother even than glass. Three of those walls were purple: the ones behind him, in front of him, and to his left. The wall on his right, however, was pink. A color he'd rarely seen in the empire, except on the blushing faces of a few fair-skinned Roman women. The floor was an untarnished white. A white table before him, a white chair beneath him, and a white ceiling high, high above him.

A man stood on the far side of the room with his back to Balthazar. A man with long gray hair and matching gray robes. He looked to be pouring something from a clay jug with his left hand and holding a wooden walking staff in his right.

The gray-haired man turned, a wooden cup of water in his left hand. His face was older than Balthazar had expected. Almost unnaturally old, with deep bags beneath his cloudy eyes. His skin had clearly seen its share of sun over the years; his hands had known their share of labor. The old man shuffled across the clean white floor and took a seat across the table. He searched Balthazar with those cloudy eyes for a moment, then slid the cup across the table.

'Drink.'

He did. The cool, clear water was, perhaps, the best he'd ever had. And when he'd had his fill, Balthazar wiped his mouth and spoke. 'Who are you?'

'A messenger.'

'Whose?'

The old man smiled at him. It was a familiar smile. One Balthazar loathed more than any other. The smug, self-satisfied smile of a man who thinks himself wise.

'Fine,' said Balthazar. 'Then what's the message?'

'You mustn't leave the child to die.'

After being torn inside out on top of a pyramid, seeing

fish boil in a river of blood, and running from the shattered moon, Balthazar had almost forgotten about the baby.

'I didn't leave him. I saved him.'

'Not yet. You have to stay with him a while longer.'

'I don't "have" to do anything.'

The old man considered him through those cloudy eyes.

'If you do, you will never have to steal again, so long as you live. You will be wealthy.'

What's that – a bribe? Dangle a little gold in front of the thief and watch him run? If you think I can be tempted that easily, you're—

'How wealthy?'

'Wealthier than Herod. Wealthier than Augustus himself.'

You must think I'm stupid. No man could ever be that rich. And even if he could, there's no way you could possibly make a promise like—

'How long do I have to stay with him?'

The old man smiled. 'Until you let him go.'

'What the hell does that mean?'

'What I'm asking isn't easy. Armies will come after you.'

'I can deal with armies.'

'Not just the armies of man.'

Balthazar furrowed his brow and pursed his lips. 'What other armies are there?'

The old man smiled again. But this one was different. Less smug, more ominous. A 'you'll see' sort of smile.

Balthazar changed his mind. He hated this smile the most.

'I said what other type of armies?'

'Why don't you have another drink?'

Balthazar stared the old man down. He didn't like being toyed with. Then again, another drink of that cool, clear water sounded like the cure for all that ailed him. He looked down at the half-empty cup on the white table. But when he reached for it, it was with someone else's hands. Hands that were covered in brown spots, with dark blue veins bulging beneath thin, baked skin. Balthazar startled – pushing his chair away from the table and trying to stand. But his body was weak. Old. When he looked up for an explanation, the old man was gone.

He looked down at his hands again, shaking and discolored. His eyes barely able to see beyond the length of his arm. There was something in his right hand. Something gold. Balthazar raised his arm, slowly. He knew what it was, but he didn't dare believe it. Not until it became clear in the palm of his shaking hand. Not until he saw the thing he'd spent half his life searching for.

The pendant.

III

The patient would live. He'd been unconscious for nearly two days, sweating through the last of his fever, but he was starting to come around. Zachariah had saved him.

Balthazar had been lucky. He was still young and strong, and the blade had only just broken the outer sac of his lung. Had it gone any deeper – even a few centimeters deeper – there would have been nothing to do but watch him drown. As it was, Zachariah had been able to drain the air and blood trapped in his chest, and suture the wound shut with a bone needle and flax thread. It was healing nicely, thanks in part to the myrrh the patient had been traveling with.

Balthazar was sitting up on his own. His color had returned, and his appetite with it. Zachariah sat at his bedside in the glow of a candle. The house quiet around them. He watched the patient drink from the cup in his hands, wipe his mouth, and politely say no to the question he'd asked moments before.

'Please,' said Zachariah, 'tell me what you saw.'

'I told you . . . I don't want to talk about it. It was just a dream.'

Balthazar had mumbled in his sleep. Mumbled about flying. About the moon, and the pink walls, and the roots of a tree being ripped from the earth. Zachariah had seen other patients do this over the years, and he'd always found their visions fascinating. The way their minds interpreted what was happening to their bodies. Their vividness.

'Even if it was strange or absurd. Tell me what you saw.'

Balthazar looked at the bearded old man. The man not unlike the one in his dream. The man who'd saved his life. He supposed that he owed him at least that much. It was just the two of them, after all. The others were asleep.

And so he did. He told him about flying over the desert. About the mountain and the people dancing around the great golden something. He told him about his body tearing itself apart and falling down the side of the pyramid. About the statues on the shores of the Nile. He told him about the fish going belly-up in a river of blood, the moon breaking apart into pieces and falling from the sky. About the room with pink and purple walls and the man with the wooden staff who offered him a drink and told him to go to Egypt.

But not about the Man With Wings. That he kept to himself.

When he was done telling his story, Zachariah sat silently for a long time. Thinking. Balthazar thought he saw the old man's eyes filling with tears.

'I believe,' said Zachariah at last, 'that you have been chosen by God.'

Here we go . . .

In the two days since the surgery, Zachariah's house had been full of storytelling. He'd learned who his patient really was. How he and the other fugitives had run into Joseph and Mary in the stables. How he'd saved them when Herod's men had stormed into Bethlehem. His niece, Mary, had told him about visions of the angel Gabriel and her miraculous pregnancy. This had prompted Zachariah's wife to admit something she'd kept from him for six years: that the same angel had visited her during her own miraculous pregnancy and told her that their son, John, would be the Messiah's prophet. And now, Zachariah had just been told about the most astonishing dream. A dream he believed to be a message from God himself.

'I believe,' he said, 'that you have been instructed to walk the path that Moses walked. The path of Exodus. I believe that you have been chosen to take the child and his parents to Egypt.'

It made sense. Egypt was relatively close, and beyond Herod's political or military reach. And while it had technically been a Roman province for the last thirty years, the Romans had little influence over local affairs.

'Do you want to know what I think?' asked Balthazar. 'I think I had a bad dream.'

'Will you take them?'

The voice hadn't come from Zachariah. Balthazar turned toward the door and saw a boy. He had no idea who this boy was or how long he'd been standing there.

'Will you take them?' the boy repeated. 'Take them to Egypt?'

'My son,' said Zachariah. 'You must forgive him. He sometimes mistakes himself for a grown man.'

Balthazar didn't like children, generally speaking. He especially didn't like the way this one looked at him. There was no fear in his eyes.

'If I take them,' he said, turning back to Zachariah, 'it's only because I'm headed in the same direction. Not because I believe that some god sent me a message.'

'It doesn't matter whether you believe or not,' said Zachariah. 'As long as God believes in y—'

'Stop.'

He wasn't about to hear any more of that zealot garbage. Not even from the man who'd saved his life.

'I said I'll think about it.'

It was nearly 200 miles to Egypt if they took the route Balthazar had in mind. South past Aijalon, then through the desert to Hebron, where they would rest and resupply before making the final push south to Egypt. Normally, he could make a trip like that in five days. But with his current entourage, and the fact that they'd have to stay off the main roads, he expected it to take nearly twice as long.

It had been five days since the surgery, and Balthazar was beginning to feel like his old self again. Up, around, and ready to go. Gaspar and Melchyor had seen to it that the camels were fed and watered. They'd packed as much food as they could carry. Their robes were new, their bodies were bathed, and their bellies were full. They were ready.

And they were waiting.

Waiting because the Jews were inside, performing another one of their ancient, pointless rituals. *If ever you need proof that religion is a waste of time, here it is. We could've been off an hour ago.*

With everything that'd happened, Joseph and Mary had almost forgotten that it had been eight days since their baby's birth. In accordance with Jewish law, males were circumcised and named on their eighth day. Normally, the bris would've been performed by a mohel – an elder designated by the father, usually a rabbi. But under the circumstances, an old physician with shaking hands would have to suffice. Joseph and Mary held hands as they watched Zachariah wield his scalpel and lean over the baby.

Both of them said a silent prayer asking God to guide his hand.

The Gift of the Magi

'I will scatter you among the nations and will draw out my sword and pursue you. Your land will be laid waste, and your cities will lie in ruins.'

—*Leviticus 26:33*

I

For a moment, it seemed like Herod was done screaming. Then he began again.

What came out of his diseased mouth was less a collection of words and more a series of sharp, anguished notes. Tired lungs forcing bursts of air through bloodied vocal cords. Sounds with no shape or rhythm. The improvisations of a madman. Herod's courtesans had taken refuge behind their pillars once again. His advisors and servants pressed their backs against the walls of the sunlit throne room, trying to make themselves as small as possible as their king circled, tearing and kicking at any object that dared cross his path, spewing those frightening, senseless sounds.

A body lay in the center of Herod's harried orbit – the body of a giant whose legs had been shredded by the enemy in Bethlehem and whose throat had more recently been cut by friends in Jerusalem.

It was the body of the soldier Balthazar had spared.

He'd been led in to see his king only moments before, two fellow soldiers helping him along as he limped down the length of the throne room, helping him down as he knelt before Herod on broken knees. With his head bowed and his body shaking from fright, the giant had delivered the news: They'd failed to kill all the male children of Bethlehem. His captain was dead, and many men with him.

'Did the men of the village rise up against you?' asked Herod. There was a faint hope behind this question. An uprising could be forgiven. Better yet, it could be crushed. He would simply send more men.

'No, Your Highness.'

'Then why does one of my soldiers come crawling back to me with his head hung low, spilling his blood on my floor? Who did this to you?'

The soldier paused, ashamed of what he was about to say. He'd considered lying to the king, saying it was thirty or even fifty men who'd defeated them in Bethlehem, making up some story about a band of mysterious fighters who came out of nowhere. Mercenaries from some nearby kingdom. But lying was pointless. Sooner or later, Herod would learn the truth. Shameful as it was, it had to be told.

'Three men, Your Highness,' he said at last.

Herod stood and walked slowly, slowly down the steps from his throne.

'Three men?'

'Three men . . . dressed in the robes of nobles.'

Somewhere at the ends of his arms, Herod's spindly fingers were balling into fists.

'They . . . killed our captain and . . . escaped with one

198

of the children. One of them gave me a message. I'm . . . supposed to deliver it to you.'

Herod was directly in front of the soldier now, his small frame rendered almost comically frail next to the giant kneeling before him.

'Then,' said Herod, 'I suppose you'd better deliver it.'

The soldier swallowed hard. All things being equal, he would've preferred being left to bleed on the streets of Bethlehem. But this duty had fallen to him, and it must be done.

'He said "the Antioch Ghost is laughing at you." He said he'll . . . "stand over your grave."'

The words took a moment to register. When they did, Herod lost the last of himself that was sane and ordered the soldier's throat cut at once. Even repeating such a thing was an act of treason. And so the two soldiers who'd helped their battered comrade kneel now drew their blades from behind. The giant, for his part, didn't resist. Not as his brothers dragged their daggers along his neck. Not even as he saw a spray of red cover their arms or felt the warmth of blood running over his chest. He'd known. He'd known the moment the Antioch Ghost had chosen him as his messenger. He'd known he would never leave Herod's throne room alive. The giant fell forward, feeling as if his head were full of wine. A moment later, he couldn't remember his own name. A moment after that, he was gone, and Herod was screaming, 'The child will die! The child will die, and the Antioch Ghost with him!'

There were no political considerations to be made. No

discussions to be had or advisors consulted. These things would simply come to pass, no matter the cost in men or treasure. They would come to pass, even if he had to kill all the sons in all of the villages of Judea.

Not even the sight of that treasonous blood spilling on his floor, of that treasonous mouth hanging stupidly open, could assuage the effect of what the giant had said. Of how the Antioch Ghost was mocking him. And so Herod circled, spewing those strange, disconnected noises with his raw throat while his advisors waited in silence. Waiting for his rage to subside – for they could no more hasten the end of their king's tantrum than make a storm blow itself out before its time. All they could do was take shelter and wait for the clouds to part. When at last they did, Herod slumped into his throne. He was shaking from exhaustion, wincing from the pain in his throat . . . but he was smiling. Smiling, because the storm had left a seedling in its wake. An idea.

Herod smiled, for here again was proof that he was blessed with the greatest gift a leader could possess:

Vision.

Where others saw arid wastelands, he saw future cities. Where others mourned the ashes, he harnessed the flames. Even now, slumped over in his throne, weak with rage, he saw an opportunity. A way to slay the child and the Ghost in one stroke, and achieve something even greater in the process.

The emperor . . .

Herod, like all provincial kings, only ruled because he enjoyed the backing of Rome. But his relationship with the empire had been strained ever since Rome's civil war, from which Augustus Caesar emerged the ultimate victor. Unfortunately, Herod had been a supporter of Augustus's chief rival, Marc Antony. And while he'd been quick to pledge his everlasting and unwavering loyalty to the new Caesar, Augustus had viewed Judea's puppet king with suspicion ever since. But here was a chance to change all of that. A chance to improve relations with Rome and protect his dynasty in Judea. Here was a chance to flatter the emperor, while using him at the same time.

With the last of his voice, Herod summoned a scribe and dictated a letter. It began:

Mighty Augustus, Master of the World,

I humble myself before your glory, and beg you condescend to advise me in a matter most dire. A matter of great consequence, not only for Judea, but for all the empire . . .

II

A fellowship of six fugitives rode south from Emmaus, divided among the backs of three camels: Gaspar alone in front, Melchyor and Joseph in the middle, and Balthazar, Mary, and the child in back. They moved slowly over the sand, far from the roads and the prying eyes of soldiers, their mouths dry and canteens nearly empty. There were no debts of honor binding them together. No pledges of friendship or shared beliefs. Balthazar had saved the lives of his companions, and they'd saved his in return. They were square in the eyes of the desert. All that united them now was a common need to escape Herod's grasp.

As the heat of the day reached full bloom on their backs, the child woke and began to cry, and Balthazar realized this was the first time he'd heard his voice since they'd escaped Bethlehem. Given everything he had been through in the last few days, the infant had remained strangely calm, strangely silent. Now his sharp, short wails rang in his ears, waking the headache he'd almost managed to forget. He was parched, fatigued, and half starved. Sharp pain pulsed from his stitches and through his body with each of the camel's footfalls. And now a baby was screaming at the back of his throbbing head.

'We have to stop,' said Mary.

'We can't,' said Balthazar.

'But he's hungry.'

'We're all hungry.'

'I have to feed him.'

'Then feed him while we ride. I won't look.'

'I can't. Not with the camel moving up and down like this.'

'Then I guess he'll starve.'

How could he say that so dispassionately?

'You would deny a hungry baby his mother's milk?' she asked.

'No, I'd deny Herod's men a better chance of catching us. We find food or water? That's when we stop. Otherwise, you're the woman – you figure it out.'

'But—'

'Look, I'll gladly let you climb down and feed him, but I won't wait behind while you do.'

Mary thought about appealing to Gaspar or Melchyor, but it was useless. They'd simply tell her the same thing. She thought about calling ahead to her husband and begging his help in convincing Balthazar to stop. But she knew it wouldn't make any difference what Joseph said. She felt tears welling up in her eyes and hated herself for it. Who were these men they'd entrusted with their lives? With their child's life? But her frustration gave way to dread when she realized the baby had stopped crying.

Maybe he's too exhausted to cry. Too dehydrated. Too hungry and weak. Maybe this is how the end begins. Maybe I have no idea what I'm doing. Maybe we should never have left Emmaus. Maybe this was all a—

'Look!'

The voice had come from up ahead. Gaspar had stopped his camel and was pointing at something on the ground. Something in the sand, catching the sunlight. It was a stream – a tiny sliver of life trickling across the desert, a foot in width and only a few inches deep. It ran from left to right, as far as the eye could see in both directions, and from what they could tell, it was almost perfectly straight.

Balthazar had traveled this section of desert many times before, but he had no recollection of there ever being a stream. In fact, he had no recollection of ever seeing water move over the sand in such a way, flowing over it, without being absorbed into the grains. He would have thought it impossible. Yet here it was, running clear and cool, from horizon to horizon.

'What do we do?' asked Gaspar.

Balthazar took in the strange sight a moment longer, then turned back to Mary.

'We stop.'

III

The young Roman officer knew an opportunity when he saw it.

It was one of his gifts. The gift of being able to sit, and watch, and wait – letting others pick the low-hanging fruit, until the right, ripe opportunity presented itself. The gift of knowing when to get aggressive. And when aggressive wasn't enough, knowing when to get ruthless.

This self-discipline was a skill in its own right. But when coupled with naked ambition, it became a thing of beauty, a weapon, which had seen this particular officer rise through the ranks faster than almost any in Rome's history. Rising through lieutenant, then captain, until he was made imperator at the age of twenty-two. Most of the recruits under his command were older than he was, but this didn't bother the officer in the least. He was comfortable with power. He'd been born to wield it.

He marched down the central corridor of the emperor's palace, flanked by two of his lieutenants. Heels clopping against the marble floor, helmets held firmly on their hips, swords rattling against their sides. In his hand, the young officer held the letter that had been delivered by a rider from the East that very morning. A letter that bore the seal of Judea's king.

In that letter was one of those juicy pieces of fruit. The young officer had known the moment he'd read it. A piece worth getting aggressive over. Here was a chance to catch someone called 'the Antioch Ghost.' A middling pest who'd caused the Roman Army no shortage of headaches over the past decade. More important, here was a chance to further impress his beloved emperor and further secure his future. He would be a general, of course. There could be no doubt. And before his thirtieth birthday, at this rate. After that? A senator, perhaps. Or a provincial governor. But those pieces of fruit were still ripening on the vine. He would pick them all in due time.

The young officer reached the large double doors at the end of the corridor, each of them twenty feet high, plated with silver and decorated with gold embellishments. A golden eagle, the symbol of Rome's military might, dominated these adornments – its outstretched wings spanning the entire width of both closed doors. The officer and his lieutenants saluted the guards who stood on either side of it. The guards saluted in return and stepped aside, ready to open the doors to the throne room. But the officer held up a hand: *Not yet.*

He paused a moment. Took a breath, composed himself. He wanted to make this entrance count. After all, he was about to ask the ruler of the world to go to war with an infant and a thief. When he felt sufficiently prepared, the young officer addressed one of the guards: 'Tell the emperor that Pontius Pilate is here to see him . . .'

Augustus Caesar was the most powerful human being who had ever drawn breath, though he was only 'human' in the strictest sense of the word.

To his subjects, he was a god. It was reflected in the way they revered him. Feared him and worshipped his likeness, whether it was stamped on the face of a gold coin or chiseled into marble. He was in his sixties, twice the average life expectancy. But he'd aged gracefully and still projected a stately, if graying sense of power. The very name his subjects had bestowed on him, Augustus, meant 'Illustrious One,' and when he appeared in public, protocol demanded that he be introduced with a number of platitudes, which included:

> *He who is beyond the reach of the gods! He before whom all kings kneel! Before whom even the mountains bow their heads!*

His kingdom reached every corner of the known world: from Hispania in the west to Syria in the east, from the tip of Africa below to northernmost Gaul above. At his command were the greatest army and navy the world had ever known. The best-prepared soldiers, with the finest weaponry the collective taxes of the earth could buy.

But all that power was nothing without vision.

It was lack of vision that had doomed his uncle, Julius. For all his military prowess, all his strategic genius, Julius Caesar had lacked vision.

Fate had delivered the world into the palm of his hand, but he hadn't been man enough to wrap his fist around it, to take it all for himself. He'd tried to be a man of the people. He'd tried to share his power with the senate. And for his troubles, he'd been stabbed twenty-three times by the very senators he'd reached out to. Stabbed in the back as he slipped on his own blood, trying to flee. Left to rot on the steps of the senate for three hours before anyone even bothered to cover his body. That had been his reward for being a man of the people.

To think he could have stopped it all, if only he'd been willing to use the weapon . . .

The world knew that Julius Caesar had transformed Rome from a republic to an empire. They knew that he was a skilled orator and general. But of those closest to Julius, only a few – including his beloved nephew, Augustus – knew the dark secret behind his power. The weapon that had given him the confidence to march on Rome and seize the empire for himself:

The magi.

Julius had come to possess this weapon during his conquest of Gaul, but not by stealing it from another ruler or by constructing it from his own blueprints. He'd come to possess it because the weapon had *chosen* him. As Julius explained in a letter to fellow general and confidant Pompey:

The campaign had been going badly. The Gauls had beaten us into retreat. One night, as I conferred with my officers, the guards presented a visitor. A short, frail man in a black robe, with a gray beard, sunken eyes, and bald head. He looked some fifty years in age, though he walked with the wooden staff of a much older man, topped with a coiled brass snake. Clearly he was some kind of priest, though I had never seen a priest who looked quite like this one. His skin was covered with strange designs rendered in black ink, and his arms bore the scars of many burns, both old and new.

'I have foreseen that the name "Caesar" shall ring through the ages,' he said. 'That he shall be worshipped as the gods are worshipped. I come to offer him my talents. My loyalty and protection. In return, I ask only a modest share of his spoils.'

'And why do I need the protection of a priest?' I asked. 'I have four legions under my command.'

'Because,' he said, 'for all your legions, you find yourself on the brink of defeat. Chased off by farmers armed only with rocks and sticks.'

My officers rose and drew their swords. To speak to a general in such a way was unthinkable. Punishable by death.

'Are you mad?' I asked.

A strange smile came across the priest's face, as if he had intended such a reaction. As if he had wanted such a question asked.

'I am a magus,' he said.

The magi were an ancient cult. Masters of a magic that had all but vanished from the earth. They'd come to power in the Age of the Scriptures, back when angels and mystical beasts had walked side by side with man, when the battles of heaven and hell had been waged on the plains of Galilee and in the hills of Hebron. The world had been different then. Time had barely begun, and the gods still mingled freely with man, whether they were the many gods of Mount Olympus or the lonely God of Abraham. And while most men lived in fear and reverence of their gods, a few sought to wield that power for themselves.

At their height, they'd numbered in the thousands, hidden away in monasteries, studying the higher forces that ordinary men feared. The dark forces. Learning how to control them, master them, exploit them. It was said that a magus could summon fire from thin air. Turn statues into living men, and living men into stone. It was said they could see things that had not yet come to pass, and influence the thoughts of men half a world away. For thousands of years, they were treated as living gods – revered, feared, and rarely seen outside their monastery walls.

But over the centuries, the Age of Miracles had given way to the Age of Man, and their numbers had dwindled, until – more than 10,000 years after the first man had called himself 'magus' – only one remained, wandering a world ruled not by gods but by Romans. The last of his kind, the bearer of a forgotten gift that no longer had any use.

But Julius Caesar found a use for it.

With the last of the magi at his side, he'd turned his campaign in Gaul around. And when he was finished, he'd turned against his allies and taken all of Rome's glory for himself.

As emperor, Julius learned to rely on the dark priest's ability to see into the future. In his ability to uncover an enemy's secrets through a kind of deep meditation and summon nature to Rome's aid, conjuring wind and lightning to drive out surrounding armies, commanding beasts to betray their masters. Even invading the minds of senators and influencing their votes. With the magus at his side, Julius had been elevated from a general to a god. But over time, he'd begun to fear his secret weapon. In another letter to Pompey, he wrote:

There is a darkness about him that unnerves me. If he is able to read the thoughts of others, what is to stop him from reading mine? If he can summon bolts of lightning from the heavens, what is to stop him from using one to strike me down? What good is a weapon if one cannot command it without fear?

Paranoid, Caesar ordered his 'weapon' sent away in 44 BC. But before his exile, the magus gave him one last piece of advice: 'The Ides of March,' he'd said. 'Beware the Ides of March.'

Caesar ignored the warning. And that very year, on the fifteenth day of the third month, he was stabbed to death on the senate floor. In the end, he'd been too afraid to wield the weapon that had sought him out. Too weak.

But this was a weakness Augustus didn't share. On learning of his uncle's murder, Augustus had summoned the magus at once and demanded his loyalty. Slowly, deliberately, he'd consolidated his power in the empire – using the magus's insight and influence to battle his rival, Marc Antony, and the Egyptian whore, Cleopatra. Using the magus's power to beat them back, until they had no choice but to take their own lives in shame. And to make sure that no further challenges to his supremacy emerged, Augustus had ordered their children put to death.

With vision and cunning, he'd succeeded where his uncle had failed. He'd taken all of Rome's glory for himself. And so long as the magus remained sequestered in Rome, Augustus Caesar knew that the empire would never fall.

But that was all in the past now, and the past was where small minds dwelled.

The future had just walked into Augustus's throne room. Here was Pontius Pilate, kneeling before him, his bowed head reflected in the polished marble of his floor.

Handsome Pilate. Loyal, beloved Pilate, bearing the request of a sickly, traitorous old king.

Herod 'the Great.' The name had always elicited a sneer from Augustus, even before he'd become master of the world. Who was this 'great' man but a servant of Rome? A torturer of his own people and murderer of his own children? Yes, Augustus had ordered children put

212

to death. But they were the children of his enemies. To murder one's *own* children? It was barbaric.

He listened as Pilate relayed the message. Something about a baby. A prophecy. Someone called 'the Antioch Ghost.' When Pilate was finished, Augustus considered it all for a moment, then said, 'He wants me to send an army across the water . . . to kill a child?'

'The Antioch Ghost is the true prize, Caesar. He's stolen untold riches from your provinces. Killed untold numbers of your men. If we—'

Augustus held up a hand. *Stop.*

'You said the people of Judea think this "Ghost" is already dead, did you not?'

'Yes, Caesar.'

'Pilate . . . what good is it to kill a man who is already dead? Where is the glory for Rome?'

Pilate couldn't help but smile. He knew his emperor well. After pausing for effect, he uttered the sentence he'd carefully crafted on his way to the palace. The one he knew he'd have to utter after being challenged on this point:

'With all respect, Caesar, this is less about Rome's glory and more about sending a message to Judea's king.'

Augustus shifted on his throne, thinking. He didn't like the idea of all this fuss over a thief and a baby.

But Pilate is right . . . there is an opportunity in this.

'Very well,' said Augustus. 'I will catch Herod's infant and his thief. But not because Herod requests it, and not because they have wronged Rome. I will catch them because Herod cannot. And in doing so, I will remind our sickly friend how small he really is.'

An ordinary emperor would have sent troops and left it at that. But Augustus had no interest in being ordinary. He would do more than send troops. He would make a real show of his power. Put the fear of death in the puppet king of Judea.

He would send the magus.

IV

Melchyor and Joseph watered the camels and filled the canteens in the desert stream, while Mary sat on the sand with the child under her robes. Balthazar knelt a ways downstream, cupping handfuls of water – first to his mouth, then over his face and chest, washing away the blood that continued to seep through his stitches.

'This is madness,' said Gaspar, who'd come to kneel beside him. 'We have the entire Judean Army after us, yet we play wet nurse to a baby. We could have been halfway to Egypt by now if we were not dragging them with us. It is too dangerous, Balthazar. We must think of ourselves.'

'I am thinking of myself. I was thirsty. We found water. I stopped.'

'You know what I mean.'

'I know,' he said, cupping another handful to his wound. 'I also know what I saw in Bethlehem. What all of us saw. You want to leave them to Herod's men?'

'Yes, I saw. And the same will happen to us if we are captured. I did not escape certain death to throw my life away for strangers.'

'I don't like it either, okay? But I didn't go back for that baby just to dump him in the desert to rot. Once we cross the border, we go our separate ways. Until then, we play wet nurse.'

Balthazar stood, shook the water from his hands, and dried them on his robes.

'Why does the Antioch Ghost care if an infant lives or dies?' asked Gaspar.

It was a stupid question, of course. The obvious answer was, 'Because I still have a shred of decency,' or 'The real question is, why don't *you* care?' But Balthazar didn't say either of these things, because as obvious as those answers were, they weren't the real answers.

Go on, tell him, Balthazar. Tell him why you care so much. Why you hate so much, kill so much, search so much, as if any of it will bring him—

'Ask yourself,' said Gaspar, shaking Balthazar out of his trance, 'would you give your life to protect theirs?'

Balthazar looked back at Joseph and Melchyor wrestling with their camels. At Mary sitting on the ground, feeding the baby beneath her robes.

'Not if I can help it,' he said, and walked away.

Pontius Pilate stared ahead at the open water of the Mediterranean. Only hours after kneeling in the emperor's throne room, he found himself standing on the bow of the *Heptares* – a heavy warship carrying over 1,000 men, leading an armada of smaller triremes from Rome. He'd never seen water rush by a bow so fast or known a sail to be fuller than the one above him. Normally, the hundreds of men sitting belowdecks would be rowing across the sea one stroke at a time. But today they could only sit with their oars on their laps, as a steady tailwind sped them along faster than mortals could ever hope to row.

Pilate wasn't sure, but he had a good idea of where this strange, steady wind was coming from. The magus was onboard the *Heptares* with them, tucked comfortably in his private quarters below. And though his cabin door was closed, he could be heard muttering to himself on the other side. Praying in some strange mix of Latin and other languages, repeating the same phrases over and over like a chant. Pilate hadn't been able to make all of it out, but as he'd pressed his ear curiously to the magus's door, he'd heard one word repeated among the others: *ventus*.

Wind.

The emperor had taken Pilate into his confidence in Rome, sharing the secret history of the Caesars and the magi, his powers and the role they'd played in creating the present-day empire, and what was known of their cult's origins and demise. And when he'd finished, Augustus had summoned the magus to his palace and introduced him to the young officer.

Pilate had done his best to hide his dread at meeting such a strange, dangerous little man. He'd been prepared for the oddity of the magus's appearance, but nothing had prepared him for the feeling of seeing those piercing black eyes for himself. He'd felt those eyes look right through him, felt as if they were peeking into his head. His thoughts. Most unnerving was the fact that the magus looked just as Julius Caesar had described him in his letter forty years earlier.

That he hadn't aged a day in all that time only unnerved Pilate more.

'He doesn't speak,' Augustus had said, 'but he will tell you everything you need to know. Listen to him, Pilate, and return him to me unharmed. I'm trusting you with my most prized possession.'

And here he was, alone on the bow of *Heptares*, the sole commander of 10,000 men and one mystic. Pilate could feel himself getting closer with every mile. Closer to his prize, his destiny. That's all this was, after all – just destiny, playing itself out, mile by mile. There were no accidents in this life. Pilate believed that the gods had a plan for all of us. And no matter which turns he took, he believed that his life would intersect greatness sooner or later. His name would ring through the ages, immortal.

Usually, if the sea smiled on you, it took seven days for a ship to sail from Rome to Judea. At this rate, Pilate would intersect his greatness in less than two.

Mary rode behind a terrible man. Yes, he'd come back for them, saved them from Herod's men, and she was grateful for that. Grateful enough to risk everything to save his life in return. But Mary was eager to reach Egypt and be rid of him forever.

The sun was growing blessedly lower in the sky,

though the heat still radiated off the sand, baking them from the bottoms of their feet to the tops of their head-dresses. At least the baby seemed full and happy for the moment, his blue eyes blinking up at her, the lids above them growing heavy. She poured water from her canteen onto her hand and ran it over the baby's scalp to keep it cool. She adjusted her robes, trying to keep the sun off of his face, while whispering one of her favorite stories from the Scriptures to nudge her son closer to the sleep his body craved:

> *And a great cry went up to Moses. 'Why have you led us here?' they said. 'Were there no more graves in Egypt? Have you brought us into the desert to wither and die?' And Moses said, 'I was commanded by the Lord to lead you here, for you were the slaves of a cruel pharaoh – and it is better to die in the desert than die a slave.'*

When she was little, Mary had whispered these stories to herself at night – a way to quiet her restless mind, to comfort herself when she was frightened or anxious. She envisioned the Scriptures as a bottomless well of these stories. A place from which she could always draw nourishment, even here in the desert.

As a woman, she was forbidden from studying the scrolls on which they were written. But she was permitted to sit in the rear of the synagogue, listening to the men read them aloud. She'd been transported by those stories as a young girl: Jonah in the belly of the whale, the folly of building a tower to heaven, Noah's test of faith before the Great Flood. And though she would never say so aloud, she prided herself on being able to quote these passages better than many of the men who fanned themselves in the heat of the synagogue and stole naps beneath their shawls. This one had popped into her head out of nowhere.

'Do not be afraid,' said Moses. 'Stand firm, and the Lord will stand with you. Be still, and he will fight for you.'

'What are you muttering about back there?' asked Balthazar.

'I'm not muttering. I'm reciting a story to help him sleep.'

'Well . . . recite quieter.'

Mary bit her lip in frustration. *Miserable soul! Uncaring, dispassionate wretch!* She sat in silence for few moments, reminding herself that every step of the camel beneath her was one step closer to Egypt. But in the absence of his mother's soothing voice, the baby began to fuss again. Soon he would begin to cry, and the insufferable man in front of her would only grow more insufferable. *Fine. If you won't let me whisper, you'll just have to talk to me.*

'Do you know the Scriptures?' she asked.

Balthazar rolled his eyes. *Here we go.* What was it about these people? Why couldn't they just keep their delusions to themselves?

'This may come as a shock,' he said, 'but not everyone in the world is a Jew.'

'No . . . but even the Romans have their sacred stories. Surely your people do as well.'

'Ancient nonsense, written by dead fools. Just like your Scriptures.'

'How can you say that, when God has spoken to you?'

'God's never "spoken" to me. In fact, I'd love it if you tried to be more like him.'

'What about your dream? Zachariah said he chose you.'

'He didn't choose anything.'

'But how do you kn—'

'Because there is no "he."'

Mary couldn't believe a man would say such a thing. It was one thing to be cruel and uncaring. But to be blasphemous?

'But . . . that's ridiculous. Who sent the plagues to Egypt? Who created the earth beneath us? The stars above us? Who created man?'

'It's too hot to argue. Especially with a woman.'

'I'm not trying to argue. I just . . . I've never met a man who didn't believe in God.'

Balthazar turned and glared at her. Mary was surprised by the contempt on his furrowed face.

'Of course you haven't,' he said. 'You're a stupid little girl from a stupid little village of zealots. This is the real world.'

'But a life without God is . . .'

'Is what? What's so great about your God? You tell me

what's so great about a God that does nothing while infants get run through with swords. Swords held by his devoted followers, by the way. You tell me what kind of God that is.'

Mary had no answer.

'Either I'm right,' he continued, 'and he doesn't exist, or you're right, and he's the kind of God who watches children die. The kind of God who sits around while men like Herod build palaces and good people starve. Either way, he's not worth worshipping.'

Mary sat in silence. She'd never heard anyone denounce the Lord. Of course he existed. To think otherwise would be to admit that everything she believed was a lie. Worse, it would mean that she was crazy. But Balthazar's words were confusing.

'All men need something to believe in,' she said at last.

Without looking, Balthazar reached down and pulled his sword out of its sheath.

'Well . . . you have your weapon,' said Mary, 'and I have mine.'

Balthazar put the sword away and turned back to the desert ahead.

'I like mine better,' he said.

V

Night had come to the desert.

Ten thousand Roman soldiers stood in formation, flames reflected in their polished helmets and shields, all of them facing a makeshift altar of piled stones. As Pilate predicted, they'd reached the shores of Judea in less than two days. Faster than most of the assembled men thought possible. Some were calling it a miracle. But it was only a taste of the extraordinary things to come.

Two great pyres burned before them – one on either side of the altar, where the magus stood over the body of a sacrificial lamb. Its throat had been cut and its blood drained into a bowl. As the men watched, the magus dipped his finger in the blood and used it to draw a line across his own forehead. He dipped a second time and traced it along the brass serpent that topped his walking staff.

'*Nehushtan . . .*' he whispered.

To the Romans, it was nothing more than a strange word. They wouldn't have recognized it from the Book of

Exodus, nor known that the brass serpent they were looking upon – *the Nehushtan* – had been cast by Moses himself. Created to adorn the walking stick he'd used to guide his people through the desert. It was a relic of untold age and power. How the magus came to possess it was a mystery.

He raised the bowl to his lips and drank a mouthful of the lamb's blood, then walked to the pyre on his right, so close to the flames that his robes billowed in the heated air. He held the staff out in front of his body, until the snake was fully enveloped in fire. The lamb's blood on its surface blackened, then burned away. The magus chanted to himself, his words growing faster, as Pilate and his fellow officers looked on from the side of the altar.

Did the snake just . . . move?

At first, the men thought it was a trick of the light. Until, to their amazement, the brass snake slowly uncoiled itself and wound its way onto the magus's arm. A few of the enlisted men broke ranks and fled, terrified by what they saw. *What darkness is this? What gods are at work?* But Pilate stood his ground, even as the Nehushtan wound its way down the magus's body and onto the desert floor. He didn't know how it was possible. He didn't care. He only knew he was one step closer to his prize.

The magus stood before the altar with his eyes closed, reciting an ancient incantation over and over, guiding the beast at it slithered off into the desert . . .

Hunting.

Balthazar sat near the mouth of a cramped cave, keeping watch over the vast expanse of desert. The others were sleeping behind him. All except one.

'Get some sleep,' said Joseph, who'd come to join him. 'It's more important you be rested than me. I can keep watch for a while.'

Balthazar considered the faint, moonlit outline of Joseph's face. The young, bearded face of a village woodworker. They were about the same age, but they couldn't have been more different.

'I'll stay,' said Balthazar. 'No offense, but I wouldn't be able to sleep knowing it was you keeping watch.'

Joseph smiled and sat beside him.

'You think I'm weak.'

'I think you're naïve.'

'And what have I done to make you think this?'

'You believe the impossible.'

Ah . . . this again. The man who mocks others for believing the word of God.

'So I'm naïve because I believe the Scriptures?'

'No . . . you're naïve because you believe her.'

It took a moment for Joseph to untangle what Balthazar had said and get his meaning. When he did, his face darkened, and his mind wandered back to what had been the hardest few days of his life. The days back in Nazareth, when his happiness had been shattered and his faith tested to its limit. And all because his young bride-to-be had come to him with a tearful confession.

'I didn't, you know,' Joseph said at last.

'Didn't what?'

'Believe her. Not when she first told me, anyway. I wanted to, of course. Desperately. But . . .'

'But?'

'I'm a patient man, but to believe such a thing . . . like you said . . . it was impossible.'

'What did she tell you?'

Joseph thought about it for a moment. *What was it she'd said again?*

'She told me,' said Joseph, 'that she had woken to the whispering voice of a man.'

'Not a promising start.'

'She told me that she'd followed the voice outside, only to find that the night had turned bright as day. And yet the streets of Nazareth were barren. There was no sound. No rustling of olive trees or birdsong.'

'A dream.'

'But as real as any dream she'd ever had. As real as the two of us sitting here in this cave. Mary told me that she'd seen a man approaching. A shimmering, radiant man who seemed to step out of the sun itself and walk toward her. A man not of this earth . . . a man with wings.'

Balthazar tried to hide the chill that touched his spine on hearing those words.

'And before he even opened his mouth,' said Joseph, 'Mary told me that she knew – knew with absolute certainty – that his name was Gabriel, archangel of the Lord.'

'Gabriel?'

'"Rejoice, you highly favored one," he told her. "The

226

Lord is with you. Blessed are you among women. Behold, you will conceive in your womb, and bring forth a son. And the holy one who is born from you will be called the son of God."'

'That's it? That's what she told you?'

'I knew it was a lie. I knew. I thought, "*No, it's worse than a lie. A lie could be forgiven. This was blasphemy! God born of a woman!*" I could see only two possibilities: one, that Mary had known another man, whether by her choice or not, and invented the story to explain her condition. Or two, that she suddenly dreaded the idea of being my wife and was trying to scare me off. But I thought, *if she dreaded me that much, why has she seemed so happy until now?* It didn't make sense.'

'Women never do.'

'But then I realized that there was a third possibility: that Mary had gone mad. That she actually believed what she'd told me. And the more I thought about it, the more I felt in my heart that this was the real answer. She'd told her story with such conviction. Her face had never wavered; her eyes had never lied, even as her lips did. Maybe it was just that I wanted to believe anything other than the thought of, you know . . .'

'I know.'

'But what could I do? If I turned my back on her, I knew exactly what would happen. I'd seen it before: adulterous women dragged out of their homes, made to stand against a wall as the men gathered up stones. I'd seen those women with their skulls cracked open, with their brains dashed out, left to die alone. As much as I refused to believe Mary, I couldn't condemn her to death. I thought, "*I could always tell them that I was the father.*" But to admit that we'd been together before marriage? We would've been exiled from the only home we'd ever known. Shunned by the people we loved.'

'So you married her anyway.'

'No. I mourned. I mourned the life that could've been. Everything had been perfect, you understand. But in the space of one cursed day, my future had been narrowed down to three possibilities: either I would be the husband of an adulteress, the keeper of an unwilling bride, or the guardian of a madwoman. Three possibilities – each one worse than the last. But then? A miracle.'

This time, Balthazar had to consciously keep himself from rolling his eyes.

'That night,' said Joseph, 'as I wrestled with these three possibilities, the angel Gabriel visited me and showed me a fourth possibility: that what Mary had told me was true. That the Messiah was growing in her womb and that I was to be his guardian.'

Balthazar sat in silence for a good deal of time. Clearly, the carpenter was also out of his mind. Yes, he'd probably had some kind of vision – a vivid dream brought on by desperation. A desperation to believe *anything* but the painful truth. Balthazar had experienced visions of his own. Things he would've *sworn* were real at the time. It had happened to him as a boy, when he'd dug up bodies on the far side of the Orontes. It had happened to him while he suffered through his recent surgery. The difference was, he had the ability to discern dreams from reality. Visions presented themselves all the time. Dreams came, fully formed. But they were just that – dreams. Nothing more. And the carpenter was naïve for thinking otherwise.

'Well,' said Joseph, 'let me know if you change your mind about getting some sleep.'

With that, he excused himself and retreated farther into the cramped cave – disappearing into the darkness. Balthazar flirted with the idea of calling after him. Of keeping him close by so he could spend some more time mocking him for his stupidity. But what was the use? No . . . leave the little man to his little delusions. It wasn't worth the energy.

Balthazar sat alone at the mouth of the cave, searching the darkness with his eyes and ears. Looking for the low stars of far-off torches. Listening for the distant beating of hooves and the clanging of armor.

But not the slithering of a brass snake rendered living by an ancient darkness.

If Balthazar had, by chance, turned his attention to the desert floor, he might have seen the Nehushtan slither past him, then off into the black desert with its message:

I've found them . . .

8

Miracle of the Bowing Palms

'They shoot from ambush at the innocent;
they shoot suddenly, without fear.'

—*Psalm 64:4*

I

Herod was feeling much better.

Though it was nearly midday, he was still in his bedchamber, his head propped up on silk cushions, his chest shining with scented oils. He was awake, but his eyes remained peacefully closed as he breathed deeply of the healing vapors, just as his physicians had instructed him to do. Herod was usually loath to follow their advice. They'd proven useless in ridding him of his cursed disease, after all. Despite all of their so-called remedies and potions and rituals, his skin remained covered in oozing lesions, and his ribs stuck out of his emaciated chest like dunes in the desert sand. Even so, Herod had to admit that his physicians had done well in ridding him of the raw throat he'd given himself while screaming. He was feeling so good, in fact, that he'd decided to stay in bed on the 'pleasure' side of his twin palace today. His 'business' palace, with all its duplicitous courtesans, unsettled disputes, and ceaseless bad news, would wait. Today would be a day of rest. Of pleasure. He deserved it. He deserved something new.

And here she was.

Sitting on the bed beside him. A girl he'd never seen before. A girl of twelve, thirteen at the most, her body not yet a womanly shape. Here she was, sitting beside her sickly king, dropping dried figs into his mouth, one at a time. Herod savored each sweet specimen, chewing them slowly, loudly between his blackened teeth – his eyes closed all the while. He'd stolen a glance at this nameless little beauty when she'd entered, carrying her basket of foods and ointments. She'd been fully clothed then. Now her robes sat in a heap around her waist, her bare breasts red from where Herod had playfully pinched them between his fingers. He continued to feel his way around her body, his eyes closed. Chewing his figs with a faint smile on his lips. But it wasn't the feel of her young, warm secrets that made him smile. It was knowing that he had Augustus Caesar, the world's most powerful man, right where he wanted him.

Herod's instincts had proven themselves once again. Only days after his messenger had left for Rome, letter in hand, no fewer than 10,000 Roman soldiers had landed on Judea's shores. This in itself was something of a miracle. Even Herod couldn't have imagined such a quick response. But that was Rome. Decisive. Overwhelming. You had to hand it to them – right or wrong, they were never perfunctory.

Herod wasn't stupid. He'd known that the emperor didn't like or trust him. Just as he'd known that Augustus wouldn't be able to resist his letter and the chance it gave him to make a show of his might. *He'll want to frighten*

234

me, Herod had thought before sending the letter. *Remind me that I'm nothing more than a sniveling little puppet king who's lucky to have his throne.* But far from feeling frightened or inferior, Herod now found himself filled with a deep sense of accomplishment and pride.

He'd killed two birds with one stone: He'd flattered Augustus, and at the same time, he'd turned the Ghost and the infant into Rome's problem. Let the emperor think what he wanted to think. What mattered were facts. And the fact was, Herod was sitting here in bed, being hand-fed by a naked girl while the Romans were dragging themselves through the desert looking for his fugitives. He couldn't help but smile at the thought. A legion of the emperor's best troops, running Judea's errands.

Your little 'puppet' has outsmarted you, Augustus.

There was, however, one little piece of the puzzle that Herod hadn't anticipated: this 'dark priest.' There were rumors of a soothsayer traveling with the Romans, a magician of some kind. Rumors of a ritual in the desert. A bloody sacrifice, a brass snake. Herod's advisors had come to him with these rumors. They'd warned him that the Romans had brought something strange across the sea. Something that had frightened many of the men who'd witnessed it. And while Herod had been surprised to hear of Romans appealing to the gods for anything, he hadn't allowed himself to share in their concern. So what? The Jews had their prophets. The Greeks had their oracles. Let the Romans have their priests.

She wants me . . . I can feel it . . .

Herod opened his yellowed eyes and took her in. The fear on her face. The tears. *Why do they cry, even when their bodies are joyous at my touch?*

In some kingdoms, it was customary for young girls to lie with their king. In some kingdoms – and Herod had heard these stories firsthand, so he had no doubts as to their veracity – all girls were sent to live in the royal harem when they came of childbearing age. They were forbidden from returning home or taking husbands until they'd first given themselves to their king. The Romans called it *ius primae noctis* – 'law of the first night.'

Herod knew the Jews would never stand for such a custom. Even if they did, Judea was a big kingdom. There were too many girls, and he was only one king. So he'd been selective instead, sending his men into the city streets, into the villages to find the most fetching creatures, to bestow upon them the honor of serving their king. And here was one of the honored now, feeding him on his silken bed.

He ran his spindly fingers through her brown hair, then pulled her close. Closer, until he could feel her hurried breath against his face. He could feel her trembling. They usually did. But that fear was good. It was normal for a common girl to fear her king. To be excited by his touch. Honored by his attention. She held a fig to Herod's lips, but he pushed it away.

'Enough of that,' he said.

He drew her in. Kissed her deeply. He could feel her pulling away as his tongue felt its way around her mouth. Felt her struggling against his grasp. This was the part he enjoyed most. The resistance. They all resisted. They all tried to run.

But in the end, they were all his.

II

An ibex looked up, mindlessly gnashing the dry grass in its teeth – the flavorless blades it was somehow compelled to seek out and pull from the hot earth, from morning until night. Something was wrong. It'd caught another glint in the corner of its eye, felt another tiny, almost imperceptible vibration beneath it. And now it watched – its eyes unblinking, its body tense and ready – as three camels passed the herd, a hundred yards distant. Close enough to raise concern but not close enough to send them scattering. Not yet.

The ibex had no memory of ever seeing a camel before, although it had, on countless occasions. It watched as the larger beasts moved from left to right across its field of view – five humans on their backs, one of them carrying something small in its arms. They moved slowly, purpose-fully in the direction of what the ibex, for lack of knowing the proper term, called 'the thing over there.' The big, smooth thing that all the humans hid behind. The one it and its herd mates dare not approach.

Confident there was no danger from the camels or

their passengers, the ibex lowered its head and resumed the hunt for dry blades. The hunt that it had been compelled to begin the moment it had emerged on wet, rickety legs and would continue until its dying breath. By the time it pulled another flavorless patch of grass from the desert floor, it had forgotten the camels were ever there.

Just as it'd forgotten the thousands of Romans who'd marched past an hour before.

Joseph stared back at the ibex. A large herd had taken note of them, watching closely as they passed, their curled horns held high, their mouths mindlessly chewing cud. They were stupid little creatures, to be sure. But they were a welcome sign of life in a desert that had enveloped them for hours, empty and eternal.

Hebron was finally in their sights, though there were a few miserable miles to go before they reached its smooth outer walls. They would be silent miles, for Joseph, Mary, and the others had hardly passed a word for hours. They were all stiff from a night spent tossing and turning on the floor of a cave, all weak for lack of food and water and sick from the unrelenting heat. And the baby – the baby had grown eerily quiet again. Too dehydrated to cry for his mother's milk.

God knows how long they'd ridden. Eight hours straight? Ten? They'd set out before dawn, and while the sun finally seemed to be falling toward its western cradle, its rays were still murderous as they beat down from the heavens, baking their faces and the tops of their feet, turning their skin a painful pink.

Patience, Joseph . . . God will provide . . .

It'd become his desert mantra. The only thing keeping doubt outside the walls of his mind, where it had laid siege months ago, waiting oh so patiently to starve him out and slaughter his sanity. Joseph felt the presence of doubt all around him, just as he had when Mary first told him about her dream. Its sabers rattling outside his city walls, ready to accept his offer of surrender. *Admit it, Joseph, she's a liar. Admit it, Joseph, this was a mistake. Admit it, Joseph, he's not the Messiah.* And yes, in times of weakness and fatigue – times like now – these voices had a way of growing louder. But then they'd crested the hill and spotted the walls of Hebron in the distance, and Joseph had breathed fully of the desert air. He'd never seen anything so beautiful in all his life. His desert mantra had never rung truer.

God will provide . . .

Hebron had suddenly and completely revealed itself before them – a walled oasis in the desert. Not quite big enough to be called a city, but too substantial to be called a village. It was surrounded by almost perfectly square walls of beige brick. Behind those walls, there would be markets where they could resupply. Baths where they could wash the dust from their faces. Beds where they could spend the night, restful and replenished. God, as always, had provided.

240

A few silent miles later, as they neared Hebron's north gate, the fellowship passed a small hill on their left. On its peak, a dozen wooden posts had been driven deeply, permanently into the earth at even intervals. To the unknowing eye, they looked like the naked anchors of some unfinished structure. But to Balthazar and his fellow thieves, they seemed like claws reaching out of the earth, ready to grab them if they strayed too close.

Crucifixion was among the bloodier innovations the Romans had brought from the West, and it had quickly become a favorite method of execution throughout this part of the empire. The condemned were attached to beams by having spikes driven through their palms and into the wood. After those beams were hoisted up, men simply hung in agony for hours, sometimes days, humiliated by their nakedness, covered in the remnants of their own filth. As hunger and thirst set in, they were taunted with unkept promises of food and water. Pelted with stones and poked at with spears.

Some had their legs shattered by the clubs of earth-bound soldiers. Sometimes this was done to hasten death. More often, it was done to make their final hours even more wretched. When at last they did die – usually from blood loss, exposure, shock, starvation, or infection – their stinking, discolored bodies were left to wither in the heat for weeks . . . a warning to men thinking of committing similar crimes. A warning to men like Balthazar.

Thankfully, there were no men affixed to those posts today. Balthazar had witnessed the suffering of crucifixion before, and he never wished to see it again.

Still, as he left the hill behind and led the others through the north gate, he couldn't help but feel a chill swim through his blood. There was something about those posts. Something about how they'd looked. Naked, and eager for company. Hungry.

Almost like they were looking at us.

Something was wrong. Balthazar suddenly had that feeling. The feeling of eyes on him. It was undefined and instinctual, but it was real. Maybe he'd caught a glint of something in the corner of his eye; maybe he'd felt some tiny, almost imperceptible change in his surroundings. Whatever it was, Balthazar decided, silently, that they wouldn't be spending the night in Hebron.

Through the gate and into the bustle they went. Directly in front of them, a wide, central street ran straight and clear to the other side of the village, packed with people and lined with tall palm trees on either side. To their left, a bazaar rang with the blended noise of merchants, customers, and animals. To their right, dozens of Jewish pilgrims swarmed toward a massive square monument in the distance – a clean, windowless cube of white stone blocks, with walls eighty feet high and six feet thick. Joseph had never seen it before, but he knew at once what it was.

'The Cave of the Patriarchs,' he whispered.

It was one of the holiest sites in all of Judea. Second only to the Great Temple to some. For as plain as its white stone walls were, those walls protected something

242

extraordinary beneath: the final resting place of Abraham. The father of Judaism.

Legend held that Abraham and his wife, Sarah, had asked to be entombed in a cave beneath Hebron. For thousands of years, the faithful had come to the cave's sealed mouth to offer their prayers to the man who'd communed with God, the woman who'd borne Isaac and Ishmael.

Herod had ordered a monument built over the site – another selfless gift to his Jewish subjects. And while many felt the monument defaced Abraham's grave, men still traveled days to offer their prayers at its walls. To pray over the bones of the man from whom all Jews were descended, from Isaac to Moses to David. Joseph had often thought of making the pilgrimage himself, but the opportunity had never arisen, until now.

Here he was, cave in sight. And in spite of the troubles that had led him here, Joseph couldn't resist the urge to join those pilgrims he watched streaming toward its wall, off to commune with the Lord. He said as much to the others.

'Are you crazy?' asked Balthazar. 'We don't have time to stop and pray. We have to resupply and get out of Hebron as quickly as we can.'

'If ever we needed God's ear,' said Joseph, 'it's now. Besides, to be so close and not pay my respects . . . it would be a sin.'

'Sin or no sin, I'm not going to watch you pray in front of a wall. End of discussion.'

'Then don't go,' said Mary. 'My husband and I will go by ourselves while you get supplies.'

243

'We're not splitting up,' said Balthazar. 'Not when we've got the whole world looking for us.'

'And who are they looking for?' asked Mary. 'Four men, a woman, and a baby. If we stick together, we'll only draw more attention to ourselves.'

Balthazar felt his jaw clench. He hated this woman. The way she looked, the way she talked, as if she knew everything. But what he really hated was the fact that – in this case, anyway – she was right. They would attract less attention if they split up. *But I'll sit here and glare at you a moment longer, just so we're clear on how much I despise you.*

'Fine,' he said at last. 'We meet at the south gate in an hour. You're not there, we leave without you.'

Mary glared back at Balthazar. *Just so we're clear that I'm not afraid of you.*

'South gate,' she said. 'One hour.'

After tying their camels up along the Street of Palms, the fellowship went their separate ways.

The wise men headed left toward the bazaar, where Gaspar and Melchyor would trade the last of their stolen gold for whatever it would buy, and Balthazar would work on stealing *more* gold. Joseph, Mary, and the baby went right, toward the Cave of the Patriarchs, braving a sea of faithful pilgrims to pay their respects to the ancient founder of their faith.

Joseph held on to Mary for dear life, fearful that she and the baby would be swept away in the current of bodies if he let go. The area around the monument was even worse than it'd looked – packed with bodies and filled with unrelenting noise. Musicians clanging their cymbals and plucking their harps. Merchants enticing the faithful to buy all manner of souvenirs. There were sacrificial goats and oxen braying and bleating, money changers pouring coins. Above it all, the din of a thousand voices muttering a thousand prayers.

And then there were the prophets. The screaming prophets, who could be found holding court on all sides of the monument, issuing dire warnings of God's wrath, of Herod's – even Rome's overthrow from atop their makeshift platforms. Proclaiming the day of the Messiah was at hand – the day that would see the children of Israel freed from bondage. The same thing they'd been proclaiming for thousands of years.

'He will strike the earth with the rod of his mouth! With the breath of his lips he will slay the wicked! Righteousness will be his belt, and faithfulness the sash around his waist!'

One of these prophets, who called himself Simeon, was ranting to an anemic – and by the looks of it, bored – group of nine or ten followers as Joseph and Mary tried to push their way past. It was the same fiery sermon he'd been barking for weeks:

'Herod executes those who dare speak against him! He rules through brutality, and he remains in power because we fear him! Well I say *he* has reason to fear! For it is written that the arrival of the Messiah is at hand! A king of the Jews, who will topple not only the rulers of Judea and Galilee, but also the rulers of all the world! And when our Savior comes, it will be with . . . with a . . .'

Simeon's eyes had landed on a young girl on the other side of the crowded street. A girl being led along with a child in her arms. He stepped down from his platform, not quite sure of why he was doing so, and pushed his way through the mob.

Joseph turned his head just in time to see this strange, wild-eyed man grab Mary's hand.

'You!' Joseph cried. 'Let go of her!'

But Simeon the prophet didn't move. He just stared at Mary, as if reunited with a long-lost friend . . . his face a mix of reverence and terror.

'A sword,' he said. 'A sword shall pierce your heart . . .'

As the words fell from his mouth, they seemed to come from a far-off place – as if spoken by someone else. Someone behind his eyes. Years later, Simeon wouldn't even remember saying them. And when told by his future followers what he'd said, he would claim to have no idea what the words had meant.

Joseph shoved him aside and pulled Mary along, eager to be rid of this madman. Simeon held on to Mary's hand firmly for a moment, then let it slip from his fingers. He watched her go, his eyes suddenly, inexplicably filled with tears. *Filled with joy.* Something had stirred within him. Something he couldn't possibly explain.

Balthazar hovered above the earth – watching, waiting. He stood atop Hebron's north wall, near the leaning ladder he'd used to scale it. Looking down on the bazaar that ran along it below. He needed money to buy their much-needed supplies. And to get it, he needed a pocket to pick.

'C'mon,' he muttered to himself. 'I know you're out there . . .'

There weren't as many targets as there would've been in the markets of Jerusalem or Antioch. Hebron's bazaar was a decidedly smaller affair, with fewer goods to buy and fewer overstuffed coin purses to steal. He scanned the earth from his perch, a mere sixteen feet from the ground, yet above it all: above the people shoving past each other, moving up and down the dirt street that ran through the market's center. Above the men haggling with merchants, the women dragging uncooperative children behind. He could see Gaspar arguing with a man over the price of dried fruits, as Melchyor stood fatly and faithfully behind him. An old woman with a clubfoot limping blindly along. A dog pushing its nose through the dirt, sniffing around for anything that might've—

'There you are.'

Balthazar locked onto a heavyset man in sweat-soaked robes. From the quality of his clothing and the size of his belly, he was well-to-do. And from the unevenness of his gait, he was carrying something heavy on his belt. Balthazar guessed it wasn't a weapon. *No, you're not a fighter. You're not a fighter or a farmer or a slave trader . . . You're a* money changer. *One of the larger specimens I've seen too.*

Large was good. The bigger they were, the less aware of their bodies they tended to be.

Balthazar reached for the ladder, ready to climb down and follow his target through the crowd. Following, waiting for the right time to make his move, setting up for a bump. *A bump. Bumps are always good with bigger targets.* When the time was right, he would 'accidentally' knock into the money changer. It would have to be a good jolt – enough to startle him but not enough to hurt. *You never want to hurt them, no. Never want to make them angry.* As he had a thousand times, Balthazar would apologize profusely for his clumsiness and be gone before the money changer realized exactly what he'd lost at the moment of impact. His plan in place, Balthazar put one foot on the ladder, ready to climb down and—

There's that feeling again.

The feeling of eyes on him. The feeling that something was wrong. But where the first instance had been vague, unattached to any particular evidence, this one was validated almost at once. In stepping onto the ladder, Balthazar had turned his body away from the bazaar, ready to climb down. Now he lifted his eyes and looked out over the top of the wall and into the desert that lay beyond. And as he did, Balthazar felt his heart sink, for he knew that there was a very slim chance they would make it out of Hebron alive.

Romans.

Thousands of them, massed in the desert, less than a mile north of Hebron. They were lined up in ranks. But they weren't charging toward the north gate, sabers held high. Nor were they limping along, as if they'd been tracking Balthazar and the others through the desert all day. They were simply standing still. In fact, these didn't look like soldiers who were in pursuit at all. They looked like soldiers who'd been . . .

Waiting. They were waiting for us.

Balthazar and his companions had been lured into a trap. Made to feel safe and alone as they rode into Hebron, only to be surrounded on their arrival. Imprisoned by its almost perfectly square, smooth walls. The 'how' of it all would come later, if ever. Right now, Balthazar had to find the others.

Pilate was a patient man.

Though he still wasn't entirely sure how, the magus – or rather, his snake – had tracked their prey to a cave south of Emmaus. And though he wasn't entirely sure why, he'd decided to take the magus at his word when he reported having a vision of six fugitives walking down a street lined with tall, uniform palm trees on either side. If this vision was accurate, then the Antioch Ghost was headed to Hebron. It made sense. Hebron was on the way to Egypt. A perfect place to rest and resupply. The question was, what to do with this information.

Pilate knew he couldn't storm Hebron and slay a seemingly innocent couple in cold blood.

What, run their baby through with a sword in the light of day? Only a madman like Herod would do such a thing. Besides, the Jews would start a riot.

Nor could he challenge the Antioch Ghost in the open desert. Not with 10,000 of his men lumbering along, kicking up dust. They'd be spotted miles off, and the fugitives would have too much time to escape.

A trap. That was the smart move. The patient move.

Pilate would race to Hebron, but he wouldn't enter it. He would hold the bulk of his men outside the city walls, keeping the emperor's treasured magus safe and keeping a respectful distance from the pilgrims who'd come to see the Cave of the Patriarchs. At the same time, he would dispatch horsemen to cover all possible exits – every gate on every side of the city. A small detachment of foot soldiers would take position on the streets adjacent to the Street of Palms, closing in and attacking only if something went wrong. He would let his targets ride into Hebron, thinking they were days ahead of their pursuers. *Thinking they're safe.*

Pilate had watched, his spies scattered among the masses, his men perched on rooftops. He'd watched all those who rode into Hebron from the north, until at last he'd spotted three exhausted camels making their way through the north gate, three swordsmen, a couple, and their child on their backs. He'd watched as the Antioch Ghost and his companions had split up, the Ghost and his fellow thieves to the bazaar and the couple and child to the Cave of the Patriarchs. And while this split had been unexpected, it was manageable. Pilate dealt in the unexpected. He watched from a second-floor window overlooking the Street of Palms . . . knowing that he and fate would soon find each other, one way or another.

Joseph had paid his respects, braving the throngs to lay a hand on the monument that covered the Cave of the Patriarchs. He'd stopped only long enough to say a quiet prayer for the dead, while Mary waited with the baby nearby. His prayer finished, he'd taken her hand and led her back the way they'd come.

All in all, it hadn't been the experience he'd hoped for. The site had been too crowded. The monument too plain. And when he'd finally worked his way close enough to feel the stone against his palm and send his thoughts to God, Joseph had felt rushed. Unable to concentrate. Not because of the noise of his fellow pilgrims or the worries of recent days. It was something else. Even now, as they pushed their way through the crowds, Joseph felt the presence of something sinister outside the walls of his mind, and he didn't know why.

He and Mary fought the current of bodies until they reached the Street of Palms, walking south down its center, toward where they'd tied up their camels. They would reach the south gate in plenty of time to meet the others.

And then Joseph beheld a miracle . . . his heart full to bursting.

The palm trees that lined the street were bowing their heads. Bowing in reverence as they passed. *Could it be? Do they bow for us?* Joseph turned to Mary, wondering if she saw it too – but her eyes were fixed squarely on the child below. *The child*, thought Joseph. *They bow for the child!* Before he could fully grasp what he was seeing, a passage suddenly unveiled itself in his mind. A passage

251

from the Scriptures. A prophecy of the coming of the Messiah:

> *The trumpeting of angels shall herald his coming. His name shall be praised from the mountaintops, and the heavens and the earth shall bow before him . . .*

And here it was. The prophecy realized. Here was nature, bowing before an infant. Here was a vindication of everything he believed, and a total destruction of the armies of doubt that had laid siege outside his mind. The visions, the rescue from Herod's men, the stream in the desert, and now this? Now trees bowing their heads? No, there could be no doubt! His son was indeed the Messiah! God be praised!

And then the arrows came.

They came from the tops of the bowing palms. Descending from the heavens – so numerous, so dense that their black bodies looked like a swarm of insects flying in formation. Insects that had caught sight of them, of he and Mary and the baby, and begun their attack. And in the seconds that those arrows hung in the air, Joseph's eyes drifted back to their source. Only then did he see why the palm trees *really* bowed. Not in reverence to their newborn king, but because they were laden with archers. Assassins, who'd climbed to the tops of the trees and lain in wait.

An ambush.

Joseph stood in awe of the sight. A sight Mary was still blissfully unaware of.

This can't be. Why would God take us this far, only to strike us down?

Joseph was frozen, waiting for God to tell him what to do. Waiting for him to provide, as he always had. But doubt was rattling its sabers once again, louder than it ever had. He and his young wife would die where they stood. Their child – their ordinary, insignificant child – would die beside them. Right here on this street, only yards from where Abraham and Sarah had been laid to rest. Only, their bodies would have no shrines built above them. No pilgrims would come to pay tribute to their legacy, because they would have none. They would be filled with arrows, and forgotten.

'GET DOWN!'

Joseph suddenly felt his body bolt sideways as it was struck by some unseen force. Only later would he piece together what had happened in those next few seconds: how Balthazar had tackled the three of them just before the arrows arrived. How Melchyor had come running behind him, how he'd swung his sword and cut several arrows out of the air before they could reach their targets.

The baby was screaming, but Mary couldn't find breath to comfort it. She and Joseph lay on their sides, face to frightened face, still unsure of who or what had brought them to the ground. Unaware that Roman soldiers had begun to pour in from the side streets where they'd been hiding, swords drawn. They heard screams go up along the street as the veil of confusion lifted, and the people of Hebron began to understand. As mothers grabbed their children and hurried them away from the path of the arrows, and as fathers met the advancing Roman soldiers with their fists.

Balthazar and Melchyor were quick to their feet and pulled the others up with them. Balthazar kept one hand clenched around a piece of Mary's robes, determined not to lose hold of her in the panic, for there was a good chance she and the baby would be trampled if he did. With the other, he held his sword and readied himself for whatever came his way in front, while Melchyor did the same and covered their backs.

Gaspar watched his fellow fugitives from a distance, reluctant to join them. He could easily slip away in this commotion. He could run away and no one would care. *But what about Melchyor?* Poor, helpless Melchyor would be lost without him. No, Gaspar wouldn't be able to live with himself if something happened. Besides, there was no honor in betraying a loyal friend. *But there's no honor in throwing your life away either. Look, Gaspar – look at how many soldiers come from the side streets . . .*

Nearby in the bazaar, commerce ground to a halt as word spread that something big was happening on the Street of Palms. Curious customers began to walk, then run in the direction of the screams coming from just beyond the market. Merchants gathered their wares and closed their stands, wary of the looting that often followed this sort of excitement.

They'd seen it before. Arguments among the religious pilgrims had spilled into the streets; animals had thrown off their riders and trampled unlucky bystanders. In a small city, chaos was the order of the day. Most of the few dozen men making their way from the bazaar expected to find a familiar disturbance waiting for them on the Street of Palms. Instead, they were greeted by a sight they never could've fathomed:

The Roman Army had declared war on Hebron.

At least, that's the way it looked. There were Roman archers shooting at unarmed citizens from treetops, Roman soldiers bludgeoning the fathers who fought to protect their women, and women using their bodies to shield their children. A mighty army, attacking the good and gentle people of Hebron. Specifically, it looked like they were after a few helpless souls at the center of the fray, including a young woman and an infant. The men of the bazaar took this all in for a moment. There was an unwritten rule in occupied Judea: 'Fighting the Romans only brings more Romans.' It was best to let them go about their business and move on. But this wouldn't stand. The men rushed into the chaos of the street, determined to help their brothers and sisters drive back the aggressors. They picked up stones and flung them at the treetop archers, pelted and punched the soldiers as they advanced deeper into the riot.

Balthazar was fighting his way forward, dragging Mary along, when a lone soldier broke through the riot and came at them, sword held high. Balthazar swung and hit the side of the soldier's helmet with a clang, stunning him just long enough to swing again. The second strike found the soldier's jaw, leaving a deep, bloody gash clean through his right cheek, deep enough to take a piece of tongue with it. The resulting spray struck Mary's face.

She gasped but resisted the urge to bring her hands up and wipe it away. She simply held on to the baby as the red droplets ran down her cheeks. Balthazar turned and caught a glimpse of her shocked face, just long enough for a thought to flash in and out of his mind:

Tears of blood.

No sooner had the first soldier fallen than two more came on his heels, side by side. Balthazar couldn't fight both of them off, not with one hand behind his back, pulling Mary along. He wouldn't be able to block both of their blades. Balthazar saw exactly how this would play out: He would raise his sword to meet the attack, blocking the first soldier's blade. Then, as he held it there in the air, the second soldier would run him through his belly. *Unless, by some miracle, they both swung their swords at the same time.*

But there would be no miracle. The first soldier raised his sword and brought it down on Balthazar's head. Balthazar, naturally, raised his own sword to block it, even though he knew this would leave him exposed. Their blades met in the air with a clang, and Balthazar held it there with all of his strength, fully expecting that the other soldier would run him through at any moment. But the second attack never came. Only when Balthazar looked down did he realize why: the second soldier was too busy grabbing at his own belly, trying in vain to catch the blood pouring out of it.

Gaspar had attacked him from the side.

Now, with one soldier bleeding and the other disoriented, Gaspar attacked again, running Balthazar's soldier through his middle and joining his fellow fugitives in pressing forward. Balthazar wondered what had taken Gaspar so long, why he hadn't run with them when the arrows had started flying. But those questions could wait. For now, they fought through the chaos around them: the Street of Palms a mess of soldiers, angry men, and panicked women. Balthazar and Melchyor took the front; Joseph and Gaspar took the rear, all of them protecting Mary and the baby in the middle.

The camels.

'The camels!' he yelled to the others.

Balthazar knew it was their only chance: to fight their way to where the camels were tied up and ride off into the desert. But even if they could reach the animals, he knew the plan was almost certainly doomed to fail. He had seen how many Romans there were waiting beyond those walls. He'd seen their horses. Still, a long shot was better than no shot.

Mary glanced to the side as Balthazar pulled her along. She caught a glimpse of a young father – *Joseph's age* – fighting with a Roman soldier, grabbing on to the sides of his helmet with both hands and trying to bring him to the ground. She saw the young mother – *my age* – cowering behind him, protecting two small children with her body. Mary watched in horror as the soldier brought his sword down on the man's forearm, splaying it open and exposing the bone beneath. He cried out and grabbed the wound with his other hand, freeing the soldier, who struck him again, this time in the skull. The blade burrowed deep into his brain, and a spout of dark blood shot into the air above his head, pumped out by the racing heart that would soon beat its last. His young wife screamed twice first at the sight of her husband's body hitting the ground, and then as the soldier raised his sword a third time. The young mother held a defensive hand out in front of her body, only to have it split in half as the sword came down between her outstretched fingers. Mary turned away. She couldn't bear any more.

But the horrors were everywhere. As Mary looked forward, she saw Melchyor drenched from head to toe, his face shimmering with blood. He led his fellow fugitives through the melee, his gifted blade catching glints of sunlight as he twirled it faster than the eye could see, cutting down the unfortunate Romans who powered their way through the panic, only to find themselves face-to-face with the most skilled swordsman in the empire.

Mary saw two soldiers break through the crowd and charge at them from the front. She watched Melchyor swing his blade through the air, taking the first soldier's head clean off and catching it by the hair with his free hand before it hit the ground. At first, she thought this was merely showing off, until Melchyor lifted the severed head and used it as a shield, blocking the second soldier's blade before running him through with his own. It was such an impressive feat that Mary almost forgot how gruesome it was.

Yet for all Melchyor's talent, even he was having trouble keeping up with this onslaught. These soldiers were better trained than the Judeans they'd faced in Bethlehem, and there were more of them. Many more, pouring in from the surrounding streets on foot and horseback. Hacking their way through an innocent mob to get to a child and a thief. The Romans were even landing a few blows, leaving gashes on Melchyor's stout little arms.

And he wasn't the only fugitive spilling his blood on the Street of Palms. A cry went out as a passing horseman drove a spear into Gaspar's shoulder blade. It wasn't a mortal wound, but it was enough to make him drop his sword and double over. The Roman was about to take another stab at Gaspar's back when his horse suddenly whinnied and reared. Balthazar withdrew his sword from the horse's hindquarters and yanked the Roman off his saddle. The horseman fell to the street, and Balthazar drove a blade into his back. The wounded horse took off on its own, cutting a path through the mob. As fate would have it, that path was in the general direction of their camels.

'This way!' yelled Balthazar, grabbing Mary's hand and pulling her again.

Melchyor threw his arm around Gaspar and helped his injured friend along, both men dripping blood as they followed Balthazar down the horse's path. The fugitives stepped over a mess of dead and dying bodies as they went. Most belonged to the men who'd come from the bazaar to join the fight. They'd made a fearless charge, but they were paying the price for that bravery with their lives. The citizens of Hebron were outnumbered and underequipped, and they were being slaughtered all along the Street of Palms, their bodies trampled against the cobblestones.

The fugitives were fifty yards from their goal when Balthazar spotted a strangely familiar face in the crowd. An officer, headed straight for them, cutting through the mess of citizens and soldiers with patience and precision. He was young for an imperator – *younger than me, if I had to guess*, thought Balthazar – but this wasn't what made him remarkable. Balthazar had never seen him before, but he felt a strange connection with the man coming straight toward him, his eyes unwavering. *You*, he thought. *You're the smart one. Smart enough to lure us into a trap instead of coming at us head-on in the open desert.*

He wasn't sure how he knew, but Balthazar was suddenly and completely sure that this was the man who'd kept his troops back, hidden – knowing that the sight of Roman patrols would've scared his targets away before he had a chance to strike. The man who'd anticipated their path through the city and set up the ambush. Somehow, Balthazar knew he was looking at the architect of their troubles. And somehow, he knew that this officer still had a very important role to play in his life, though he had no idea what it was or why he was so absolutely certain of it.

'Keep going,' Balthazar told his fellow fugitives, and handed Mary to her husband.

'But where are you—' Joseph asked.

'GO!'

Joseph led her toward the camels, Melchyor and Gaspar hobbling along behind them. Balthazar readied his sword as the officer drew closer . . . almost on him now. Strange, he thought. *It's like we're both supposed to be*

260

here. Like we're supposed to face each other here on this street, at this moment.

Before Balthazar could think any further, the officer was upon him, and the two were fighting away – each knowing, somehow, that they'd been moving toward this moment their entire lives, two boats on two rivers, winding their way toward the same sea. There was no outward acknowledgment of this feeling. They simply met in the middle of the panicked street, raised their swords, and tried to kill each other. And while the great painters would likely commemorate the occasion in grand fashion, with both men striking impressive poses in impressive outfits, the reality was far less attractive. Balthazar and Pilate were both covered in dirt and sweat and flecks of blood, both doing their best to beat the others' brains out, punching and grabbing and pulling at each other.

While Balthazar was the better swordsman, Pilate was the better fed and rested, and before long, the Antioch Ghost was on his heels, holding his sword out in front of his face, blocking Pilate's repeated strikes. *Just a few more and I'll have you on your back*, thought Pilate. *And then I'll go after the infan—*

A roar went up behind them. The roar of furious men charging into battle, their cries echoing down the length of the street. Pilate and Balthazar ceased fighting and turned toward the source of the noise.

Hundreds of screaming, devout Jews were pouring into the north end of the street, as if a dam holding a sea of bodies had suddenly broken. Word of the Roman attack had finally reached the Cave of the Patriarchs, and pilgrim and prophet alike had thrown off their shawls and rushed to help, ready to give their lives to defend the sanctity of Abraham's final resting place.

How dare the godless Romans defile such a sacred city! How dare they slaughter the innocent!

The faithful began attacking the Romans with anything they could find. Some fought with their bare hands; others used canes and rocks. The bazaar had given dozens of men to the effort. The Cave of Patriarchs had given *hundreds* – each one believing his cause righteous.

It was exactly what Pilate had feared. Exactly why he hadn't marched into the city with his banners flying. Now he would have to pull his men back or risk a real catastrophe, risk seeing the riot spreading to the rest of the city. *All of this*, he thought, looking at the madness before him. *All of this for a baby and a thie—*

Pilate remembered the Antioch Ghost and spun around with his sword raised, ready to fight again . . . but the Ghost was gone.

It doesn't make sense, Balthazar thought as he ran toward the camels. How had the Romans known where they were going to be? Why had he felt such a strange kinship with the officer?

It didn't matter, he supposed. What mattered was that no city or village was safe from now on. No road passable. No strangers could be trusted to keep their secret. Not with the Romans looking for them in such numbers.

They wouldn't be able to stop again. Not until they reached Egypt. But they wouldn't make the Egyptian border without supplies. They'd have to take a different route. An unexpected route. They wouldn't be able to venture out in public anymore, not even in disguise. It was too dangerous.

What they needed was a place to hide for a while. Resupply. Somewhere unexpected. Somewhere safe. And despite every oath he'd ever sworn to himself, Balthazar knew exactly where they needed to go.

The Return

'For it was not an enemy that reproached me; then I could have borne it: neither was it he that hated me that did magnify himself against me; then I would have hid myself from him: but it was thou, a man mine equal, my guide, and mine acquaintance.'

—*Psalms 55:12–13*

I

The door opened, and there she was, as wickedly beautiful and dangerous as he remembered.

'Hello, Sela,' he said.

How long had it been, eight years? *No, it has to be more. Could it be more?* Balthazar was too tired to tax his mind with the math. Besides, it didn't matter how long it'd been. Here they were, and here she was – a sight for six pairs of sore eyes. Here was the face they'd all crossed an ocean of sand to find, without food or rest, leaving Hebron with their camels in a full gallop, as day became freezing night became glaring morning and scorching day. Here was the reason they'd kept riding, half dead, toward the promised land of Beersheba, the last waypoint of note before the Judean Desert's long march into Egypt. The last chance to replenish. Riding with nothing to guide them but the faint hope that Balthazar's information was up to date. That the rumors he'd held on to were true. And always with the knowledge that the Romans weren't far behind.

But on reaching the city walls, the fugitives had found

the promised land of Beersheba a wasteland. At first they thought the Romans might've beaten them again, for there was hardly a man or woman to be seen on the streets. Fires had been left to burn themselves out, and malnourished dogs roamed the streets in search of scraps. But it was famine, not Roman swords, that had laid waste to Beersheba. For its crops had been decimated by the only thing farmers feared more than drought:

Locusts.

They'd come as a black cloud. A living storm, half the size of Judea, eating its way across North Africa. Tens of millions of soulless eyes and insatiable mouths, flying from field to field, leaf to leaf, consuming everything they touched. And though months had passed since they'd come through Beersheba, leaving ruin in their wake, the ground was still littered with their withered molts. The dead shells that each locust had cast off, renewing itself before moving on, leaving the city a dead shell, suddenly and totally transformed but not renewed.

The once-vibrant streets were now eerily quiet. Empty. With the crops had gone the traders and merchants, and with the traders and merchants had gone the slaveholders and their slaves. They'd all moved on in search of food and commerce, leaving only a skeleton crew of faithful denizens behind. Seeing all of this on their arrival, Balthazar's faint hope had just about snuffed itself out:

She won't be here. She'll have moved on like the others.

But here she was.

Here she was, standing at the door of a two-story house, its smooth white walls and red-tiled roof distinctly

Roman. Here she was, clearly stunned to see his face.

Of course she's stunned. Here I am, after all this time, after what happened, after the way it ended.

Sela stared back at him for what seemed like ages, her expression unchanging. Her hair black as ink. Her body long and lean, with skin a polished copper, same as her eyes. *Ten years. No, it's definitely ten.* She would be twenty-four now, give or take a year, but she looked almost exactly as he'd left her.

Balthazar smiled. That sad smile she used to love. *The one she could never resist. Not for all her anger, not for all her sadness and distrust.* Those things had never mattered when it came to Balthazar. They'd always just seemed to melt away when she looked at him. Back when they were young, and in the kind of love that only the young can be in. The first love. The sick-to-your-stomach, lying-awake-all-night-counting-the-hours-until-you-saw-each-other-next kind.

Did she ever think this day would come? Did she half expect to see me standing here every time she opened this door? Has she thought of me as often as I've thought of her? Has there ever been someone else? More than one someone? Is there someone now?

Balthazar opened his mouth to pay her a compliment. It wasn't fully formed yet, but he was leaning in the direction of praising her beauty. Something like, 'The years have been kind.'

No, that's stupid. Of course they haven't been kind.

'You haven't aged a day' popped in next, but it lacked the poetry he was going for.

'You're just like I remember?' *No, that evokes the past, and we definitely don't want to bring up the past.*

With his mouth fully open and his time up, Balthazar settled on the innocuous but safe, 'It's good to see you.'

But before the words could roll off his tongue, a fist was in his mouth.

It was driven there with so much force that his own teeth were briefly weaponized and turned against him, cutting clean through his top and bottom lip from the inside. Balthazar nearly passed out as his brain rattled around in his skull, and he staggered backward into the cobblestone street, struggling to keep his balance.

At first he didn't realize he'd been hit. There'd been no windup, no change of expression to warn him it was coming. One minute she'd been there, beautiful and clear, and the next, there'd been three of her – her faces floating behind a thick sheet of cloudy glass. By the time the first packets of pain began to arrive from his mouth, slicing their way through the fog, he'd been hit again. First with another fist, and then with the bottom of a sandal, as Sela kicked him square in the throat.

For a moment, it had all been beauty and reminiscence. The music of love's long-delayed reunion. Now Balthazar was clutching his throat, gasping for breath and barely clinging to consciousness, fists and feet coming at him without mercy. His arms hung stupidly at his side as his face was struck again and again. Fist, sandal, sandal, fist. The only thing keeping him from passing out was curiosity. His mind was so wrapped up in trying to sort out just what the hell was happening, that it refused to shut down. Even as another kick found his chin, snapping his head back violently and sending Balthazar to the ground with a dull thud.

Somewhere, across a shapeless, cavernous space, the others were looking down at him, stunned and silent. One of them was yelling something. Something like 'Wait!' or 'Stop!' or 'What are you doing?'

Is that the carpenter? Is that the carpenter telling her to stop? I can't te— gahhhhhh, my face hurts . .

With Balthazar rolling on his back, clutching at his already-swollen lips and nose, Sela finally stopped and got a good look at the other people outside her front door: three men, a girl, and an infant. All of their jaws hanging open. All of them looking at her, wondering if they were next. With her chest rising and falling with each heavy breath, Sela brushed aside the hair in her eyes, and said, 'Come in.'

II

He was fourteen when he first saw her. Only two years older than he'd been when he'd robbed his first grave, but 100 years wiser.

He could remember the day, the hour, her clothes, the light. He'd been walking home from the forum, where he once picked pockets amid the noise and madness, risking so much for such paltry rewards. But not anymore. Things were different now. There was no need to pick pockets, to pay off accomplices and reward tips with part of the profits. These days, Balthazar visited the forum to spend, not earn. And there was plenty to spend, thanks to his stroke of genius, his realization that it was easier to steal from the dead than the living.

Nearly every night after that first plunder, Balthazar had waded through the dark water, returning to the shallow Roman graves on the far side of the Orontes. Nearly every night, so long as the moon hadn't been too bright or the sentries too close, he'd dug up the freshly buried corpses of the condemned. He'd been frightened at first, yes, especially when he unearthed some of the more gruesome specimens. Those who'd been beheaded or stoned to death. Being so recently buried, their blood was often wet, the expressions on their faces still fresh. Alone in the dark, Balthazar's young imagination had gotten the best of him in the early weeks: He'd seen their eyes pop open, felt their cold fingers grab at his arms. But as the months wore on, these hallucinations had grown less frequent, and the fear had grown weaker and weaker, until one day, he realized it had disappeared altogether.

In the two years since his stroke of genius, Balthazar had gotten so fast that he could process ten corpses in a single night, assuming the executioners had been that busy – digging them up, looting them, and returning them to the desert without the Romans ever knowing he'd been there. Filling his pockets with their rings and necklaces, with their silver and gold and silk. And all without a single accomplice. So much more reward, with only a fraction of the risk.

A month after he began operations, Balthazar had stolen enough to move his family into a new neighborhood. A year after that, he'd moved them again – this time into a house that had once belonged to a Roman nobleman. His sisters had new fabrics to sew. Abdi had new clothes and toys. And his mother had everything a mother could want: a new house to care for, plenty of food to cook, a new stove to cook it in, rugs to sit on, oil lamps to light her way. And while Balthazar knew she had her suspicions about their newfound wealth, she never asked him where the money came from or where he disappeared to each night. The closest she ever came was just before they moved into the nobleman's house. Upon seeing it for the first time, Balthazar's mother pulled him aside, looked him squarely in the eye, and said, 'Before I sleep under this roof, promise me one thing.'

'Anything, Mama.'

'Promise me that our happiness doesn't come at the expense of another's.'

He looked at her for a moment, silently wrestling with the prospect of lying to his mother's face. More specifically, wrestling with how he was going to do it convincingly. On one hand, their happiness was certainly coming at another's expense. If you wanted to get right down to it, people had paid for their happiness with their lives. On the other hand, she'd left him a fairly sizable loophole. Technically speaking, he was taking valuables from people who no longer had any use for them. Having a necklace or a gold ring wasn't going to change the fact that they were dead, was it? He wasn't making them any less happy than they'd been when they died, was he? Therefore, he could technically say in all honesty, 'I promise.'

Balthazar had been tempted to tell her, just as he'd been tempted to tell his fellow thieves. But he'd kept his mouth shut. He hadn't spoken a word of his dealings with the dead. Not to his family and *especially* not to his fellow pickpockets. It wasn't that he feared their condemnation, although he knew that some would surely condemn him for violating the old superstitions. What he really feared was their competition. Balthazar knew he wasn't the only boy who'd be able to see his way past a few social mores and dead bodies. Not when there was that much money just sitting there in the sand, ready for the taking.

No, he'd stumbled onto a treasure vault that constantly replenished itself, and he wasn't about to share it. Not when the Romans were sending so many men and their jewelry to the executioner. Not when everything was going so perfectly.

And then he saw her, and it all went to hell.

He'd been walking home from the forum, carrying a bag of grain along the cobblestone streets of his new neighborhood. A neighborhood that was home to the 'better' families of Antioch. *Families like ours.* Typically, he spent these walks staring at his feet, his mind wandering through a series of disconnected thoughts and images.

Something funny Abdi said it's cloudy out today bodies will there be tonight my feet are killing father felt anything when he died.

But on this day, at this moment, he decided to look up. And when he did, he was struck by an otherworldly image. At first he thought it was a ghost. The ghost of a beautiful girl, rendered as real as the hallucinations he used to have in the graves. She was sitting alone on the front stoop of a one-story brick villa – one of the nicer homes in the neighborhood.

She was the most beautiful thing he'd ever seen, and she was crying her eyes out.

The most unlikely little sliver of sunlight had cut through the clouds and fallen on her back, making the edges of her black hair burn and giving her that ghostly, otherworldly look. She was a native Syrian, like him. But Balthazar knew at once that she wasn't like him at all. This was a girl who hadn't grown up stealing for a living. Who'd never known hunger.

But you haven't had it easy, either. No, you've had a terrible time on this earth. And somehow that makes you twice as beautiful, although I'm not sure why, or even if it's possible for you to be ANY more beautiful than you already are.

As it happened, Sela looked up at precisely the same time and found a boy standing in the middle of the street with a bag of grain over his shoulder, staring at her like a dumb animal. His body frozen, his mouth hanging open as he watched her cry.

'What are you looking at?'

'I . . . uh—'

'You think it's funny, standing there and looking at me?'

'No! No, I—'

'Leave me alone!'

She turned away, crossed her arms, and waited for the boy to leave. And waited.

'No,' he said.

Later, Balthazar would only remember pieces of what happened next: Sela looking up and glaring at him through her tears, wickedly beautiful and dangerous. He remembered dropping his bag on the ground and working up the courage to sit beside her. He remembered asking her what was wrong. He remembered her resisting, then relenting. And once she began to tell him everything, he remembered that she didn't stop until long after night had fallen. It was a variation of a story he'd heard so many times before. Another tale of woe at the hands of the Roman occupiers.

Sela was an only child, her mother having died when she was very young. Too young to remember her face, her voice, or her touch. But her father, a successful importer, was able to provide her with a comfortable upbringing. He was a quiet, kind man. And though he never spoke of his departed wife aloud, Sela knew that he never stopped mourning her. He doted on his only daughter, and, in turn, she devoted herself to his happiness – eschewing the usual childhood pursuits to be by his side. It was all very pleasant-sounding, Balthazar remembered now. Pleasant days passing pleasantly by, blending together until they formed a relatively pleasant, if uneventful childhood.

And then, like a scorpion stinging the foot of a passerby, Sela's pleasant days had been suddenly and violently ended. Her father had found himself on the wrong side of a business dispute with a member of the Roman provincial authority. An assistant to an advisor to the Roman-appointed governor of Antioch. And while he couldn't remember the details of the dispute – something about price promised versus price paid – Balthazar remembered the outcome:

Sela's father had been roused from sleep that night by a banging on his door, dragged from his home as his daughter scratched and pulled at the faceless soldiers around her. That very night, he was sent to the executioner without trial, beheaded and tossed in a shallow desert grave. All on the whim of some nameless, middle-ranking foreign bureaucrat. All over a business dispute. Just like that. That's how fast these things happened.

Balthazar remembered the chill that had gone from his toes to his fingertips when she'd told him this. And while he would never tell her of his dealings with the dead, not on that or any night, Balthazar would often wonder if her father had been among the bodies he'd dug up on the other side of the Orontes. If some small part of his happiness had come at her expense.

A year had passed since her father's death, and here she was. Fourteen. All alone in a big house. Struggling to get by as best as an honest girl could, but not doing a very good job of it. Here she was, wiping away her tears and saying something to a boy she'd only just met. Saying it like she absolutely believed it: 'I swear . . . before I die . . . I'll watch all of Rome burn to the ground.'

Balthazar remembered thinking, *Now, there's a nice image . . . all of Rome in flames. A beautiful girl laughing as she watched it burn from a hill above the city – the warm winds kicked up by the fire below, making her hair dance around her face.*

Balthazar said he believed her. Though silently he doubted that any army, let alone a single person, could pull off such a feat. But there was no doubting her resolve. He could feel the anger radiating off her body, just as heat radiates from the stones around a fire, long after the flames have died out. And it was intoxicating, that anger. Anger and beauty, sadness and loneliness, all mixed up in one face.

He remembered a kiss and knowing that he was hopelessly and forever in love.

Pleasant days had blended pleasantly together after that. Balthazar had chipped away at the honest, sheltered girl he'd found on the stoop, teaching her how to fight, how to steal, how to do a better job of getting by. Showing her a side of Antioch she'd never known in the comfort and isolation of her youth. He'd doted on her, provided for her, spending his every free moment by her side, often with Abdi tagging along. Sela, for her part, fell into a familiar role, devoting herself to his happiness. Forcing Balthazar to unfurrow his brow. Forcing him to laugh. Showing him a side of Antioch he'd only recently discovered but never really known.

They'd been the kind of days that shone golden in the memories of the old. Days when it had all been promise and forever ahead. Days spent confiding in each other, whispering things they'd never dared to whisper before. And nights, those impossibly warm nights, spent walking the Colonnaded Street, hand in hand. Sneaking off to the banks of the Orontes, disrobing by the light of the stars. Wading into the water and standing face-to-face, pressed against each other beneath the surface. Feeling each other's nakedness in the black water. The same water Balthazar had waded through, back and forth between the living world and the dead. But these things were far away when he was with her. In these moments, it was just perfect, and it always would be, as if destiny had delivered them to exactly this place, if you believed in stupid things like destiny. Like he'd been sent to rescue her from being alone. To look after her. And like she'd been sent to rescue him back. And, God, it had been so stupidly giddy and erotic and perfect.

And then, like a scorpion stinging the foot of a passerby, it had all been brought crashing down in a single moment.

Just like that.

III

It was a big house by any measure, especially for a woman living alone. The first floor had two bedrooms, one where Sela had slept alone for the last five years and one where she'd worked when there was work to be found. They were centered on a large kitchen and common area, with a table and chairs and rugs covering every square inch of floor. There were three smaller bedrooms upstairs. The previous owner had filled them with children. But Sela had never had any use for them. Not until tonight.

Darkness had only just begun to fall outside, but most of the fugitives had excused themselves and disappeared upstairs for the night, eager to be rid of the strained silence that had hung over the house since their arrival. Balthazar sulked alone in one of the bedrooms, nursing wounds of the face and ego and quietly cursing all those giddy and erotic and perfect memories that had flooded into his rattled mind after their extended absence. He lay on his back, staring at the ceiling through a pair of black eyes. He could hear Gaspar and Melchyor's muffled whispers through the wall on his right and Joseph's deep, rhythmic snores on his left. He didn't know which sound he hated more. Or if he hated them at all. Or if he just hated everything.

I shouldn't have come. I should've known *she'd react like this.*

It was all so stupid, so juvenile. He was a killer. A thief. The Scourge of Rome. And look at him now. Caring for a baby and a couple of zealots. Beaten bloody by a woman. A hole in his chest. The Roman Army on his heels.

Of the six fugitives, only Mary and the baby remained downstairs after sunset. Sela sat with them at the table in the common area, watching the fifteen-year-old girl across from her – *not much older than I was when I met him* – bathe the tiny, wrinkled creature in a bowl of warm water. His blue eyes were wide open, darting around, looking at everything without really looking at anything. His head was propped against one shoulder to relieve the burden of his tiny neck, and the remnants of his umbilical cord had blackened and shriveled over his belly button, threatening to fall off at any moment.

Sela sat in silent fascination, watching him. Listening to the involuntary little *hics* and *coos* come out of his body as his mother gently washed the dust of the desert off his fragile scalp. She'd never had a sibling, never had cousins to care for. She'd never even held a baby, best as she could recall. *Abdi was the closest thing I ever—*

'Do you take boarders?' asked Mary.

It was a reasonable question, given that the house was

much bigger than most single women would need or be able to afford without some form of income.

'No,' said Sela. 'But I work. Down here . . . in one of the rooms.'

Mary was suddenly embarrassed that she'd brought it up. *Of course.* She knew what line of 'work' Sela was in. *A beautiful woman with no husband, no children? A beautiful, sophisticated woman who seems to have plenty of mon—*

'I'm not a whore, if that's what you're thinking.'

'What?' said Mary. 'No! No, I didn't think . . . I didn't think that.'

Sela watched the girl's cheeks turn bright red. *No . . . of course you didn't – that's why you're blushing and indignant.*

'I read fortunes,' said Sela.

'Oh . . .'

'Farmers pay me to predict the weather; women pay me to tell them how many children they'll have. We sit, I conjure, they pay. Though business has been a little slow since the locusts came. Nobody needs a fortune-teller to tell them things in Beersheba are going to be bad for a long, long time.'

'And you . . . know these things? These answers they're looking for?'

'I know what people want to hear.'

The blush drained out of Mary's cheeks, and she tried to keep her face from betraying her disappointment. Fortune-telling wasn't much better than prostitution, especially when the 'telling' part was outright lying. Religiously speaking, it was worse. The Scriptures expressly forbade such things. In the eyes of God, Sela was a false prophet. *And false prophets are heretics. And heretics, well —*

'Are you all right?' asked Sela. 'You look troubled.'

Mary continued to wash the baby's skin, staring vacantly off into a dark corner of the room as Sela's eternal damnation played out in her mind. She suddenly felt as though she were standing across the table from a leper. As if Sela's sin was contagious. There was a palpable urge to snatch her baby up, to protect him from that sin. To wash it off his body. Given the circumstances, the least offensive thing she could think to say was, 'It's just . . . I couldn't lie to people, I guess.'

'Why not? You lied to me.'

Mary looked up sharply. Visions of damnation gone in a flash. 'I did not.'

'Sure you did.'

'Why would you say—'

'When I told you I wasn't a whore, that's *exactly* what you'd been thinking. But you insisted it wasn't. "No, no, no – I would *never* think that!"'

Mary blushed again.

'Look at me and tell me I'm wrong.'

'I . . . I was trying to be polite.'

'Uh-huh. You do it to be polite. I do it to give hopeless people a little hope and make a little money while I'm at it. Either way, we're both liars.'

Mary didn't like this woman. She didn't like being here. She didn't like any of this. For the thousandth time since she and Joseph had left Nazareth, she felt the pangs of homesickness. She longed for the familiar faces of the village, the foods and sounds and smells. She longed for the comfort of family. For the spiritual lift that came with being surrounded by the fellow faithful. She and her husband were alone in the great big world. A terrible world, filled with murderers and heathens and famine, with bullying thieves and contagious sin. They were alone, and they were the bearers of an impossible burden: to protect the most important thing that had ever lived from the most powerful men in the world. And, God, he was so small . . .

IV

Herod looked down at the deathly white body beneath him. Silent and still. Her eyes open and bulging. Spit drying on the corners of her mouth.

It wasn't your fault, he thought. *You were simply in the wrong place when the news reached me. You were simply there when I needed something to kill.*

Herod supposed he regretted killing her, if only because he wouldn't get to enjoy her again. Her wetness and warmth. But he'd done her a service, in a way. Think of all the misery she would be spared. Even if she didn't eventually grow sick from his touch, think of all the disappointing years that lay ahead. Years of growing older, of taking a husband. Bearing his children. Her body betraying her, her beauty leaving her as she aged. But she would be spared all of that. This little one would be beautiful for all time.

Besides, who could blame him for reacting the way he did? It had been unwelcome news. They'd had them. The Romans had surrounded the Antioch Ghost and the child in Hebron, Herod had been told. They'd had archers

286

lying in wait on the Street of Palms and men hidden on adjacent streets. But when the ambush was sprung, a riot had broken out. Zealots and pilgrims had attacked the Romans as they flooded in, holding them off before they could reach their targets.

Why didn't they just take them in the open desert? Or arrest them quietly once they entered the city walls? Why do the Romans always have to make such a show of everything?

But as unwelcome as these developments were – as angry as they'd made him – they hadn't made him kill. No. It was fear, not anger, that had cost this little girl her life. Fear that had summoned Herod's hands to her throat and made them squeeze the life out, until her bulging eyes glazed over and foam ran red from her mouth. Herod had killed her because for the first time since these troubles began, he was frightened.

To any rational mind, the facts demanded fear. The Romans had been close enough to touch the Antioch Ghost. Close enough to touch the baby's belly with the tip of their swords. All the might of the empire had descended on a single street, with a single purpose: to kill a wretched little thief and the helpless little infant he harbored. And what had happened? The impossible. One man – one injured, exhausted man – had slipped through their fingers.

When Herod had been told the details of Hebron, he'd known. This was no longer a simple matter of old prophecies and ancient superstitions. This was the God of Abraham taunting the King of Judea. Laughing in the face of Herod's power. Of Rome's might. There could be no more doubt: The child was indeed the Messiah. And if allowed to live – if allowed to reach Egypt and disappear beyond the eyes of Judea and Rome – then he would topple the kingdoms of the world. Perhaps even the empire itself.

The emperor won't believe a word of it, of course. No matter what the evidence is, or how many miracles deliver the fugitives from the hands of his troops. But I know . . . and it's time I got directly involved.

Herod thought about his next steps, lying beside a girl who would never know the miseries of age. He would honor her memory somehow. When this was all over, he would do something to make up for his outburst. Perhaps he would order a statue of her made and added to the collection in his courtyard so that he might enjoy her beauty again whenever he went for a stroll outside.

But first, he would enjoy her body one last time.

V

The cool light of early morning invited itself through the windows, the house still quiet and asleep. Balthazar sat alone at the large table downstairs, a knife in his hand. The wound on his chest had finally healed enough for his stitches to come out, and he was carefully cutting them one by one. Pulling the loose threads from his skin, until a shadow cut across the table in front of him, drawing his eyes up.

Sela was standing in the doorway of her bedroom, her hair a mess and her eyes half asleep. *But still so beautiful it isn't fair.* She was quick to look away and continue in, as if she'd expected to find him sitting here so early, bare chested and knife in hand. Balthazar, for his part, had been quick to resume cutting his stitches out, pretending she wasn't there at all.

It had been this way for three days. No words had passed between them since their painful reunion. Balthazar had made a point of avoiding her, keeping mostly to his room upstairs, nursing his swollen eyes and cut lips. Coming down only when he knew she was away or asleep and relying on Joseph to bring him his meals. But with today's departure weighing heavy on his mind, he'd tossed and turned until it'd become useless to resist. And so he'd come downstairs, thinking he'd be the only one up at this hour.

She probably thought the same thing. And now here we are.

Balthazar had experienced these tense silences with other women. Silences where the air seemed to become flammable. Where a single spark could ignite it all. That's why it was best to say nothing. No good could come of words. Not when a single misplaced syllable might spark, might light the air on fire and get you blown to pieces.

Balthazar watched as she walked to the opposite side of the room, toward a water jug that sat on the sill of an open window. Pretending to cut away at his chest, he stole little glances at her as she wet her hands, washed the sleep from her face, and smoothed her hair over her scalp – all in unfairly beautiful silhouette against the fluttering curtains.

'I'm sorry,' she said, her back to him. 'You know . . . about your face.'

He was surprised to hear her voice at all. Let alone hear it issue what sounded like a genuine apology. But Balthazar said nothing in return. He just sat at the table, half stitched. *No good can come of words.*

'It's just . . . seeing you was a little . . .'

What, upsetting? Surprising? So unbelievable that you needed to kick and punch me a few times to make sure I was real? Wait, why are you talking? Don't you know the air in here might catch fire and kill us both?

Sela shook the excess water from her hands, opened the drapes, and stared out into the empty streets of Beersheba.

'After you left,' she said, 'there were days when I would go and stand on the banks of the river. Stand there for hours, looking out into the desert. Wondering if you were out there. Wondering where you were, what you were doing. If you were even alive. Sometimes . . . sometimes I would hold my hand out in front of my body . . . lean forward and close my eyes. My arm stiff, my palm facing out – listening for you. I would stand there . . . as if I could feel you with my body. As if I could send you a message. Send a thought through that outstretched hand and ask you to come home. And it was so stupid, all of it.'

She turned. He saw tears massing in the corners of her eyes, threatening to fall.

'It was so stupid and naïve, but I'd go out there, day after day, convincing myself that sooner or later one of those thoughts would reach you.'

They did . . . I thought of you every—

'You destroyed me, Balthazar.'

I know.

'You showed me how good life could be, and then you left.'

And you of all people should know why I had to.

'You left, and over time . . . I forgot. I forgot that feeling. I even forgot your face.'

What was there to say? How many times had he been over this in his mind? How many times had he imagined having this very conversation, on the remote chance he ever saw her again? And now, here he was, and there was nothing to say.

'Your mother is dead, Balthazar.'

It took him a moment to hear this. When he did, he swore he heard the *hisssss* of all that dangerous air seeping out of the room.

Oh, don't be so surprised, Balthazar. Don't you dare get all weepy eyed, as if you didn't already know. Of course she's dead. You knew she would be by now. You chose this, Balthazar. You knew you could never see her again – not after Abdi. Not after you left.

'I'm sorry,' she said. 'I should've told you sooner.'

Balthazar found tears threatening to fall nonetheless. He couldn't help but think of his mother alone at the end of her life. All alone, with so many unanswered questions, so much grief over the things she'd lost. He couldn't help but picture her face. *'Promise me . . . promise me that our happiness doesn't come at the expense of another's.'* But of course it had. It had come at a terrible expense. *Her expense. And now I'll never get to see her and tell her how sorry I—*

Balthazar turned away, not wanting her to see the tears that had made good on their threats. Sela walked closer to the table, wiping away tears of her own. He half expected to feel her hand on his shoulder. Even a kiss of condolence on his forehead. He wanted those things more than he knew how to express, but only if she was willing to give them. They weren't his to take.

'Balthazar . . . if you still care about me at all, you'll promise me something.'

He wiped his eyes and looked up at her.

Anything.

'Promise me that after you leave, I'll never see your face again.'

With that, she left him to pull the last few threads from his chest.

VI

Morning was giving way to midday, and still no sign of Gaspar or Melchyor. Balthazar paced back and forth, his face and lip almost completely healed now, his movement enough to stir the curtains that had been drawn to ward off the sun. *Where the hell are they?* They'd gone for food and supplies shortly after breakfast, leaving their fellow fugitives with Sela to pack up the camels and prepare for their departure. They had a long ride ahead. If they pressed themselves, stopping for only a few minutes at a time and making camp in the open desert, they could reach the Egyptian border in two days.

Mary was in the next room, feeding the baby beneath her shawl, while Sela topped off their canteens, taking care not to spill a single precious drop. Joseph was praying again. Kneeling in the corner of the room, muttering to himself. Though his words were barely above a whisper, they'd slowly built to a crescendo in Balthazar's ears. *We have real problems. Real problems here in the real world, and he sits there and mutters to God.* Finally, it was all he could take.

'Could you just . . . not do that?'

Joseph stopped muttering, though his eyes remained closed.

'You pace when you're anxious,' he said. 'I pray. Of the two of us, I'd say my method was less annoying.'

'Of the two of us,' said Balthazar, 'I'm the one with the sword, so I'd shut up and go do something useful before I cut your tongue out.'

Joseph's eyes opened. He rose to face Balthazar. 'Why does my prayer bother you?'

'Because! It goes on and on and on and on and on and on! I've never heard someone babble to God so much in my life!'

'Well . . . I have much to be thankful for.'

'Like what? The fact that the whole world wants your baby dead?'

'Like you.'

Joseph's answer had the desired effect of stopping Balthazar's rant in its tracks.

'You rescued us in Bethlehem,' he said. 'You led us through the desert, led us here. And you nearly gave your own life doing it. I thanked God for sending you, because if he hadn't, we'd be dead.'

'In the future, instead of thanking God, you can save yourself the trouble and just thank me directly.'

Joseph smiled. 'I know men like you,' he said. 'Men who believe that God has forsaken us. That he's grown tired of our imperfections. These men are burdened by sin. By weakness, and temptation, and guilt. And so they think *all men must be this way And if all men are this way, why would God want anything to do with man?*

'And I know men like you,' said Balthazar, 'who believe that every drop of piss is a blessing from "almighty God." Men who spend their miserable little lives shaking and mumbling, reading their scrolls and setting their goats on fire – afraid they'll eat the wrong thing, or say the wrong word, or think the wrong thought, and SMACK! God's fist will fall out of the clouds and flatten them. Well let me tell you – and I speak from experience – God doesn't care, okay? He doesn't care about you, or me, or what we do or say or eat or think.'

'He cared enough to send me his son.'

This time Balthazar made no attempt to hide the roll of his eyes. *You've got to be kidding me . . .*

'Right, right – the Messiah. And let me ask you a question: Of all the thousands of years, of all the thousands and thousands of Jews he had to choose from, God chose a poor carpenter and a little girl to raise him? Why not a king, huh? Why not let him be the son of an emperor? Give him a real chance to change things?'

Joseph thought about it as the baby began to cry in the other room. In truth, the best he could manage was, 'I don't know. I just know that he did.'

'See?' said Balthazar with a smile. 'That's the problem with your God. He doesn't think big enoug—'

'BALTHAZAR . . . OF . . . ANTIOCH!'

The voice had come from outside, cutting off the rest of Balthazar's insult. An unfamiliar voice, from in front of

296

the house. Balthazar felt the strength leave his limbs. The blood in his fingertips froze, just as they had when he'd seen the Roman legions in Hebron.

They've found us.

Silence followed. A deathly silence as Balthazar and Joseph shared a look of dread, their argument already long forgotten, and moved toward the nearest window to sneak a look through the curtains.

Here were the empty houses of Beersheba. In front of them, standing in neat formation in the street, were Roman soldiers – led by a young officer atop a brown horse. Beyond the soldiers and empty houses, a long, dark cloud hung near the horizon, silent and still. *Sandstorm*, thought Balthazar. *Big one.*

'That is your name, isn't it?' asked the officer. '"Balthazar"?'

The baby's cries were suddenly behind Balthazar's ears. Mary and Sela had come running into the room, drawn by the commotion. As soon as they saw Balthazar and Joseph kneeling by the window, they knew. *They've found us.*

'Can we get out the back?' asked Sela.

'Doubt it,' said Balthazar.

He was smart, this officer. This time he would've taken care to surround them first. To make sure there was no chance of escape. These discouraging thoughts were still forming in his head when Balthazar spotted two men standing beside the officer's horse. But these weren't Roman or Judean soldiers. They were liars and thieves. Cowards and traitors.

Gaspar and Melchyor.

'I can see why you don't use it,' the officer continued. '"The Antioch Ghost" is much more colourful, more menacing.'

Balthazar glared at his fellow wise men across the wide street. 'How long?' he yelled. 'How long have the two of you been working for these dogs? Is this how they found us in Hebron? Did you lead them right to us?'

'On my life,' said Gaspar, 'we did not.'

'Your "life"? Your "life" isn't worth the spit in your lying mouth! You only *have* a life because I spared it! I saved you! Both of you!'

Here it was. Here was a vindication of everything Balthazar believed. Here was proof that men were dogs and that all hearts were empty vessels. *It's too bad I won't live long enough to rub this in Joseph's face.*

'You have to understand,' said Gaspar, 'they caught us in the market! They . . . they recognized us. We had no choice but to—'

'Lies!'

Balthazar was right. Gaspar had been considering this betrayal for days – especially in the wake of their near-capture in Hebron. And when he'd watched the mighty Antioch Ghost get beaten senseless by a woman, the last of his faith in their fearless leader had evaporated. Better to strike a deal and live than cast their lot with Balthazar, whose luck had clearly run out.

'They offered us pardons,' said Melchyor, so stupidly and apologetically that it was hard not to feel for him.

This part, at least, was true. When Gaspar had

approached the Romans, he and Melchyor had been offered pardons in return for the Antioch Ghost and the infant.

'They offered us pardons if we led them back to—'

'Led them back to what,' cried Mary, 'an infant? You're no better than Herod's men! Both of you!'

Melchyor looked away, clearly ashamed.

'I'm sorry,' said Gaspar.

'Go to hell,' said Balthazar.

As far as insults went, it left a lot to be desired. Especially since Balthazar didn't even believe in such a place. But under the circumstances, it was the best he could muster. With an entire legion of Roman troops staring him down, surrounding the house. There would be no angry pilgrims to help them fight this time. This time they would either be captured or—

'Balthazar!'

Sela was looking out a side window, clearly distressed. Or at least, more distressed than everyone else under her roof. Balthazar and the others hurried to her and peered through the curtains and saw why.

They're going to burn us.

A handful of Roman soldiers stood ready with flaming torches in their hands, awaiting the order. Their young commander sat atop his horse, his eyes darting between the house they'd surrounded and the long, dark cloud hanging low to the horizon. *Sandstorm*, he thought. *A big one, and growing closer.*

For all the fugitives' fears of charred flesh, Pilate had no intention of burning them out. There were Jewish zealots in there, and he knew how zealots thought. *They would rather give themselves to God as burnt offerings than surrender to a godless Roman like me.* No, if he ordered the house set alight, he would only be able to watch as they martyred themselves in the flames. And what good would that be? And the Antioch Ghost? What glory was there in burning him? Pilate wanted to present his emperor with a living, quivering specimen, not a heap of charred remains. Unlike Herod, he wasn't comfortable having the blood of women and infants on his hands. This campaign had taken on a dark enough tenor already.

It was a dark thing to hunt a newborn child with swords and spears. But Pilate had comforted himself with the idea that he was merely delivering his targets to their judges. He wasn't responsible for what happened after that. What Pilate *wasn't* comfortable with was the magus. The way he frightened the men with his strange little rituals. With his very appearance. The power he seemed to have to conjure visions from the air, to breathe life into places it didn't belong. The way he seemed to know exactly where their targets were going. This was an altogether different kind of darkness. One that any rational man would know to fear. But in this case, Pilate's hands were tied. Augustus wished it, and so it must be done. But Pilate had tried to keep the emperor's little mystic on a tight leash – keeping him sequestered 'for his own safety.' Under guard, alone in his tent. Miles from where they now stoo—

Stop.

Pilate caught his mind wandering and reined it back

in. The image of the magus had just popped into his head out of nowhere, distracting him from the task at hand. Regaining focus, he noticed the torch-bearing solders beginning to advance on the house, their faces uniformly blank. Their movements stilted and awkward, as if they had strings attached to their limbs, being pulled from above. At first he thought it was some kind of joke.

'What are they doing ?' cried Pilate to his officers. 'WHAT ARE THEY DOING?' But when he got a better look at their faces, Pilate knew. *They have no idea what they're doing.*

'STOP!'

But it was too late. The torches were laid at the foot of the house on all sides, and in seconds, the flames had taken hold. They climbed the walls, hastened by the dryness that permeated all of Beersheba. And though he would never have the opportunity to prove it, Pilate would go to his grave believing that the magus was responsible for it all: flooding his thoughts to distract him. Sitting cross-legged in his tent, eyes closed, muttering some strange old chant. Controlling his men, all the while thinking, *This is what you get for trying to keep me on a short leash, you insignificant little nothing.*

Inside, Balthazar and the others backed away as the flames climbed through the windows, filling the room with blistering air and setting the curtains ablaze in the process. Smoke began to pour in almost immediately, crawling across the ceiling and forcing the fugitives to crouch. As Mary covered the baby's face with her robes, Sela hurried to the wall farthest from the fire, grabbed a washbowl, and threw its contents at the burning curtains. But this had all the effect of spitting into a volcano. The flames were spreading too quickly, the smoke already too heavy to be beaten back. They were faced with the unsavory choice of burning alive or running out of the house and being captured by the Romans.

Before Pilate could order his men to storm the house and take the fugitives alive, his eye was drawn away from the conflagration by a darkness in the west. The low cloud had risen from the horizon and doubled in size in the few moments since he'd last looked at it. Pilate had never seen a sandstorm – or any storm – move so fast. But that wasn't the only strange thing about this cloud. It was shrieking. The sound had been barely perceivable at first, but it was unmistakable now. The cloud was shrieking. Emitting a constant, otherworldly sound – like the ceaseless scream of an angry animal. The scream of an angry god. A million voices raised in unison, growing closer by the second.

'Sandstorm,' said Gaspar. 'We should take cover.'

'It's not a sandstorm,' said Pilate, his eyes fixed on the shrieking cloud.

It's a swarm.

Locusts. Millions of them, flying in a cloud so dense that it choked out the sun. Moving so fast that it defied nature. They'd crossed into the city, washing over the dead streets and abandoned houses like a wave, heading straight toward them. There were no crops left to eat in Beersheba . . . but still they came.

Pilate's men saw it too. They heard the shrieking of the

millions of locusts, saw the wave washing over the city. Like their leader, they turned away from the flames that climbed the wall of the house and stared in rapt wonder at the cloud. *This is no sandstorm . . .*

Some of them began to break ranks and run for cover, but it was too late. By the time they took a few steps of retreat, the leading edge of the cloud slammed into the Romans with enough force to knock men over. Pilate's horse reared up in fright, throwing him to the street. Dazed and hurt, he covered his face with his arms and curled his body into a ball as the shrieking swarm washed over them. All around, men held their shields up to their faces to protect themselves from the onslaught, insects clanging against them like stones from a slingshot. Locusts flew into the mouths of those who'd had the misfortune to leave them open, lodging themselves in men's throats twenty and thirty at a time, choking soldiers with their armored bodies, biting them from the inside until blood ran from their mouths and nostrils.

What had been an orderly siege was suddenly chaos. An endless swarm poured over the Romans, drowning them. Blinding them with their numbers, and in some cases, blinding soldiers by feasting on their eyes in groups. Men tried to swat them away, to crush the locusts in their fists. But for every bug killed, ten more seemed to take its place. The soldiers might as well have been swatting at boiling tar.

Still balled up on the ground, Pilate saw a man crawling past him, completely covered by locusts. The man pulled himself for a few feet, then stopped – and the locusts covering him flew away en masse, leaving behind a mess of ripped skin and exposed innards. His lips were gone, leaving his teeth exposed in a ghastly eternal grin, and his eye sockets were nothing more than empty holes in his face. His carcass looked like it had spent a week being picked apart by crows. But it had taken only seconds.

Pilate heard the crunching of winged bodies everywhere as soldiers ran for cover in adjacent houses or rolled around on the street, trying desperately to brush thousands of insects off their arms, legs, and faces. He saw one soldier sitting upright, his palms pressed to his temples and his body writhing as something feasted on the inside of his skull. The man let loose a muffled scream, then fell over, silent and still. A moment later, Pilate saw locusts crawl out of the soldier's mouth and eyelids before rejoining the swarm. These weren't the mindless, dead-eyed bugs that had eaten their way across half of Africa, leaf to random leaf. These had been possessed by something. Given orders.

Pilate turned toward a pair of nearby voices and found Gaspar and Melchyor pulling themselves along the ground, looking for refuge as locusts covered them like a blanket. It was strange . . . the bugs seemed to be targeting some of the men but avoiding others completely. *Like me – so far, anyway.* In Gaspar's and Melchyor's case, they seemed less interested in killing than torturing – biting at their flesh, feeding on them one microscopic bite at a time.

Pilate watched the thieves crawl along, wondering

what all of this meant. Wondering if the magus or some other magic was behind it. *And if not the magus . . . who?* He might have kept watching and wondering forever, or at least until the locusts changed their mind and began eating his eyes, had one of his lieutenants not grabbed his arm and dragged him into one of the adjacent houses. As he was pulled inside, Pilate saw that the flames that had engulfed the front of the fugitives' hideout had begun to retreat, beaten back by the bodies of locusts that willfully flew into the fire, sacrificing themselves to put it out, and in doing so, buying the people inside precious time.

Inside, Mary had turned away and buried her head in Joseph's shoulder, terrified by the otherworldly shrieking and horrified by the sight of men being eaten alive. Balthazar turned away too – less horrified than dumbfounded, and found himself confronted by a smiling little face. Despite the chaos in the streets, despite the sounds of men having their skin torn away, the baby was back to his calm, curious self. Resting in his frightened mother's arms, looking – *no, beaming* – at Balthazar. Sela hurried around the room, drawing the curtains over every window, as if the thin fabric would be enough to stop the swarm from entering. *But they won't enter*, thought Balthazar. *They won't even try . . . because they're not here for us.*

Somehow, he knew. The strange, almost blinding comet in the sky above Bethlehem. The clear, cool stream in the barren desert. A swarm of locusts, beating back the Roman Army. On their own, any one of these events was strange. Any two were nearly impossible. All three?

Almost too much for even the staunchest realist to ignore. It was an interesting feeling, watching something that couldn't possibly be real. And Balthazar reveled in it for a moment, watching the screaming Romans, before sense caught up with his senses, and a single word struck him with the force of a fist from the clouds above:

Go.

10

The Dead

'Dry bones . . . I will make breath enter you, and you will come to life. I will make flesh come upon you and cover you with skin; I will put breath in you, and you will come to life.'

—*Ezekiel 37:4–6*

I

They'd all lived through sandstorms, had all felt the stinging of fine grains against their skin, the dry desert blowing over squinting eyes. But this was unlike anything they could've imagined.

This storm was *alive*.

Each grain of sand had been replaced by a locust. Their eyes lifeless and black, their spindly legs and hard shells the color of desert sand. The bugs flew at them like debris in a tornado, their bodies forming a cloud that surrounded the fugitives, blinding in its density, deafening from the fluttering of its millions of wings. And while at a distance it seemed like the locusts were flying under their own power, in the cloud it was clear they were being blown along by something powerful. Something angry.

Balthazar's hunch had proven right so far. The locusts didn't seem interested in the five of them. Nor directly, anyway. Not in the way they'd been interested in the Romans, choking them with their bodies, biting at their eyes and flesh. But while they weren't the target of its wrath, the fugitives still had to contend with the millions upon millions of bugs flying past them toward Beersheba, pelting them like living hail and leaving marks on their arms and faces as they marched against its current. This continued until the darkness of the locusts around them began to give way to the darkness of the sky, and the cloud evaporated at last.

As the sun vanished behind the horizon, painting the last of itself in the pale sky, the fugitives stopped to rest and take stock of what they'd seen. Joseph cradled a bundled robe beneath his head, grabbing a few precious minutes of sleep on the ground. Mary, in turn, cradled the baby, feeding him beneath her robes.

Sela sat a stone's throw from them, drinking from a canteen and looking at her arms and legs in the fading light. Examining the small bruises from the constant beating of tiny bodies against her skin, and examining the thoughts that had been beating against the inside of her skull for days now.

Here I am.

Once again, Balthazar had managed to turn her life upside down. The first time, he'd done it by leaving. This time, he'd done it by showing up.

She'd been perfectly unhappy in Beersheba. Perfectly alone. Now that her misery had company, she was worse off than ever: stuck in the desert without a possession left in the world. Stuck with two strangers, a baby, and an old flame she'd learned to hate in the absent years. Even if she *could* go back to Beersheba, what was there to go back to? Her home had been burned. Her city abandoned. If they were caught, the Romans would kill her just as quickly as the others. She was one of them now, like it or not. A fugitive. And while there'd been a time when she would've found that a romantic, adventurous notion, now it was only deeply annoying and troubling.

Sela took another drink, sifting through her limited options. She would go to Egypt with them, yes. Going south made sense, and besides, there was safety in numbers – even if they weren't the numbers you would've picked if given the chance. But she wouldn't linger there. She would continue on by herself. Maybe across the north of Africa to Carthage or across the sea to Greece.

You rebuilt your life once before; you can do it again.

She had no interest in playing odd woman out to a Jewish couple. Nor did she have much interest in hanging around with the man formerly known as the love of her life. From the looks of it, Balthazar had no interest in her, either. He was off on his own, watching—

A herd of ibex grazed in the distance. It was a smaller herd, only a dozen or so. Not the hundred or more they'd spotted outside Hebron as they walked into an ambush. Balthazar sat a good distance from the others, watching the ibex mindlessly, stupidly chew their cud. Taking comfort in it.

Blissful, simple little things.

They spent their abbreviated lives flitting around, moving from place to place, taking what they needed to survive. Always searching for the next little patch of green to keep them going, always running away when it got too dangerous, never stopping until they were either hunted down or simply faded into nothing. Forgotten.

Balthazar could think of a million explanations for what they'd seen in Beersheba, none of which made much sense. Just as he could think of a million reasons why a stream might appear out of nowhere in the desert or a riot might break out at exactly the moment they needed it to. But he could no longer outrun the nagging feeling that had been following him through the desert for days:

There's something about that baby.

There had to be. Why else would all these people want him dead? A tiny, brand-new creature who had never so much as uttered a word. A creature who still bore the half-open eyes and misshapen head of his birth. And why did the child always seem so calm? Like it knew exactly what was going on? Why had the old man in his dream shown him an image of Egypt? Why did nature itself seem to come to their rescue when they were in need? And how?

Balthazar was filled with new questions. New doubts. Doubts of his old doubts. And this swirling pool of questions and doubts made him confused. And being confused made him angry. And here he was, sitting apart from the others, watching the sky slowly darken over the desert. Angry and alone.

Sela had been watching him sit there for some time, when a disembodied voice gave her misery more unwanted company:

'Why don't you go and talk to him?'

She turned to her left and found Mary walking toward her. The baby still feeding beneath her robes.

'Sorry, what?'

'Why don't you go over there?' said Mary, sitting beside her. 'Sit with him. Talk to him.'

'And why would I do that?'

Mary looked confused. *Isn't it obvious?*

'Because . . . you love him.'

Sela was sure she'd gone cross-eyed. *Love him?*

'Did you see the way I greeted him when he showed up at my door?'

'Yes. And if you didn't care, you would've turned your back on him. Closed the door in his face. But the very sight of him made you angry. Violent. Those are passionate feelings. You don't feel those things if you don't care about someone.'

'It's a little late for passion.'

'If there was love, real love, between you, who can say if it's—'

'You know,' said Sela, cutting her off, 'I think we have more urgent things to talk about, like the fact that we're alone in the middle of the desert. Or that a whole army's trying to find us and kill us.'

Mary realized she'd gone too far. 'I'm sorry,' she said.

'It's fine.'

'No, you're right. It isn't my place.'

'Really, it's fine. Let's just leave it—'

'I was only trying to help. Give you a little advice.'

Sela couldn't help but smile.

'What?' asked Mary.

Just say 'nothing,' Sela. Don't insult her – just leave it alone.

'I just . . . I think it's funny, that's all.'

'Think what's funny?'

Leave it alone, Sel—

'The fact that I'm getting relationship advice from a fifteen-year-old girl. And one who freely admits that her baby isn't her husband's.'

A considerable silence followed.

'It's different,' said Mary at last. 'It's God's child.'

Sela smiled again. 'I thought we were all God's children.'

And now another considerable silence, and a tinge of regret from Sela. She could see that she'd really wounded the girl with that one.

'You think I'm a joke,' said Mary at last.

Sela rolled her eyes. *Here we go.* This was exactly the conversation she didn't feel like having. Not now. This wasn't two girls talking about boys anymore. *Just move past it.*

'I don't think you're a joke. I just . . .' *How to put it?*

'You just don't believe me,' said Mary.

Look at this face – this earnest face . . . this fifteen-year-old who thinks she knows everything.

'No,' said Sela. 'I guess I don't.'

Mary turned away, toward the ever-darkening visage of her sleeping husband. Her exhausted husband, bruised from shielding her through the storm. *Poor Joseph*, she thought. *Poor, noble Joseph.*

'I understand,' Mary said. 'Sometimes I ask myself,

why, of all the girls in the whole world, did he choose me? Should I not love my baby as a mother is supposed to? Should I not hold him when he weeps? Comfort him when he is frightened? Scold him when he misbehaves? Or should I worship him, even now?'

'I can see how that might get a little complicated, sure.'

'I didn't ask for this burden. I didn't appeal to heaven or beg of God for any honor. But this is the path that's been chosen for me by God, and I have to walk it.' She turned back to Sela. 'I can either walk it alone,' said Mary, 'or walk it holding the hands of the ones I love. Either way, it's the same path.'

Sela looked at Mary intently and smiled. She supposed this fifteen-year-old knew more than she let on. Mary turned away from her and stared straight into the desert, toward the fading image of their broad-shouldered protector.

'He doesn't believe me, either,' she said, looking at Balthazar.

'Yeah, well, don't take it personally. He doesn't believe in much of anything.'

'He's a strange man. He'll fight to protect my child, but he won't so much as look at him, hold him. And I wonder how a man can be so angry – so cruel, so violent. And how this same man can risk his life for a child he hardly knows.'

Now it was Sela's turn to sit in silence for a while, considering. Maybe it was the guilt of having insulted Mary, or the need to show a little girl who thought she knew everything how little she actually knew. Maybe it was the need to sort it all out in her own head, to remind herself of how this had all begun. Whatever the reason, Sela decided right then and there to tell Mary about the day Balthazar died.

'We were still in Antioch,' she said.

II

And we're fifteen again, and in hopeless, hideous young love. There's Balthazar and I kissing on the banks of the Orontes, and it's beautiful and golden and forever, and it always will be. And there's Balthazar's little brother, Abdi, following us everywhere we go. Four years old and still wearing that gold pendant around his neck. The one his big brother stole for him but won't tell me from whom or where. There he is, proudly imitating Balthazar. My God, he loves his big brother. And my God, Balthazar loves him more than any object or idea or feeling in this world. We both do. He's our constant companion. Our shadow. Our son. A practice son, for the ones we'll have together when we're married.

But not marriage – not yet. First, Balthazar teaches me how to live again. How to fend for myself. Teaches me how to fight. How to pick pockets in the forum. And Abdi looks on as he teaches me. Imitates his brother. Idolizes him. He wants nothing more than to be Balthazar.

And there's Balthazar taking me to the forum when he thinks I'm ready to try my pickpocketing skills on a real target. There he is playing my accomplice. And there's Abdi, who we've told to wait for us across the forum. 'Don't move from this spot,' says Balthazar, 'until we come and get you.' But there's Abdi moving anyway, wanting so desperately to be like his brother. Sneaking off on his own, trying to pick a pocket all by himself. He's watched us practice so closely, so often. He's sure he can do it. But he's not yet five years old, and he doesn't know it isn't a game. And there he is, following a man through the forum. A man who looks like he'll have a great deal of money hidden away. There he is, mimicking the way Balthazar slips his hand into the target's robes, pulls out his coin purse. And there's Abdi reaching . . . and there's Abdi taking . . .

And there's Abdi caught in the act.

His hand seized as it grabbed at an overstuffed coin purse. Seized by a man who towers over him, looking down with a pair of harsh, unforgettable eyes as he squeezes that thieving little hand. Squeezes it until its little bones threaten to break. Squeezes it until Abdi has no choice but to scream out. And the towering man leans over this little thief. This little Syrian rat. The very picture of everything that's wrong with this wretched city.

And the man is a Roman centurion.

And the centurion's bodyguards surround him now. And a crowd of locals forms around the centurion and this suddenly very, very frightened little boy — not yet five years old. And a few of the locals, the men, beg the centurion to let him go. 'We'll make sure he's punished,' they say. 'We'll beat him until he bleeds,' they say. And the little boy is terrified, of course. Screaming out to be let go. Screaming out because his hand hurts so, so much. Screaming out because he suddenly knows this isn't a game. And the centurion pulls out his sword. And some of those in the surrounding crowd gasp and cry out in protest. And the men redouble their promises to punish the child themselves, even though they know they're helpless to interfere.

'Let this be a warning!' the centurion shouts. 'A warning that crime will not be tolerated in Antioch! By ANYONE!'

And he squeezes Abdi's hand even tighter, eliciting another anguished cry. But there's Balthazar to answer it. Here's the heroic big brother who would never, ever let any harm befall Abdi. There's Balthazar, drawn by his brother's anguished cries — running right at the centurion, with me on his heels. We've been summoned by that familiar voice. And Balthazar is going to tackle this Roman before he can do what he intends to. He's going to tackle him and beat him bloody while Abdi and I escape. And chances are he'll pay for this with his life, but he doesn't care.

But the centurion's bodyguards care. They block Balthazar before he reaches his target. They form a barrier in front of their fellow Roman, grabbing Balthazar's arms and legs and holding him in place, even as he struggles and screams. Even as his eyes meet Abdi's, and the little brother suddenly realizes that the big one can't save him after all.

And the centurion pushes his sword into Abdi's belly. And the boy cries out as his tender flesh gives way but doesn't break. So the centurion pushes harder, and the skin tears, letting the blade in. Letting it through his little belly and out the back.

And we stop now for a moment. We stop right here in this little piece of time, because our eyes have deceived us.

319

Because, we tell ourselves, this isn't what happened at all. It can't be. It can't be, because men don't run little children through their little bellies with sharp swords. It can't be, because Abdi is going to grow old and have a whole life with us. A whole, rich life of his own, filled with all the beauty and discovery, all the love and opportunity a little boy with a warm heart deserves in life.

But it is real.

The centurion withdraws the blade and lets go of the boy's half-broken hand. Lets him fall into a seated position, where he remains a moment, before falling over on his side and silently clutching at his stomach. Clutching as the blood runs over his fingers. And as Balthazar watches this in some other world where it can't possibly be true, he imagines Abdi tugging at his leg and crying, 'Bal-faza . . . Bal-faza . . . you stay right here . . .'

And the anguish. The screams of his big brother. His big brother – still too small, too young to fight off the guards who hold him by the arms and neck. Who beat him into submission as he struggles and screams his throat raw. And the crowd is shocked. Silent. Helpless. It's not their place. They don't want to end up on the other side of the river, in one of those shallow graves.

I'm watching all of this, right beside Balthazar, but miles away from the agony he feels. He's all alone in that, and I know it. Even then, in the first seconds of it. I turn away from my screams, toward his. I watch as Balthazar undergoes a transformation right there in the forum. I watch him fall to his knees. I watch him pick up his brother's lifeless little body, holding it in his shaking arms. Holding our practice son. And I drop to my knees, too, feel the sickness crawling up the back of my throat.

And now the centurion's eyes meet Balthazar's, and he knows. He knows this is a relative. A brother. And he smiles at Balthazar, because he can. Because he's above the reach of the law. A god. And the centurion decides to leave his mark on this Syrian rat, dragging his blade across Balthazar's right cheek twice, leaving a bloody 'X' behind. And like that scar, the centurion's face will stay with Balthazar forever.

Adding insult to murder, the centurion takes the pendant that hangs around the boy's neck – rips it off his neck while he gasps for the breath he can't find – and hangs it around his own.

'Probably stolen anyway,' he says to the assembled.

And with that he's gone. Whisked off into the busy forum by his bodyguards.

Just in case, *I think*. Just in case we aren't as afraid as you make us out to be, and we decide to rise up against you.

But we are. We're too afraid, and we let him slip away into the safety and anonymity of Antioch's ruling Roman class. And with the centurion gone, never to be seen again, we turn our attention back to the two brothers he's left behind. One big, one small. One dead, one wishing he were.

And we witness this together. Gawking at this deeply private moment. Intruding into this mourning with our eyes, unable to offer any comfort. Together, we witness the end of the being who went by the name 'Balthazar' and watch the birth of a new being. The one who they'll call 'the Antioch Ghost.' An angry, murderous creature.

It isn't good enough to rob the Romans anymore. He wants to kill them. No, not wants. 'Wants' is too weak. It's merely a desire. But even 'needs' is insufficient to describe what courses through him now. He'll kill the centurion. He knows this as surely as he knows his own name. Like me, he wants to burn Rome to the ground. But unlike me, he knows he's actually going to do it. Not today, not in a year's time – but someday. He knows he'll stand over Rome as it burns to the ground. He soothes himself with this knowledge. And though he isn't a praying man, he prays for this. He prays as earnestly as any man ever has. A silent prayer, right there in the forum:

Give me this, O Lord . . . give me this. Let me see my enemy's face again. Let me strike him down for what he's done. Let me do this before my life on this earth is ended. Let me do this, whatever awaits me across the gulf of death. No matter the consequences of time or punishment.

He's shaking now, sobbing as Abdi's body bleeds into his lap. Rocking him back and forth as he kneels on the cobblestones of the forum. And for some reason, my eyes are drawn to Abdi's robes, and I see that he's wet himself. And this is what brings the tears at last. For it reduces him to the child he is; it speaks to the fear he must have felt and takes the last shred of dignity from him. And the crowd is already thinning, frightened that the Romans will come back and punish all of us for making too big a scene of so little a murder.

Balthazar sobs and screams and rocks his brother – our

son – *to sleep, just like he used to on the banks of the Orontes, when Abdi would nap in his arms in the shade of their scarred tree. And I'm on my knees beside them, rocking and sobbing myself. But there's nothing I can do. I'm already useless, and I know it.*

Forget me or his mother or anyone else. Balthazar is alone. But worse – so much worse than that – is what he knows in his heart. He knows that this is his fault. All of it. It's his fault for being so irresponsible. For teaching a little boy how to steal. For being a bad example to a good soul. And he knows that somehow, some unseen power is punishing him for what he's done with his own life. All of the unforgivable sins he's committed. He's knows that God hates him. Here is proof in his arms. What God could do this? Only a God who hates.

And smooth, singular purpose washes over him. He's dead now. There are no more consequences in life. He's dead, and the dead have license to kill the living. He's dead, and God hates him. Here's the proof – right here, bleeding into his lap. But Balthazar won't settle for being hated by God. He'll hate God right ba—

III

Sela stopped in midsentence. The desert had grown almost completely dark, but she could feel Balthazar standing over her. She looked up, and there he was, looming over the two sitting women and their tear-streaked faces, silhouetted against the last of the pale sky and the first stars to welcome the night.

'Go on,' he said. 'Don't stop there.'

Sela tried to tell herself she didn't care what Balthazar thought. But she couldn't help but feel a little ashamed at sharing his darkest secret with relative strangers. Mary was right. She still cared enough to feel a twinge of guilt over having betrayed something so deeply personal.

'Go on,' he said again, in a tone that sounded less like a suggestion and more like a threat.

'Balthazar, I—'

'Tell her,' he said. 'Tell her what happened next.'

Sela sighed. There was no point in arguing. The damage was done. *The damage was done a long time ago.* She turned back to Mary, and continued.

'He spent weeks searching all over Antioch, asking

questions. Spying on Roman barracks, hoping to get a glimpse of the man who'd killed his brother, a glimpse of the pendant that hung around his neck. I barely saw him anymore, and when I did, he hardly said a word. And then one day, he found what he'd been looking for. A clue. Someone who'd seen the centurion pack up and leave Antioch, headed to a new post in another part of the empire. He left that night without a word to his mother. Or me.'

'Then what?' asked Mary.

'You'll have to ask him,' said Sela, looking up at Balthazar. 'That was the last time I saw him until three days ago.'

'After that,' said Balthazar, 'he spent every waking minute looking for the centurion. Looking for vengeance, or justice, or whatever you want to call it. Following rumors from city to city. Stealing to survive. Killing. Until one day, for no real reason at all, he woke up and realized that it was all pointless. Life isn't fair. There *is* no justice – there's only what's taken from you and what you take back, and that's it.'

'If it's meant to be,' said Mary, 'God will deliver the centurion to you.'

'God had nine years to deliver him to me.'

'Maybe this was his plan for you all along.'

'Don't talk to me about "God's plan," okay? What about the plans Abdi had? What about the children who died in Bethlehem? The babies who were hacked to death before their lives even began? What plans did their mothers have for them?'

'What about the plans I had for us?' asked Sela.

Balthazar turned to her, stared at her for a moment. Then another.

'Hurry up and finish feeding that thing,' he said to Mary at last. 'We have to get moving.'

With that, he disappeared into the darkness again, determined to soak up a few more minutes of being angry and alone. Sela stood and disappeared, too, determined to do the same.

Mary found herself alone in the last of the dying light. She looked down at the baby in her arms, asleep but nursing. Seeing him there, so helpless and trusting, brought the full horror of Sela's story rushing back. She imagined the grief that Balthazar's mother must have felt at losing two sons in one day. She imagined the face of the centurion as he squeezed Abdi's hand to the breaking point. She didn't know how a person could do such a thing to a child. Nor did she know how anyone could go on after witnessing something so violent happen to someone you loved.

She only knew that the terrible man didn't seem quite as terrible anymore.

IV

Herod never expected he would live to see such a thing. A Roman legion, laid to waste. Licking their wounds in the desert of Judea. And not from the work of Gauls or Visigoths, either, but from insects. It was impossible, of course. Yet if you believed the accounts, that's exactly what had happened.

And why wouldn't you believe them? Who would lie about such a thing? Who would admit to being vanquished by a swarm of bugs?

Herod watched through the curtains of his lectica, his slaves bearing its burden on their shoulders fore and aft. He'd traveled all day and half the night, trying to catch up with the Romans he'd set loose like dogs in his own kingdom. The Romans who'd proven no more effective than his own troops had. He realized that he'd been a fool to involve Rome. Yes, there was the benefit of flattering Augustus Caesar. Of giving Rome the credit for victory. But Herod hadn't considered the alternative: that they might fail. And if that happened, the blame would rest squarely on his shoulders.

The fires of the camp burned on either side of him, filtered through the curtains of his traveling chair. Roman camps were usually filled with energy and music and conversation. With the camaraderie of rested, wine-soaked soldiers. But this camp was like a graveyard. The men sat quietly around the flames, frightened. Clearly they were beginning to realize what Herod already had: *We're dealing with more than a thief and a baby here.* They were coming to terms with the fact that the Hebrew God had taken sides. That he was mocking them. And even though it was only the Hebrew God, being the enemy of *any* deity was a tactical disadvantage, to say the least.

Herod, however, was used to this feeling. The Hebrew God had been mocking him for years now. Belittling him with every drop of blood that dripped from his open sores. With the painful, yellow discharge seeping from places he'd rather it didn't. And this mockery was getting stronger with time, his body growing weaker. Herod knew it, though he preferred to push these thoughts to the shadows. *You've lived this long, and it hasn't killed you yet. Nothing will.* Sometimes he wondered whether this God had it in him at all.

Can a man be bigger than a god?

Herod's lectica was gently lowered to the ground and its curtains opened by courtesans. They helped their frail king to his feet and pulled politely at his robes, removing the wrinkles of a day's travel, then led him toward the unremarkable tent in the center of the camp – its flap guarded by a pair of Roman soldiers in full armor and flanked by torches on tall posts. And though Herod didn't see them, one particular pair of wounded men went to great lengths to make themselves scarce as he approached.

Gaspar and Melchyor peered around the corner of Pilate's tent, both of them nursing wounds from the tiny jaws of locusts.

Pilate's tent was a simple affair. More Spartan than Roman, in Herod's opinion – a few chairs for holding court with his officers; a bed that looked unused; and a polished helmet and breastplate neatly laid out on a dress-ing table, with a sword beside them. A few hanging oil lamps cast dancing shadows around the interior. But there were none of the usual comforts Herod demanded during his own travels: no rugs or pillows, no couches to recline on. More importantly, no young girls to recline on them with.

This was no way to go to war.

Pilate stood ready in his formal lavender robes, their seams adorned with patterned leaves in gold thread. He greeted the puppet king of Judea with a deep bow, taking care not to let his eyes linger too long. He'd heard reports of Herod's sickly appearance, but when confronted with the real thing – with the rotted flesh and blackened teeth, the yellowed eyes and sores   Pilate was quietly shocked. Breaking with protocol, he decided against kissing Herod's extended hand and instead touched his lowered forehead to it – a rarely used but acceptable alternative.

'I have come to help you,' said Herod.

'I'm honored,' said Pilate, rising to his full height. 'And may I ask what it is Your Highness has come to help us with?'

'With the thing you were brought here to do. To capture a common thief and an infant.'

'If I may,' said Pilate, 'there's nothing "common" about him.'

Herod showed a bit of those blackened teeth. 'No,' he said. 'I suppose there isn't.'

Pilate motioned for the king to sit, and he did. The wooden chair creaked beneath him, and for a fraction of a second he thought it might break and send him to the dirt floor. His arms shot out to his sides on their own, and he felt the rush of adrenaline that accompanies a near fall, followed almost immediately by relief and the fervent hope that Pilate had missed this brief show of weakness.

'Do you find it strange, Your Highness?' asked Pilate, who'd seen the king's momentary panic but showed no sign of it.

'Find what strange?'

'Well . . . the Antioch Ghost or "Balthazar" or whatever you prefer. He's known to be a heartless murderer, as you say – a man who places no value on life, who prefers to work alone.'

'So?'

'So . . . do you not find it strange that such a man has cast his lot with a pair of Jews and their baby?'

'A man like that thinks only of himself. He travels with them only because there is some advantage in it – I guarantee you. But I'm not concerned with the Antioch

Ghost, Commander. I'm concerned with your inability to catch him.'

'With all due respect, Your Highness, we've been battling forces beyond our control.'

'With all due respect, your men were just beaten by a creature that I could crush in my fingers.'

Pilate was too political to say the words that sizzled on his tongue. Too professional to give Herod the slightest hint of a telling expression. Herod stood, determined to make his point while looking down at the young officer.

'In thirty years of ruling over Jews, I've come to believe in one very simple truth,' said Herod. 'That their time on this earth is almost at an end. All they have are old stories. Old traditions. All they have are tales of ancient leaders and kings, ancient magic, and a messiah who keeps promising to arrive but never does. Everything about them is old. Everything about them is the past.

'I'm interested in new traditions. New empires. I build new things, and they protest. I pass new laws, and they protest. But I don't listen to them, because I'm the future. And I certainly don't fear them, or their God. Because the time of Moses and David has passed to dust. The world belongs to Caesar now. To men. And I'm here to make sure it stays that way.'

'All the same, Your Highness, my men are frightened. They fear the wrath of this power. This God.'

'If I were them, I would fear the wrath of Augustus more.'

Vision. It was the most important quality a leader possessed. It's why Herod had reigned as long and successfully as he had. He'd already summed up this young officer. This 'Pilate.' He was a leader, sure. Aggressive and thorough. Cautious enough to avoid kissing a diseased hand but clever enough to find a suitable alternative in a fraction of a second. But he lacked imagination. He lacked vision. And this would keep him from achieving the heights his cleverness made him aspire to. As always, it would be up to Herod to make sure things ran smoothly from here on.

'They're headed south, yes?' asked Herod.

'Yes. To Egypt.'

'And the fastest way to Egypt is through the Kadesh Valley . . .' *Vision, boy. I'll show you the meaning of it.* 'I understand you have a shaman traveling with you,' said Herod. 'Some kind of . . . seer.'

'The magus.'

'I'd very much like to talk with him.'

V

'What is it, an earthquake?' asked Joseph.

Balthazar remembered hearing a similar sound as a boy in Antioch. A low rumble. The slow groan of the earth moving beneath your feet. But these rumbles were usually accompanied by violent shaking, followed almost immediately by the screams of a panicked citizenry. Neither followed in this case. Yet that slow, low complaint of rock moving over rock persisted. And the five fugitives found themselves looking for the source of the growing noise, which seemed now to be coming from all around them.

'What is it?' Joseph repeated.

The desert had funneled them into the Kadesh Valley – a long, lifeless passage between two mountains. Long ago, a river had snaked over the dry ground they now walked upon, and the early Egyptians – believers in the power of water to carry souls into the afterlife – had buried their dead on both sides of its banks in tombs of all sizes and lavishness. There were still remnants of those long-forgotten tombs all around them, some chiseled into the rock of the ravine, others made of piled stones, their riches long since taken by grave robbers.

After looking for the source of the rumbling, Balthazar's eyes at last found the culprit:

The tombs.

The first one he spotted was nearly 200 yards behind them. It was one of the bigger tombs, chiseled into the side of the hill to their left and adorned with carvings that had been worn away by the desert winds. The tomb's large stone slab was sliding open, revealing the long-suffering darkness within and producing the low groan of rock moving over rock, not unlike the rumbling of an earthquake. And Balthazar now saw the whole, stupid truth of the matter:

They were being ambushed.

Knowing they were headed to Egypt, the Romans had overtaken them – *again*. They'd lain in wait – *again*. And here they were, popping out of their hiding places – *again* – with their swords and arrows, utterly pleased with themselves for pulling off such a clever ruse.

Enough already.

It was exhausting. Balthazar was sick and tired of being surprised, and somewhat surprised that he was surprised at all.

Of course they're ambushing us. That's all they've done. Why don't they just attack us head-on and save everyone the trouble?

Sure enough, one of the Romans stuck his head out from behind the open door and began moving quickly but awkwardly toward them, moving over the rocks of the ravine like an oversized insect. But on closer inspection, Balthazar once again found himself awash in doubt. For the being that was crawling toward them – *too fast . . . it's moving too fast* – wasn't a Roman. It wasn't a soldier. It wasn't even a man.

It was a corpse.

More groans joined the first as slabs were pushed open all around them. The dead emerged from the shadowy depths of tomb after tomb. Dozens of them. The mummified remains of men, women, and children stepping into the long-lost sunlight, finally free from the prison of sleep, and moving toward the fugitives with unusual speed, crawling insectlike across the ravine.

Their bodies were in varying states of decay, but they all had the brittle, leathery look that comes with centuries of decomposition, their eyes and brains rotted out of their skulls. Skin stretched tightly over their faces and teeth exposed in sickly grimaces. They moved deliberately, forming ranks and closing in, as if controlled by a single, unseen mind, just as the locusts had been. But unlike the locusts, the fugitives sensed this swarm was very interested in doing them harm, and it was less than 150 yards away.

'Balthazar?' asked Joseph.

'I know.'

'What do we do?'

'Give me a minute . . .'

'But they're getting clo—'

'I said give me a minute.'

He had to focus himself, had to pull his mind back

from the edge of panic and come up with a plan. But all he could do was watch as a wave of resurrected beings crept closer, and fear washed over him. All he could do was watch the horde moving toward them, faster than nature intended most men to move. *Too fast for the others to outrun.* Their dry sinew cracking with every movement, loud enough to be heard clear across the ravine.

Balthazar had been wandering through his own mind a lot in recent days, trying to sift through his doubts. Trying to reconcile what his beliefs told him with what his eyes and ears had been telling him in recent days. It had been a rambling walk. Aimless. Inconclusive. But now he'd reached a fork in the road.

Either he had to accept that he was dead or dreaming, in which case nothing mattered and there were no consequences, or he had to accept that what he was looking at was real. In which case, everything he believed was wrong, and he was probably cursed to spend eternity in the flames of hell. But eternity would have to wait. It was decision time.

Better to pretend it's real and be wrong, right? Plus, I'm sure something miraculous will happen when all hope seems lost. I'm sure we'll make another last-second escape. Isn't that how it's been lately? Maybe it'll be a flood this time. A wall of water from nowhere crashing through the valley, washing these things away but somehow sparing us. In fact, I'm sure that's what it'll be. A flood.

Balthazar turned to the others.

'Run,' he said.

But they didn't. Joseph and Mary were paralyzed with fear, watching the dead stagger ever closer – inside 100 yards now. Sela seemed frozen, too, until she lunged toward Balthazar and pulled a dagger from his belt. She did this so suddenly, so violently, that at first he wasn't sure what her intentions were. *Maybe this is the opportunity she's been waiting for*, he thought. *Her chance to kill me for abandoning her.* But Sela had no intention of stabbing him. She stepped closer and pointed at the horde.

'I'll stay with you,' she said. 'Help you fight them off.'

Balthazar grabbed her hand. 'No.' He pointed to Joseph, Mary, and the baby. 'Without you, they're as good as dead.'

'Without me, you're dead!'

'You know how to fight, Sela, how to survive. Get them to Egypt.'

'There's no way you can—'

'Shut up!'

He grabbed her arm, hard. Seventy yards . . .

'Run, now, while you still have a head start. Don't stop; just keep going. I'll buy you a little time.'

He pushed her away. Sela turned back toward the frightened carpenter. Toward the little girl and the sleeping baby. She knew Balthazar was right. They were as good as dead without her.

'Sela,' he said.

She looked back at him, frightened but still so beautiful it wasn't fair, and for a moment, they were back in the waters of the Orontes, all golden and forever. Balthazar had a sudden urge to grab her, to kiss her one last time just for the hell of it. What did he have to lose? He was probably moments away from a grisly death, and besides, something about the look on her face told him she was thinking of doing the same thing. But before he could work up the nerve to do it, the wail of the approaching dead shook the past away and summoned Balthazar's eyes to the urgent now.

'GO!' he yelled. And they did.

With the others making their hasty retreat south behind him, Balthazar turned back to the mass of hideous rotted flesh. There were about forty of them, he guessed, less than fifty yards away. He saw one corpse dragging itself along the ground with long yellowed fingernails, having lost its legs in life or death. Another's torso had been horribly twisted, forcing it to move backward – which didn't really matter, since it didn't have eyes anyway.

They don't need to see, thought Balthazar. *Something else is doing the seeing for them.*

Sela was right, of course. He was as good as dead. If for no other reason than he had no idea how to kill what he was about to fight. For all he knew, his blade would bounce off these creatures like they were made of stone. For all he knew, he would burst into flames the moment his skin met theirs. Nothing would surprise him. Nothing could anymore. But it didn't matter. Even if it meant the most painful, hideous death a human being had ever experienced, they weren't getting the baby, and they weren't getting her. Twenty yards . . .

He gripped the handle of his sword tightly . . . breathed deep of the desert air.

Okay, Balthazar . . . let's die.

He charged. And as he neared them, and their faces came into crystal focus, Balthazar saw just how wretched they were: pockets of embalming fluid trapped under their hardened skin, the black rot of their teeth, the patches of hair clinging to their scalps in grays and blacks and browns.

Upon meeting the leading edge of the swarm, he was greeted with good and bad news: the bad news was, these creatures were faster and stronger than they looked from a distance. The good news was, his sword seemed to work just fine.

He went to work, chopping away at limbs and necks. Hacking away at the leathery skin and hardened sinew that held them together and trying not to focus on the terrible, chemical smell of the long and leathery dead – at the demons grabbing at him with their dry fingers. Their bones cracking, their skin ripping as they moved.

He was suddenly twelve again. Back in the shallow Roman graves, digging up the freshly slain bodies. Looting them. Fighting off the fear, the terrifying, almost real visions of the bodies coming to life. Visions of the dead grabbing at his clothes and hair. Pulling him down into the graves with them. But those had only been visions. The monsters were real now. They moved without blood in their veins, without hearts in their chests. They had no lungs or vocal cords, yet they each emitted a strange sound. A wheezing, guttural moan that sounded to Balthazar like an endless last gasp. Together, they created a chilling chorus.

There's something about that baby.

Maybe he would find out what it was on the other side of death. Something waiting for him. And what of the dreams he'd had when he lay dying from a stab wound? What of those strange visions of old men in pink and purple rooms? And what of the Man With Wings? The man whose face had made Balthazar weep at the sight of it?

Abdi's face.

That's who it'd been, hadn't it? Abdi, the grown man he never got to be? A man with wings, holding on to his big brother and soaring over the desert of Judea? Guiding him through an ocean of time and space? Balthazar had thought of them as visions. Nothing but the vivid dreams of a dying mind. But now, staring death both literally and figuratively in the face, he accepted that they might have been something more. In fact, he hoped they were.

Balthazar slashed and kicked and pushed at the corpses, but they were massing around him faster than he could fight them off. One terrible face after another. One brittle set of mummified fingers after the next – their ancient fingernails scratching at him. Grabbing at his clothes. *If I only had a torch, I could set them alight. They're so dry that they'd go up like a sunbaked grass roof.* But all he had was a sword and a pair of quickly tiring arms to wield it with.

They're winning.

There was no doubt about it. And as they swarmed

over him, Balthazar screamed. Not from any fear but from knowing that this was his moment – his last chance to make his presence known on this earth. He screamed until he could taste blood in the back of this throat as the swarm of dead fully enveloped him.

Peace at last . . .

And as he screamed, the dead suddenly and uniformly dropped to the ground, as if the strings holding their limbs aloft were cut in one swoop. And with a dull, dusty thud, they were nothing but sinew and bone again. Silent. Balthazar stood there, breathing heavily. In awe of the sight. Somewhat in awe of himself.

He'd won.

By some miracle, he'd been spared. Just as he'd predicted, some unseen force had smiled down on him at the last possible moment. If the Jews called it God, so be it. Whether it was God, or luck, or something else, it didn't matter. What mattered were the others. He could catch up to them now. Take them the rest of the way to Egypt and be done with this. *Thank God. Or whatever.*

But just as he was allowing himself one little victory, one little moment of open-mindedness, another sort of rumbling shook the optimism right out of him. Balthazar looked around, sure that he was about to catch sight of a second wave of rotting beings emerging from their tombs. But there was nothing. Nothing except the rumbling. *A different kind of rumbling, now that I think about it. A much more . . . familiar . . . kind of—*

It was the beating of hooves against the desert floor.

Balthazar looked past the lifeless bodies on the ground

before him – up, up – until he saw what seemed like a thousand horses riding at him down the center of the narrow valley from the north. He couldn't see the faces of the men on those horses, but he imagined most of them bore the smug, self-satisfied look of men who'd pulled off another clever ruse.

The Romans were coming.

The small horde of dead had been replaced with a gigantic horde of the living. It wasn't an improvement – not numerically, anyway. But at least Balthazar knew how to kill the things riding toward him. Once again, he raised his sword and readied himself for a reckless, suicidal charge, all in the name of buying his friends – *now there's a word that just popped in there and I didn't expect but seems fitting* – a little time.

Let's die . . .

He was done running. He'd spent so much time moving from place to place – searching for the pendant, stealing to survive, killing to live. It was good to die. If his death could buy his friends a little time, then so be it. *You deserve to die, after all the things you've done. After all the lives you've taken. After all the things you've stolen – the objects, the futures.*

He would meet them head-on, take as many of them as he could. For the second time in as many minutes, Balthazar charged toward certain death, his sword held high. Screaming. For the second time in as many minutes, he crashed headlong and hopelessly into a tidal wave of bodies. Into the blinding wall of flailing limbs and clanging armor.

The last thing he remembered was a brief struggle, a sharp pain. Then . . . peace at last.

And Abdi with his arms around him, telling him it was going to be all right.

11

No Accidents

'I in turn will laugh when disaster strikes you;
I will mock when calamity overtakes you –
when calamity overtakes you like a storm,
when disaster sweeps over you like a whirl-
wind, when distress and trouble overwhelm
you.'

—Proverbs 1:26–27

I

Herod reclined with his eyes closed, enjoying the gentle swaying motion of his traveling chair. A baby being rocked to sleep. He was on his way to his summer palace, a favorite retreat on the shores of the Mediterranean, where the onshore breezes carried the cooling mist of crashing waves, and the songs of seabirds calmed any nerves that might have been frayed in the lion's den of Jerusalem. And though he couldn't hear the waves beating against coastal rocks just yet, Herod knew they were getting close, for he could already smell the salt in the air. He breathed deeply of it. Savored it. It was, perhaps, the sweetest thing he'd ever smelled.

All was right with the world.

Somewhere, on the other side of his chair's wine-colored curtains, the prisoner was being dragged across the desert, naked. Humiliated and bloodied. He was being urinated on by Roman soldiers as his body scraped over grains of sand and patches of dry grass. He was being pelted with rocks and insults alike. Soon, he would be submitted to the most unimaginable suffering the empire could conjure, before being exiled to the wasteland of death. The 'Antioch Ghost' would be just that. And this was good Without their protector, the remaining fugitives would soon be captured. And this was also good. But it wasn't nearly as good as what was going on *inside* Herod's traveling chair. Inside, something extraordinary was happening.

A miracle. That's the only way to describe it.

For the first time in years, Herod the Great was getting . . . better. He could feel it happening by the minute, mile by mile. The oozing lesions of his skin – those old familiar bloody scabs and pus-filled nodules – were receding with unnatural speed, and his skin had begun to trade its sickly pallor for a healthy olive hue. His hearing was clearer, his muscles stronger, his hair already a shade darker, his teeth a shade whiter, and his mind a notch sharper. His eyes, clouded over for so long, were suddenly as clear and wet as the day he'd taken the throne.

I was blind, but now I see.

It was a miracle. But not a miracle of any god. This was the magic of man, freeing him from the false imprisonment of nature. It was more than a miracle; it was a confirmation of everything Herod believed. Confirmation that the time of the old myths and old gods was at an end. That the New World was a place where miracles would be performed by men.

A world in which there was no more need for gods.

348

Back in the Roman camp, Herod had approached the magus with a simple proposition. One that had popped into his head, as if in a dream.

His decision to involve Rome in his domestic troubles had turned disastrous. But there was an opportunity in every crisis, and once again, Herod's mind had revealed the silver lining in the clouds around him. He'd been careful to make this proposition away from the eager ears of Pontius Pilate – for Herod knew that the faithful Roman imperator wouldn't like what he had to say.

Unaccompanied by his usual cadre of courtesans and guards, Herod had let himself into the magus's large, lush tent. There, he'd found the dark priest alone in his sleeping gown, sitting with his back facing the tent flap, lit by the glow of oil lamps and engaged in the rather unmagical act of stuffing his face with cooked lamb.

'Augustus doesn't appreciate you,' Herod began.

The magus stopped in midbite. He dabbed his mouth and turned toward Herod, slowly. *Yes . . . be sure and turn slowly, for I've caught you being human, and you need to reassert that mystique.*

'Don't take it personally,' said Herod when the magus had completed his slow, mystical turn. 'He doesn't appreciate me, either.'

He stepped all the way inside and let the flap close behind him.

'I'm not saying I blame him. Let's be clear about that. It's not an easy thing for a powerful man to put his faith in others. Even I can be too self-reliant at times, too stubborn. It's part of being a leader of men. But the

Romans . . . the Romans have a particular gift for believing themselves superior to *all* men. Look at their myths. Even their gods can't help falling in love and bedding down with them. It's obnoxious.'

He stepped closer, hoping to better gauge the magus's expression through his cloudy eyes. But there was no expression to gauge. The magus remained statuesque and cautious.

'Do you know who I am?' asked Herod.

The magus gave a slow, almost imperceptible nod.

'Then you know how much I have to lose by saying what I'm saying.'

The magus studied him a moment or two, and then gave another, even smaller nod. Herod smiled and helped himself to a seat, taking extra care to steady himself this time. *No signs of weakness . . . not now.*

He knew how to speak to these mystics. On the outside, they wore their piety like a crown, eschewed the trivial pleasures of earthly life and cultivated an air of mystery around themselves. Take the magus. He didn't speak – not for some ailment or want of a tongue, but for the aura it created around him. Yes, there was all that nonsense about ancient vows of silence and keeping one's voice pure for spells and so on. But really, being a mystic was no different than being a king: The more powerful people believed you were, the more powerful you were. And this little gimmick worked, because most men were weak-minded. Most men were sheep.

But not Herod.

Yes, the magus knew a few tricks. Yes, it seemed that

he could bend the rules of nature to his will. And there was value in that. But in the end, he was a man – and men were men. They had the same weaknesses and desires, whether they wore the robes of kings, peasants, or priests.

'You and I,' said Herod. 'We're men the world no longer needs.'

He waited for a reaction. A raised eyebrow, a squint of puzzlement. Anything. But the magus gave him nothing.

'The world doesn't care about magic anymore,' he continued. 'It doesn't care about priests or withered old kings and their little kingdoms. All it cares about is Rome and its emperor. The world exists to serve him. *We* exist to serve him. And so long as we do, whatever power we have belongs to him.'

There was no going back now. This was treasonous territory.

'Alone,' Herod continued, 'the two of us, we're . . . nothing. Me, a king who's lived through two Caesars, who's ruled my little kingdom with Rome's permission. You, a conjurer who's been kept locked away like a suit of armor. Trotted out only when Augustus needs protection from his enemies. But neither of us were ever allowed to test the limits of our powers, and certainly never allowed to use them for our own benefit. No, such a thing would be a threat to the emperor's own power. Alone, a king and a conjurer are nothing compared to Rome. But together . . .'

Here it comes . . . make him see it. Make him understand how glorious it could be.

'My kingdom? Your talents? Together, we could build

something glorious. A force that could challenge Rome. Perhaps even become the new empire of the East. An empire ruled by two kings – you and I, side by side. Augustus might not appreciate you, but I do. He fears your power; I welcome it.'

He went on, flattering the magus's mastery of the elements, promising him the things that all men wanted: power, wealth, sex. And above all, *recognition*. A chance to step out from the emperor's shadow, from behind the veils of secrecy and piety. When he sensed the magus was thoroughly enticed – which was only a guess, really, for he gave no outward sign of enticement – Herod went for the close:

'Everything I have is yours, if you'll take it. My crown, my army, my fortune, my palaces, and all the treasure and women in them.

'Rule with me. Rule with me, and we can both free ourselves from servitude. We can build something that will echo through the ages.'

The magus took this all in for what seemed an age. Then, his mind made up, he turned back to his dinner without so much as a shake of his head. For a moment, Herod felt it all slip away.

I've overreached . . .

Now, not only would Herod be denied what he'd come for, but he would also be branded a traitor to the emperor and exiled to the wasteland of death. Thankfully, it wasn't cold lamb that the magus had turned back for – it was parchment. Herod watched anxiously as he scribbled something down, turned back, and passed the sheet to him.

And for you?

'All I desire is your partnership,' said Herod.

The magus pointed to each of the three words again, emphasizing each one with a tap of his finger on the parchment.

And. For. You?

Herod smiled. He liked this little priest. *No bullshit; no games.* Herod took a moment before he gave his real answer. He almost couldn't bring himself to say it. They were only two little words, but there was so much attached to them. So much . . . hope. *The wine of the weak.* What if the magus was unable to do what he asked? What if he simply said no? Then the last of Herod's options would be exhausted, and his vision would have failed him.

'My health,' he said at last. 'In return, I ask for my health – that is, if you're powerful enough to give it back to me.'

Now it was the magus's turn to smile, for he'd known, of course. He'd known since the minute the puppet king of Judea had begun his pitch. He rose to his modest height, fixed his gown, closed his eyes, and muttered an incantation under his breath. A chain of indecipherable words in some long-dead language.

A moment later, Herod was hit with strange, invisible energy, a rush of warm air from a nearby fire that wasn't there. It moved through him, circulating through his body along with the diseased blood that coursed in his veins. When the warmth reached his head, he was overcome by dizziness. A brief bit of nausea.

When it passed, he was born again.

Herod examined the backs of his hands, and though he couldn't see any immediate change to their twisted shape or scabbed surfaces, something told him he would. Something told him he'd been cured. He felt his eyes well up with tears. It was all too much, too quickly. And despite whatever duplicitous schemes he'd brought into the magus's tent, he couldn't help but be truly touched at a moment like this.

'There are no accidents in this life,' he said as a tear escaped bondage and streaked down his wretched face. 'The Fates have brought us together, you and I. And great things will come of it.'

The magus offered Herod the slightest hint of a smile in return . . .

Herod was feeling much better indeed. Something like his old self. And so long as he had the magus by his side, he would only get better. Stronger. Who could say? Perhaps he needn't hand over power to his son as soon as he'd thought. Perhaps he never needed to hand over power at all. If he kept getting better – if this warm, strange feeling continued to trickle through his veins – then who was to say how long he would live? How much more he could build?

One thing was certain: He wasn't Caesar's puppet anymore. Augustus would have to deal with him now. Respect him. Perhaps even fear him. And while the

Judean Army was no match for Caesar's, the Romans wouldn't dare invade. Not as long as Herod had the magus by his side. And not as long as he played his Jewish subjects right.

They hate Augustus as much as I do. I'll whip them into a frenzy of independence. I'll call it 'a revolt against Rome,' and they'll eat it up.

These visions twirled around him, dancing and spinning beautifully. It was funny how so many years of misery and doubt could be completely washed away in the blink of an eye. Herod had resigned himself to wretchedness. Secretly, he'd hoped, of course. But hope was the wine of the weak, and he'd been ashamed to drink even the occasional sip. Yet here was his health – returned more spectacularly than he could have dreamed. He looked down at his hands. Felt his cheeks. The only thing Herod craved more than the sight of his own reflected face was the sight of this 'Balthazar' dying in the most terrible way imaginable: his fingernails torn away one by one, his genitals cut off and burned in front of him, every one of his appendages shattered at the end of a club, and his skin cut into strips and peeled away from the muscle beneath it.

A new sound greeted Herod's ears as the smell of the salt air grew stronger. It wasn't the crashing of ocean waves – not yet. But it was wet. *It's beginning to rain outside.* He peeled back the curtains of his traveling chair for confirmation and saw the first fat droplets falling from the gray sky to collide with the desert's dusty floor. It was a rare but welcome sight in the south of Judea.

The world was alive again. Rain was a blessing. And another sign that God was powerless to stop him.

II

The words 'summer palace' conjured quaint visions of a little villa by the shore. But all told, Herod's seaside compound was nearly twice the size of his twin palace in Jerusalem, though this one was contained under one roof, not two. It was one of Herod's newer projects, built with all the amenities the modern world could offer: chamber pots, glass windows, heated baths. It also contained a large silver mirror in the king's bedchamber. Of all the amenities, this was the one Herod was most looking forward to using.

The palace rose from the rocky shores of the Mediterranean, a towering mass of beige bricks, with some walls reaching a height of 200 feet. Architecturally, it was a simple affair – an enormous central cube made of limestone, surrounded by a handful of smaller brick out-buildings. 'A big, boring block on the beach' as Herod called it. There were no walls around its perimeter. No guard towers. The sea provided a natural barrier on one side and the flat, endless desert on the other three. There were virtually no locals to keep out. Just the Egyptians to the south, the sea to the west, and a few wandering Bedouins to the north and east. The sentries posted atop the palace's roof would see any man, let alone an army or navy, coming miles off.

A marble terrace ran along the base of the cube's seaside wall, where, in his healthier days, Herod had taken to sunning himself with select members of his harem. A wide marble staircase descended gracefully from this terrace all the way to the sea, where it met with a long wooden dock. Its planks were the first things to greet Herod and his guests when they arrived by boat from the north. Today, however, they were crowded with Roman warships, bobbing on the sizable waves that had been kicked up by the growing storm.

The Roman Navy had sailed south down Judea's coast to join up with its army. The fleet was led by a legendary admiral named Lucius Arruntius, who'd been instrumental in helping his friend Augustus win sole dominion over the empire. The emperor had dispatched his most trusted admiral to keep watch over his prized magus and his promising, but untested, young officer, Pontius Pilate.

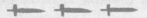

As Balthazar was pulled toward the distant palace, his wrists bound with rope, he could make out the tops of several ships bobbing up and down, their naked masts swaying like reeds in the breeze. The rain was coming harder now – each droplet providing welcome relief from the scrapes and barbs that marked his flesh. On reaching the palace grounds, he was dragged unceremoniously away from the main procession and through a small side entrance. And what had been a gray, rainy sky was suddenly an inky black passage whose darkness was permeated only by the flickering light of torches on the wall. He was in a dungeon. Never to see the sky again.

He was brought to the center of a large, dark cell, rainwater seeping through tiny cracks in the ceiling and falling to the stone floor in drops that echoed against the smooth walls of the dungeon. A rope was tied around each of his wrists and both ropes tied to a large wooden beam that ran from wall to wall above his head. When these ropes were pulled taut, Balthazar was forced to hang by his wrists, his toes dangling less than an inch above the floor. His ankles were bound together and a cloth tied around his waist – the sole concession to his modesty.

Or more likely, theirs.

In contrast to the cool droplets falling from the sky outside, the dungeon was hot. Unbearably hot. A fire raged in a brick oven that was built into one of the cell's walls. Various metal instruments had already been lined up in its flames, each on its way to glowing red-hot. Balthazar supposed they were metal pokers, brands and the like, though he couldn't tell, as only the wooden handles were visible from where he hung.

Whatever they are, I'm not going to like them at all. Not one bit.

Nor would he like any of the sharp instruments that had been neatly laid out on a small table against the wall, not far from the glow of the oven. He couldn't see exactly what these were, either, but the setting reminded him of a physician's table – with scalpels and clamps and scissors all lying neatly in a row, meticulously sharpened and ready for action. A bowl of water and a cloth had been placed beside them.

'What is it the fishermen say?' asked a familiar, gravelly voice.

The cell door swung open, and the guards made way as Herod entered.

'"The harder the fight, the sweeter the catch"?'

Herod was followed closely by a strange little man in black robes. Balthazar hated the little man at once, mostly because he suspected that he was about to use those sharp instruments to do terrible things to him. But also – and there was no way to be sure of this – because he suspected that the little man had played a role in making those corpses rise from their tombs and attack him.

The magus dipped his hands in the bowl and washed them before taking stock of the various instruments on the table before him. He made sure Balthazar had a clear view of it all, fully aware that anticipation was the most painful part of any torture. He examined the small knives and other instruments, so sharp that you could almost hear them sing. A chair was brought in for Herod, who took his seat a few feet away from the condemned. A small table was hurriedly placed beside this chair, and an assortment of orange slices and dates arranged on it. He was close enough to see every drop of blood but far enough away to avoid getting any on him. The old king reminded Balthazar of a spectator at a chariot race.

'Whatever you do to me,' said Balthazar, 'it won't get you any closer to them.'

'And what would I hope to get from you?' asked Herod. 'The knowledge that your friends are headed to Egypt? Of course they are. They're running for their lives as we speak, because they believe they'll be safe once they cross the border. But they're mistaken, you see. Egypt may be the end of my domain, but our Roman friends have dominion over the world.'

Balthazar could only glare back at him, fantasizing about getting his hands around that decaying little windpipe.

'I'm not interested in what you know,' said Herod. 'I'm interested in watching you scream.'

'Then you're going to be disappointed.'

'We'll see,' said Herod with a smile. He could see the beads of sweat running down Balthazar's face. The trembling in his fingers. Maybe it was exhaustion, but Herod thought it more likely that the mighty Antioch Ghost was quietly terrified.

'You look frightened already,' said Herod.

'And you look like a diseased dog, with Rome's leash around its neck.'

Over by the door, Pilate struggled to suppress a laugh. *Couldn't have said it better myself.* Herod glared back at Balthazar for a moment, then laughed. If he'd heard such a thing yesterday, he might've let it anger him. Even wound him. But that was before everything had changed. Before his body and his future had been pulled out of the ashes. Today, he saw Balthazar's words for what they were: the desperate swings of a dying man.

The magus chose his instrument – a scalpel – and came forward. Balthazar prepared himself for what was coming. There was a place inside. A place to which he could retreat. A place where Abdi was waiting for him. Where his mother and sisters were waiting to welcome him. And Sela. She was there, all golden and forever. Wildly welcoming and naked beneath the surface of the Orontes.

Pilate remained close to the door. He wasn't much for torture and wanted to be near the exit in case he began to feel sick. In his experience, the practice only succeeded in extracting lies. It was for the pleasure of the torturer more than pain of the tortured.

'Take your time,' said Herod as the magus stepped close to Balthazar, his blade glistening in the torchlight.

There was no need to be hasty. The public already thought the Antioch Ghost was dead. With no risk of provoking sympathy for their prisoner, they were free to be as cruel and as meticulous as they pleased.

The magus began his work, taking the knife to Balthazar's side. He'd decided to start by stripping away the victim's flesh, a little at a time. Later, they would move on to other, less surgical methods of inflicting pain. He liked to begin with the flanks – the strips of flesh that ran from the bottom of the armpits to the waist. They were rich with nerves. Excruciating when sliced open and peeled away. But removing them wasn't fatal. Others pre-ferred to start with the face and work their way down. And while removing the face was painful and shocking, it was too often deadly.

Prolonging death was akin to prolonging an orgasm. The closer you could bring the victim to the finish line without crossing it, the better it was. The trick was to take it slow. To give the victim time to recover from the shock, to keep him conscious and keep enough blood in his body to keep it alive for days on end. That was the trick. That was good torture.

Balthazar closed his eyes and pictured the boats slowly floating by. He sat with Abdi on his lap beneath their favorite tree. *The one with the scar down its side. Just like your brother's about to ha—*

Stop.

That wasn't helping. *Think of something else, Balthazar. Think of something else, quick. Get your mind out of this room. Get it away from the pain.* He flipped through a series of images, of words, of memories, of anything, looking for the one that was strong enough to wrap his arms around. Strong enough to keep him safely anchored when the pain came calling, trying to pull him back into the now. Trying to make him scream.

Balthazar looked up, past the rope that bound his wrists, past the wooden beam that held his body aloft. He looked up past the droplets of rainwater growing fat on the ceiling above and past the ceiling itself. Balthazar looked past the top of the palace and the top of the sky and the heavens alike, and he saw the thing he could cling to. The thing that was strong enough to keep him in its arms.

The Man With Wings.

He looked down again as the magus held the blade

close to his skin, teasing him with the anticipation of pain. Staring at him with those black eyes. Balthazar stared right back. He was determined to remain perfectly silent. Determined not to squirm, no matter what happened. The magus pressed the scalpel to the skin just beneath Balthazar's left armpit. With barely any pressure at all, the razor-sharp blade sank in, and then he began to drag it in a slow, straight line toward Balthazar's hip. The incision was so fine that at first it didn't bleed. Like a paper cut, it just hung there, breathing a moment, before the blood formed in beautiful dark beads that trickled down his body. And as they began to fall, Balthazar held firm, his arms wrapped tightly around the Man With Wings.

He remained silent and still even as the magus's blade returned to the top of its path and made a second incision parallel to the first, then connected the two sides with small cuts across the top and bottom. Balthazar didn't utter so much as a grunt, though his teeth were grinding themselves into powder inside his sealed mouth. He didn't squirm. And as he opened his eyes, Balthazar was rewarded for his steadfastness with Herod's scowl. Clearly, the king was disappointed with his prisoner's performance so far. The Man With Wings – Abdi – had Balthazar firmly in his grasp.

And then the magus pinched the top of the long rectangle of flesh and began to peel it downward, away from Balthazar's body. And Balthazar was peeled from Abdi's arms with it.

He screamed.

He screamed as the flank was torn away, starting under his armpit and down toward his hip. He screamed as nerves and capillaries were severed, as skin and fat were uprooted, leaving only bare and bloody muscle beneath. It was quite enough for Pilate, who quietly excused himself from the chamber and into the hall. He couldn't help but feel something for the poor wretch.

III

Ripped away, she thought.

Sela hid on a cliff just north of the palace, the waves of the Mediterranean crashing only feet from where she crouched behind the jagged rocks. Behind her, Joseph and Mary huddled close together, combining their robes to make an impromptu tent over the baby, though it wasn't enough to keep all of the rainwater off of him. Despite the intermittent droplets falling on his head, the baby slept, soothed by the sound of rain and waves.

They'd watched from hiding as Balthazar had been overwhelmed and beaten unconscious. Against their better judgment, they'd followed from a distance as the army journeyed to Herod's summer palace – dragging Balthazar with it. They'd crouched in the driving rain, watching as he was led inside. And here they stayed, huddled in a rainstorm, a few hundred yards from where half the Roman Navy was parked.

Ripped away . . .

'What can we do?' asked Mary. 'Two women and a carpenter are no match for the Roman Army.'

Sela knew she was right. There was nothing they could do for him, except get themselves killed and ensure that Balthazar's imminent death would be in vain. She'd promised him she would get them to Egypt, and that's exactly what she would do. But she owed him a moment first. A moment longer, here in the storm. Lamenting what could have been between them. Mourning what was.

Funny to get so close . . . only to have him ripped away again.

Sela paid her last respects to the wretched love of her wretched life, lost in her thoughts and the steady noise of rain and sea. Noise that masked the footfalls of the three men sneaking up on them from behind.

IV

Herod strode into his bedchamber, which was far smaller than the cavernous one in his 'pleasure palace' in Jerusalem but still a respectable thirty feet square. Soft, cloud-filtered light streamed in through a pair of glass windows on the seaward wall, casting a sleepy glow on the carpets that encircled his oversized bed and its silk pillows and making his long, freestanding silver mirror beckon.

After cutting two strips of flesh off of the Antioch Ghost, the magus had suggested they take a short break from the torture. It was important to give the victim time to recuperate after the first big shock to the system. It was equally, if not *more* important to give him a false sense of hope. Hope that the worst might be behind him, when in fact, the worst hadn't even begun. Herod had been happy to oblige, especially since the break had given him a chance to visit his bedchamber and its silver wonder.

Herod wasn't taking any chances with his prisoner. The Antioch Ghost had proven too smart and slippery for his

Judean guards. Even though he was tied up and weak, he couldn't be trusted. Before adjourning, Herod had ordered two Roman soldiers to remain in the cell with him at all times. No, he wasn't risking anything. Not when the Hebrew God was meddling with them. Not when everything was coming together so beautifully.

Herod stood in front of the mirror and removed his robes. He wanted to look at every part of himself, wanted to admire the speed with which he was healing. His lesions were all but gone; the sickly flesh that had been stretched over his skeletal rib cage was now hearty and healthy. Even his teeth, those blackened, crooked little vultures, had grown whiter. *A miracle.*

It was a little strange that none of his courtesans had complimented his appearance yet. *They're probably afraid to be too hasty. Or perhaps they're afraid to make any mention of my appearance at all.* He smiled at the thought. *I can't blame them. It's been a sensitive subject for years. But the women . . . I can tell that the women are already eyeing me differently. I can tell that they're quietly overjoyed . . . as am I.*

The magus was quietly overjoyed too. He reclined on a couch in Herod's throne room – *our throne room* – enjoying a cup of wine. A harmless little luxury. One of several he was considering taking up in his new role as ruler of Judea.

Pride was a dangerous thing. The Jews had a saying, didn't they? About pride being prelude to destruction? So be it. The magus was allowing himself a little pride today, for he'd finally succeeded in doing the impossible. With a little patience and a lot of distant persuasion, he'd manipulated two of the world's most powerful men into giving him exactly what he wanted: a chance to rebuild. A chance to pull a lost religion out of the ashes.

His fellow magi – *my brothers, requiéscant in pace* – had spent centuries locked away, studying the dark power of a bygone age. Back when miracles had been commonplace. A time of burning bushes, of plagues and floods. For centuries, they'd kept the world out, mastering this darkness. Sharing their secrets with no one. But the world had changed. Empires had grown out of the desert. Man had conjured his own magic: controlling the flow of rivers with dams, curing sickness with medicine, building towers that touched the heavens. The miracles had ceased, and try as the magi might to remain separate and pure, the world had forced its way in.

Their temples had been burned. His brothers had been hunted down, accused of heresy and put to death, until the once-thriving magi had been all but erased from the earth. Until all that remained was one lone disciple. One man with mastery over ancient darkness. And that, quite frankly, was a lonely existence.

Herod had been right about one thing: The world had no use for men like him anymore. But the king was weak. And his greatest weakness was that he thought himself wise. All it had taken was a little enchantment. A little trickery. As ancient spells went, it was relatively simple, and it worked only on those desperate enough to

370

believe its effects. Fortunately, the king was such a man.

In reality, Herod's illness was irreversible. Whatever curse had coiled itself around his innards was far stronger than anything the magus could conjure. But while he couldn't actually make the puppet king healthy again, he could make the king *think* he was healthy. In Herod's bewitched eyes, his lesions and sores were fading away, and his health was roaring back. In the eyes of the *rest* of the world, he was the same repulsive creature.

Yes, his courtesans and whores might think it strange that their king was suddenly so ebullient and spending so much time admiring himself in the mirror. Yes, they might think it strange when he skipped about with renewed vigor or remarked on his renewed appearance. But the beauty of it was, no one would dare tell him differently. And even if they did, Herod would simply think them mad.

Judea's puppet king had become the magus's personal puppet. And he would remain so, even as the disease he could no longer see or feel ate him to death.

And it will. Soon. Unless Augustus kills him first. Kills him for stealing his prized magus away.

And when Herod was gone? The magus would be there to take full ownership of the throne. A kingdom all to himself. An army, guided by ancient darkness, to challenge Rome. And a chance to rebuild an ancient brotherhood that had been all but lost to history.

A strange silence permeated the dungeon, broken only by the sound of rainwater seeping through the ceiling and falling to the stone floor, the crackling of the clay oven and its suffocating heat. Balthazar hung limply from the wooden beam above, trying to take his mind off the agony that radiated from the two strips of raw, exposed muscle on his sides. Even the slightest movement of air caused a severe pain that tensed his body and took his breath away.

He looked up through strands of wet hair and saw that the room was empty, save for two Roman guards posted on either side of the door. His torturers had excused themselves. *Apparently, watching a man suffer is hard work.* Water dripped steadily from the ceiling, seeping through the cracked mortar between the bricks, where it clung in defiance of gravity until each individual droplet grew fat enough to fall. Some of those droplets ran down the rope that held him aloft by his wrists. Some fell onto Balthazar, running down his body, mixing with the blood on his skin and aiding it on its way to the floor, where puddles had begun to form.

Balthazar was having trouble focusing his eyes through the mixture of seeping raindrops and the involuntary tears that came when the waves of pain crashed ashore. He heard the cell door creak open and saw the ghostly white outline of a large man enter.

'So, here he is,' said the man, taking off his cape and handing it to one of the guards. 'Here's the great "Antioch Ghost" in the flesh. I had to come and see for myself.'

He was older. Grayed, though still upright and muscular. He was an officer of some kind, a general maybe. A career soldier in the twilight of his fighting years.

'I was stationed in Antioch some time ago,' he said, moving forward. 'I found it to be a filthy place, truth be told. And, please, I mean no offense.'

Soon would come the slight hunch, the withering of muscles. Next, the weight would fall off of his bones with alarming speed, dark spots would appear on the tops of his hands, and he would use a cane to carry himself a few last wintry steps to the grave. But not yet. There was still power left in this man. Balthazar could tell, just by the way he carried himself.

'The river, the Colonnaded Street . . . the forum. Antioch had its charms.'

There was something flittering and gold under his chin. Something that caught the torchlight and threw it back in all directions.

'It's just that . . . as beautiful as it was, I could never get over the people. They reminded me of . . . rats. Thieving little rats.'

Balthazar felt whatever strength he had left retreat. He felt his breath leave his chest and his body go numb.

It was a pendant.

Abdi's pendant.

V

Sela didn't know whose knife it was. She only knew it was pressed dangerously, painfully against her throat.

'To your feet, slowly,' said the voice. 'You so much as twitch, and I'll cut your throat.'

She rose, damning herself for being caught unaware. Damning herself for staying long enough to get caught in the first place. They'd held freedom in their hands, but they were all dead now. *Ripped away*. And for what? A moment of stupid sentimentality. She never should have led them here. She should have done what she promised Balthazar and hurried them to Egypt. 'Don't look back!' he'd told her.

She was standing up tall now, still unable to see the man who had a knife to her throat. In the corner of her right eye, she could see Joseph and Mary being forced to stand in the same fashion, with knives to their throats – Joseph with his hands held high over his head, Mary holding the baby beneath her robes and muttering, 'No, no, no' again and again.

No, thought Sela. *Not like this*. They'd gotten

Balthazar. They'd gotten Abdi. They could have Joseph and Mary for all she cared. And they could have her. But they didn't get to have the baby.

Not a chance.

She exploded, grabbing the wrist of whoever held the knife and forcing it away from her neck. In the same motion, she spun around so that she was facing her attacker, a Roman sentry – *no surprise there* – and brought her right knee firmly up into his testicles, so hard that she was sure she'd rendered them forever useless. The soldier couldn't help himself. He dropped the knife and brought both hands instinctively to his groin. And as he doubled over in the customary fashion and vomited, Sela brought her knee up again, this time to his face, where it jarred several of his front teeth loose and turned his nose into a mere suggestion of its former shape. He fell, unconscious, and Sela quickly picked up the knife he'd dropped.

This, of course, had drawn the attention of the other two sentries, who left Joseph and Mary and rushed at Sela, their blades out front. But while two of them rushed her, only one made it more than a step – for Joseph jumped on the back of the second and put him in a headlock, choking him from behind. Sela moved out of the other sentry's path just in time, his knife grazing her face. He tried to regain his footing and come back for another attack, but he slipped on the wet rock and had to put one hand on the ground to keep from falling over.

In that vulnerable moment, Sela thrust her knife into his kidney. She was surprised how easily it went in and how quickly the sentry went down, screaming out

375

and clutching at the wound. She looked down at the two soldiers she'd just sent to the ground, then spun around and saw the third, red-faced and about to pass out for lack of oxygen. Joseph remained on the sentry's back, choking him with all his might, even as he thrashed and pulled at the carpenter's hair.

'Run, Mary!' he said. 'RUN!'

Sela froze, not knowing whether she should help Joseph or speed Mary and the baby away. She looked down at the bloody knife in her hand and thought about charging at the sentry Joseph was choking. *But if I missed? And why is Mary just standing there, looking at me and pointing?*

'Sela!' cried Mary. 'Behind y—'

Sela's eyes crossed, and the sound of rain and waves grew suddenly distant. She stood perfectly upright as the whole world tilted on its axis, bringing her face to the ground with a thud. She'd been struck on the head. She knew this somehow, even though the pain had yet to register, and her hair had yet to become matted with the blood that poured from her skull. A pair of sandals came into view, jumping over her and half running, half limping toward Joseph. Though Sela couldn't see his face, the limp told her that the sandals belonged to the first soldier. The one she'd rendered childless.

Despite his injury, it seemed he'd summoned the strength to rise, clobber the back of her skull, and rush to the aid of his fellow Roman. She watched as he tackled Joseph, bringing all three men to the ground. She watched as he pummeled the carpenter with a series of

376

punches. And as Sela watched these sideways events transpire, helpless to affect their outcome, another pair of sandals came into view – droplets of blood and rainwater running down their owner's legs and ankles.

Stabbed Kidney . . . it's the one with the stabbed kidney.

Sela also saw the bottom of a wooden club. It disappeared from her field of view as the sentry raised it high. A moment later, everything went dark.

VI

Adbi's pendant hung from a weathered neck. The red, leathery neck of a man who'd spent many a carefree day in the sun. A man who'd been permitted to grow old. The hairs on his chest were white, as was his beard. Both stood in stark contrast to the burned pigment of the skin beneath. The admiral – *the centurion* – had changed drastically in the past nine years. But the eyes were the same. The ones that'd been seared into Balthazar's mind that day in the forum. The ones that had kept him company under the dark desert skies for all those years as he'd searched the empire for the man in front of him and for the pendant, still hanging there, as it had around Abdi's neck.

Give me this, O Lord . . . give me this. Let me see my enemy's face again. Let me strike him down for what he's done. Let me do this before my life on this earth is ended. Let me do this, whatever awaits me across the gulf of death. No matter the consequences of time or punishment.

God had delivered him to Balthazar, as Mary said he might. Only he hadn't delivered him to kill. God had delivered the centurion to taunt Balthazar. To further punish him for all the terrible things he'd done in his life. All the futures and fortunes he'd stolen.

And I deserve to be taunted.

The admiral, however, had no idea who the dirty, bloody beast hanging before him was. He looked Syrian. *Like one of the little street rats in Antioch. The thieving little pieces of garbage I had to suffer. Whose stench I can still smell.* He didn't like the way this particular rat was looking at him. *Like he knows something I don't. Like he's going to kill me. And why do his eyes go to my pendant so often?*

This likely would've remained a mystery to the admiral had Balthazar's anger not driven him to bite down on his lip. Bite down so hard that a trickle of blood ran from the corner of his mouth. And as it did, the admiral saw it. The little scar on Balthazar's right cheek. That distinctive little scar in the shape of an 'X.'

The scar I gave him . . .

'GLORY!' cried Herod, the magus at his side.

It wasn't the perfect word by any means, but it was the first one that jumped off his tongue. He looked down at the baby lying on the table, naked and crying out for his mother in the center of a crowded throne room. The fugitives had been captured sneaking around outside in the rain. It was too good to be true. Herod had expected to endure one final push in this great chase. One last obstacle from the meddling Hebrew God. Instead, the

379

Hebrew God's little messenger – this so-called Messiah – had walked right to his back door and offered himself up.

'Glory to the people of Judea! Glory to Rome and her emperor!'

Pilate watched the wretched old king celebrate, the infant's mother and father in chains, in tears – held by Roman guards near the throne room's entrance. There was another woman with them, also in chains. *Probably the same one who harbored them in Beersheba.* From the looks of it, she'd been beaten to within an inch of her life. His sentries had done well, and they were being treated by the king's personal physicians. He was told two would live, though one – the one who'd been stabbed – would likely die of infection. *At least he'll die a hero.*

Herod reached down and slid his fingers under the infant's back. *My fingers . . . no longer blistered. No longer twisted and aching.* He picked the child up and held him aloft for all to see. Held him as a temple priest holds an offering to heaven.

And I'll burn *him as an offering,* he thought. *I'll burn a god . . . hear his screams. I'll watch his flesh melt away and his bones blacken.*

He wanted the Hebrew God to get a good look at this. If this baby was destined to topple the kingdoms of the world – if it was truly, as the Jews said, the 'son of God' – then what did that make the king who held him in his hands? He walked around the room, displaying the child for the assembled courtesans and officers.

Yes, a man could be bigger than a god. Here was proof.

Here was a king holding a god in his hands. *My hands . . . which move without pain for the first time in years.* He handed the child to a Roman guard.

'Take him to the dungeon and wait for us . . . I want to put him in the oven myself.'

These words brought screams of anguished protest from Mary and Joseph, which did nothing to dissuade Herod but *did* remind him: 'Kill the male,' he said before walking toward the door. Then, almost an afterthought, he turned back and gave a nod to the guards.

'Do with the women what you will.'

The admiral could've laughed at the wonder of it. If the man before him was the Antioch Ghost, and the Antioch Ghost was the little rat he'd cut in the forum all those years ago, then—

Then I made him . . . I made the Antioch Ghost.

'He was your . . . brother,' said the admiral. 'The boy in the forum . . .'

There was no condescension in the way the admiral said this. On the contrary, there seemed to be genuine sympathy behind the words. A sadness. The admiral was, in fact, touched by what was happening before him. He was overwhelmed with all sorts of emotions, sadness among them. He marveled at the fates. Of all the dungeons in the world, he'd been sent to this one. Sent to face a monster that he created.

'I'm going to kill you,' said Balthazar.

'I know.'

'I swear it . . .'

'I know . . . I know you do,' he said with that same sadness. 'My God, what you must think I am . . .'

The admiral came closer still. Close enough so Balthazar could see the burst capillaries on the tip of his nose. The scars of a wine-soaked life. After taking in Balthazar's face, he stepped away and helped himself to a seat in Herod's chair. A sigh escaped him.

'I have sons, you know,' he said. 'Four of them. They're grown now, of course, but I remember feeling that fear. That fear that they would be taken from me. And if anyone had ever harmed them when they were young, well . . .'

'He was a boy . . .' Just saying the words brought fresh tears to Balthazar's eyes.

'He was a thief,' said the admiral. 'And I was an officer, in a city where a Roman couldn't walk from one side of the street to the other without having his pocket picked.'

'HE DIDN'T UNDERSTAND!'

And that's what hurts the most, when you get right down to it. That look on his face. The one I see over and over in my mind. That fear, that confusion. Why, Bal-faza? What did I do? Why is this man hurting me, Bal-faza? I looked up to you. I loved you and imitated you, Bal-faza, and this wouldn't have happened to me if you weren't so bad, Bal-faza. IT'S YOUR FAULT, BAL-FAZA. IT'S YOUR—

Balthazar gritted his teeth, trying to banish the tears. But they came.

'He didn't understand,' said Balthazar. 'He was *good*.

He would've had a good life. A beautiful life. And you took it. You took everything he would ever have. We . . . we would ever have.'

'Maybe,' said the admiral. 'Maybe he would've had a good life. Maybe he would've had a tragic life. But you . . .' He rose from Herod's chair and came forward again. 'Look at you. You've devoted your whole life to this. To killing me. And now it ends. Useless. Unfulfilled. You're a cunning man, a strong man. You could've done anything. You could have grieved for him and moved on. You could've found love and fortune, had children of your own. But you've wasted it.'

Balthazar heard a voice whispering in his ears: *How does killing honor his memory? How does it bring you any closer to having Abdi in your arms again? Isn't it better to walk away? Doesn't that make you the more powerful man?* Besides, this admiral was right. He'd wrapped up an entire existence in revenge. His entire being was devoted to a single, murderous purpose. But now that he was so close, a new, terrifying question presented itself: *And then what? What does your life mean after that? What comes next?*

'It's haunted you,' said Balthazar. 'His face . . . I know it has . . .'

The admiral looked at him with real pity. 'The truth?' he asked. 'Look at me. Do you want me to tell you the truth?'

Balthazar looked up. Glared at him.

'I've hardly thought about him.'

He's lying. He wants me to believe that. But no man is that callous.

383

'I didn't like my father all that much,' said the admiral. 'But before he died, he gave me a piece of advice. The only one that ever really made a difference in my life. "Hug your children," he said. "Kiss your mothers and fathers, your brothers and sisters. Tell them how much you love them, every day. Because every day is the last day. Every light casts a shadow. And only the gods know when the darkness will find us."'

The admiral turned away and helped himself to one of the orange slices on the platter. He sucked on it, enjoying the taste and the moisture until there was nothing left. As he did this, Balthazar made a decision.

I'm going to find out what comes next.

Blood trickled down Balthazar's wrists as he pulled down on the rope with all his strength, pulled down on the wooden beam that it was tied to. The beam began to groan under the stress, and the admiral turned. He looked up at the beam – sturdy as any beam had any right to be. He looked down at Balthazar, pulling with what limited strength he had left in his body. The math didn't hold up. There was no way a man could free himself under these circumstance. Satisfied, he turned his thoughts back to the orange slice in his mouth.

The magus grabbed his head and bolted upright from his couch in the throne room, knocking over his cup in the process. Something was terribly wrong.

'What is it?' asked Herod, standing up from his throne. By the time Herod got the words out, the magus was on his feet, shoving courtesans and advisors aside, looking for something. *Anything*. When Herod realized what he was doing, he shouted, 'Bring him something to write with, at once!'

A piece of parchment was hurried into the magus's hands as advisors tried to make themselves look busy. Herod crossed the throne room and stood over the little priest's shoulder, reading along with every letter:

Prisoner is free. Ghost fr—

'Impossible!' cried Herod. 'He's under guard!'

The magus hurriedly scribbled again, then shoved the paper so close to Herod's face that he nearly broke the king's nose.

Guards dead. Everyone dead.

Balthazar is born again. He's Samson slaying an entire army with a jawbone. He's Hercules killing the Nemean lion. David killing Goliath. He pulls his arms until they shake, pulls on the ropes that bind each of his wrists to the wooden beam above. And witness now the sound of cracking wood.

The admiral's eyes nearly leap out of his head, because he doesn't believe what he sees. The math doesn't hold up. A man can't be that powerful, especially one whose body has been so battered. Yet the beam splinters, then splits in two and falls to the stone floor with a crash, freeing Balthazar's hands.

The guards draw their swords and come at him. Balthazar charges too. He goes for the table against the wall – the one filled with an assortment of scalpels and clamps and scissors. He grabs the first one his fingers touch, unaware that it's the very scalpel that was used to cut away the missing flesh beneath both of his arms. With long ropes still attached to both wrists, Balthazar turns and swings the blade in front of his body just in time.

And as weak and battered as he is, he swings with more strength than he's ever known. His blade cuts through the droplets of rainwater that fall from the stone ceiling, splitting the ones it touches as it strikes the side of the first guard's face – flaying it open like his own flesh had been flayed. He pierces the other beneath the armpit, driving the blade deeper – deeper past his ribs and into his lungs. He withdraws it and the man falls to the wet floor, where he'll either drown in his own blood in seconds or die from infection in weeks. It doesn't matter, as long as he leaves the earth in pain.

But no time for these thoughts. Not yet. For the admiral has just realized that he's next and begins his hasty retreat toward the closed cell door. Balthazar has to cover twice the distance to beat him there. It's impossible. But not today. The world has bowed before him. Time has wrapped him in its arms. Balthazar moves with wings on his feet, sees with eyes in the back of his head. He takes a sword from one of the guards and moves across the wet floor with impossible speed, blocking the admiral's escape. And the admiral is afraid. He backs away, for he can see the truth written on Balthazar's face. He can see that this man will not fail, no matter what he aims to do. He's afraid because he knows that these are his last moments on this earth and that they're going to be terrible moments.

And he's right.

Balthazar pushes his sword into the admiral's belly. And the admiral cries out as his tender flesh gives way but doesn't break. So Balthazar pushes harder, and the flesh tears — letting the blade in. Letting it through his belly and out the back. And it hurts, and he's so afraid. Suddenly lying on the wet floor, where his blood mixes with rainwater. Pouring out of him, around the sides of the blade.

Every day is the last day, *he thinks.* Every light casts a shadow. And only the gods know when the darkness will find us.

But the admiral sees a light. A light coming for him. His breathing is labored, blood running from the corners of his mouth. He watches this warm, soothing orange light as it grows closer, dancing from side to side. And he knows it's a merciful light, though he doesn't know how he knows this.

But there's a man with the light — carrying it with him. It's the Ghost. And now the admiral is afraid again, because he knows. He knows what the light really is. The Ghost has gone and taken something out of the oven. Something metal. Hot enough to glow.

And the Ghost is above him now. He brings a bare foot down on the admiral's hair and presses it hard against the wet stone floor. So hard that the admiral can't move his head. And before he can scream, the light is forced into the admiral's mouth, shattering his front teeth — and his scream disappears behind the sizzle and smoke. He can smell his lips burning away. Feel his saliva turning to steam and his tongue cooking as the poker moves past his mouth and down into his throat — the red-hot iron blackening his tonsils and vocal cords. He writhes with what little strength he has left as the Ghost pulls the light back out of his throat and pushes it up into the roof of his mouth, searing his palate before breaking through it and entering his nasal cavity. And the Ghost can see that glowing light beneath the skin of the admiral's face now, and it's a strange, almost beautiful sight – that warm orange light making a man's face light up from the inside. But he keeps pushing, until the iron tip breaks through the bone at the top of his nasal cavity and sinks into his—

The admiral woke with a scream. Panicked at first, he examined his body, looking for blood, bruises, anything – but to his relief and amazement, he was unharmed. It had all been a strange, vivid dream. Something brought on by an illness, perhaps. The stress of being away from home for too long.

He stood on the bank of a river. It was a hot, clear day. The fishermen were out in droves, the boats drifting gently by. He could see a boy and a toddler resting in the shade of a scarred palm tree on the opposite bank.

The Orontes . . . Antioch.

He was back in Antioch, and for all its crime and rats, he'd never been happier to be anywhere in his life. The admiral turned, expecting to see the familiar desert behind him, the long, narrow mounds marking the shallow graves where the Romans tossed their dead trash. But the desert was gone. The graves were empty. And in their place was a wall of the dead – their eyes long since turned to dust but looking at him all the same.

They'd been waiting for him . . . waiting to welcome him into the wasteland they'd called home for so many years. A place where there *were* no years. They stood shoulder-to-shoulder – a semicircle that bent around him until it touched the river on both sides. Trapped, by all the unjustly dead of Antioch. And there, at the center of this mob of twisted, bloodless bodies, was a man unlike any of the others. A man unlike any the admiral had ever seen.

A Man With Wings.

He was good and beautiful. And the admiral began to sob, for he knew – somehow he knew exactly who this man was and what he'd come to do. He sobbed and shook, for he knew there was nothing he could do to stop it. And worst of all, he knew that he deserved it.

The Man With Wings walked forward and took the admiral gently in his arms, and off they went. Off into a sea of time and space – the whole of the universe reflected in its shimmering surface. Off to the place where the dead burned forever . . .

And Mary and Joseph instinctively press their backs to the wall of their pitch-black cell and shield the baby with their bodies as they hear the latch opening. Sela rises, determined to die fighting whatever comes through that door. Every inch of her is broken and bloodied; her hands are shackled. But they aren't getting that baby without a fight. Not a chance. And the creak of the cell door opening, and the lone,

impossible silhouette it reveals. And the joy and amazement of impossible reunion and the hurried tossing off of chains.

The reunited fellowship hurried down the corridor that twisted its way through the dungeon, trying to go as quietly as they could despite the two inches of rainwater on the floor. Trying to find a sliver of daylight to show them the way and running from the growing shouts in the dark behind them. A call of alarm had gone out, and every way in or out of the palace would soon be sealed off. They needed another miracle, and for a moment, Balthazar thought they'd gotten it: daylight. Up ahead, around the next corner.

He led the others quickly and quietly around the corner. But on rounding it, Balthazar froze. There was a Roman soldier blocking their path, his sword drawn. The promise of daylight behind him. The dungeon's torch-light flickering off his meticulously polished helmet, breastplate, and sword. He'd been waiting for them.

Pontius Pilate.

Balthazar stood with his sword clutched tightly in his right hand, his left arm extended, shielding Mary and the baby behind him. The two men glared at each other. Both of them dark, driven men. Both of them killers. Their fingers shifted on the handles of their swords, each man waiting for the slightest twitch of the other. Waiting for attack. But none came.

Satisfied that Balthazar didn't mean to cut him down on the spot, Pilate's eyes shifted to the other fugitives: the baby's parents. *Terrified.* The woman who harbored them. *Who risked her life to save them and fought off at least two of my men by herself.* And then there was the Antioch Ghost. *Who risks his life to protect them even now, when he could have just as easily escaped on his own.*

Pilate stood there a moment – his eyes fixed on Balthazar. On everything he'd ever wanted.

'Fifty paces,' he said. 'And then I start yelling.'

With that, he lowered his sword, passed by them, and disappeared into the darkness of the corridor.

Until his dying breath, Pilate would never fully understand why he'd done it. All he'd had to do was call for help, and he would've been a hero. Had it been the sight of Balthazar being tortured? Was it the desire to see the puppet king of Judea humiliated? Or was it just that he didn't like the idea of putting newborn babies to death?

Whatever the reason, he'd held the glory he sought right there, in his hands – and he'd let it slip away. Just like that. It was a decision that would shape his life in ways he couldn't possibly understand, and it wouldn't be the last time he faced it. Some three decades later, Pontius Pilate would encounter the infant again, in Jerusalem. Once again, he would feel a strange compulsion to spare his life. But the second time, he would fail.

The fellowship of five ran out of the palace's seaward entrance and into the stormy gray of its terrace, where raindrops collided with marble, producing a ceaseless, almost soothing noise. With the rain falling and the alarm being raised inside, the terrace was momentarily free of guards. Balthazar had a decision to make, and it had to be made in the next few seconds, in spite of his exhaustion and the breathtaking pain radiating from the exposed muscle on his sides.

They could flee through the desert on foot, but if they were spotted, they'd be no match for the Romans and their horses. They could look for somewhere to hide near the palace and hope that the Romans would be fooled into chasing an assumption through the desert – but what if they weren't? It was here, in this moment of bleeding indecision, that a vision of waving reeds caught the fellowship's attention, and their eyes descended the wet marble steps to the sea, where the masts of Roman warships bobbed up and down in the swell. All of them firmly moored against the dock . . .

. . . all of them left untended.

VII

A young girl came running out of Herod's throne room, sobbing and soaked in blood. Some of it was hers. Most of it wasn't. She pushed her way past the Roman and Judean soldiers who packed the hallways.

'The king!' she cried. 'The king has gone mad!'

The soldiers had come running only moments before, summoned by the sounds of a melee. They'd expected to find the Antioch Ghost battling it out with their comrades, trying to get his hands on Herod. But on arriving, they'd been shocked to see that it was *Herod himself* wielding a blade, using it to dispose of his courtesans and advisors, his wise men and women. The soldiers could only stand and watch as he hacked them to pieces, screaming all the while. None of them dared defy the will of a king, madman or not.

It was something out of a nightmare. A grisly scene that forced even the most cast-iron of soldiers to look away, lest they be sick. The throne room was littered with headless and limbless victims. Shards of smashed pottery and splinters of broken furniture. And in the middle of it all, Herod himself, kneeling over one of the bodies, a sword by his side . . . his face almost completely obscured by blood.

Minutes before this madness began, Herod sat impatiently on his throne, awaiting an update on the escape. The magus sat next to him, meditating silently. *Searching for the fugitives*, Herod hoped. *Hunting them with his mind.*

Minutes after the first shouts of alarm echoed through the palace, Pontius Pilate appeared with his lieutenants, ready to give the king his report. It would be nearly an hour before the Romans discovered one of the smaller ships in their fleet was missing.

'It seems,' said Pilate, 'that the Ghost and the other fugitives were able to slip out of the palace, Your Highness.'

Herod involuntarily balled his fists. *The Hebrew God . . .*

'At present,' Pilate continued, 'we have no clue as to where they went, but I have some of my men searching the grounds in case they've hidden close by.'

'SOME of your men? Send ALL of them, you idiot! Send them all into the desert! Into the mountains! Send them up and down the coast!'

Pilate hesitated, sharing a look with some of his officers. 'Your Highness,' he said, 'in light of the admiral's death, I've . . . decided to recall my men to Rome.'

It took Herod a moment to register this.

'What did you say?'

'The emperor has already sacrificed enough of his men for this folly. I won't risk losing any more or endangering his magus. Not until I'm able to make a full report.'

Herod lifted his body off the throne, his anger rising to its full height.

'"His" magus?' He walked slowly down the steps, a smile spreading across his lips. 'You can tell Augustus that *his* magus won't be coming back to Rome.'

Pilate glared back at him. *What is this?*

'You can tell him,' Herod continued, 'that his power belongs to Judea now. As you can see, he's already used some of it to restore my health. Or did you think I'd miraculously healed on my own?'

Now it was the magus who rose, emerging from his trance and taking in what had just become a very tricky situation.

Pilate was confused. So were Herod's courtesans and advisors, his wise men and women. All of them exchanged looks behind Herod's back.

Is this some kind of joke?

'Tell Augustus,' Herod continued, 'that I'm not his puppet any longer.'

'Are you mad?' asked Pilate. 'Augustus is the master of the world! What are you but a sickly little joke of a king?'

'INSOLENCE! I should have you cut down where you stand!'

The mere suggestion made Pilate's lieutenants draw their swords, which made Herod's Judean guards draw theirs. Pilate raised a hand in the air – *easy* . . .

'Do you have any idea what he'll do to you?' asked Pilate.

'Let him try!' said Herod with a laugh. 'The magus has sworn his loyalty to me! His powers are my powers!'

Pilate looked past Herod and locked onto the magus's black eyes. He wanted to know if any of this was true.

The magus, for his part, knew he had a decision to make.

Yes, Augustus didn't appreciate him. Yes, the magus wanted to strike out on his own, use his powers to rebuild a lost faith. But he was also the last of his kind. And this made self-preservation all the more important. Herod had seemed like the perfect catalyst for his transformation – a powerful man who could be controlled, used up, and thrown away. But he was clearly coming unhinged. Declaring war on the empire in the blink of an eye. That wasn't someone you wanted in your corner. One didn't need to read the tea leaves to see how it would end. He would live to fight another day.

The magus indicated something to Pilate with a nod of his head. When Pilate saw what it was, he understood.

'Go ahead,' said Pilate to Herod, indicating the full-length mirror. 'Look for yourself. Look at what the magus has done to you.'

Herod laughed and turned back to see if the magus was just as amused as he was. But instead of the slight smirk he'd hoped for, he found the magus stone-faced, and felt a sliver of dread scrape against the inside of his stomach.

'Very well,' said Herod, turning back to Pilate.

And so Herod approached the mirror, ready to admire the full cheeks and smooth skin that had greeted him these two glorious days. But when he looked this time . . .

'No . . . ,' he whispered.

The illusion was gone. His sickly pallor and yellowed eyes had returned. His sunken cheeks and lesions oozing their foul milk.

'NO! It can't be!'

'You're not a king,' said Pilate, looking over Herod's shoulder. 'You're not even a man. You're *nothing*.'

Looking back on it, the survivors would agree that this was the moment when Herod's mind left him for good. The moment he realized that everything he believed was a lie. That his vision had finally and completely failed him. He'd gone mad before, but the clouds had always parted at the end of the storm. There would be no going back from this madness.

Herod screamed and grabbed a sword from the hand of one of his guards. Pilate's men yanked their imperator back, convinced that Herod meant to strike at him. But Herod wasn't interested in Pilate. He ran clear across the throne room, defying the weakness that was the reality of his body, raising the sword high in the air, screaming all the while, 'TRAITOR!'

Herod ran up the steps to his throne and in one swing chopped off the magus's head. It tumbled to the stone floor, followed by the magus's body. Blood poured out of his neck and onto the stone floor in buckets – and with it, the last of man's mastery over an ancient darkness.

Screams filled the throne room as Herod kept

swinging his sword at anyone in his path, crying out, 'DEATH! Death to all of you!'

Pilate looked at the headless magus a moment longer, then turned and exited, followed by his lieutenants. There was nothing more to do here. He would've killed Herod himself if he'd had the authority. The only thing to do was speed back to Rome and tell his emperor what had happened. To beg his forgiveness and let the wrath of a living god come down on Judea's puppet king.

'DEATH!' cried Herod as he swung away at courtesans and advisors alike. 'Death!' he cried as he hacked off the heads and limbs of the wise men and women who dared not fight back.

'Death to all of you!'

And so it continued, until the last of his subjects had either fallen or fled, and Herod collapsed in a heap near the magus's headless body – his chest rising and falling rapidly, his tired lungs and feeble muscles burning from the effort.

The Hebrew God had made a fool of him. Herod turned his eyes toward the ceiling and shouted at the top of his gravelly voice, 'Is this my reward for defending your Jews? For building them great cities? Is this how you repay me?'

The magus was gone. And with him the promise of eternal life, the chance to build an empire. And hope. Worst of all, hope – the wine of the weak.

It was all gone. And in the space of a few brief minutes, it was all over.

Here was Herod the Great, kneeling on the stone floor

beside the magus's headless body . . . holding his cupped hands beneath the blood that still trickled from his neck . . . collecting it and drinking it in mouthfuls.

Maybe . . . maybe if he could just drink enough of it . . . maybe he could be whole again.

Maybe he could live forever.

Joseph stood on the bow of a thirty-foot Roman trireme, holding the sleeping baby while Mary searched the ship's depleted stores for food. He looked down at the tiny creature sleeping peacefully in his arms – full and loved and safe. Not yet two weeks old and already the survivor of more peril than most men would ever know in their lives.

The storm had blown itself out, leaving a flat, calm sea and a sky of broken, brilliant red clouds in its wake. The sun had dipped its toes in the western waters and was slowly sliding its way into Neptune's kingdom for the night. It was glorious, and peaceful, and unbearably sad. For as Joseph looked down at the sleeping child, he knew he would leave him one day.

And sooner than your heart will be able to bear, Joseph.

He would leave and go off into the world, because the world is who he belonged to. His beautiful, sleeping boy.

It's okay if I call him my son, isn't it? Surely God will forgive me for that, for I cannot bear to think of him as anything else.

Joseph hoped he would be able to teach the child something about being a man. Teach him the Torah and how to take a piece of wood and craft it into something useful with his mind and his hands. But all that in good time. Right now there was nothing but blessed peace. The sea hadn't parted for them as it had their ancestors, but it had delivered them all the same.

He wasn't alone in admiring the evening sky. Balthazar stood at the helm, one hand on the rudder, the other hand clasped in Sela's. She rested her head softly against his shoulder, both of them in quiet reverence of nature's power and beauty. In reverence of the moment and the miracles it had taken to get them to it.

Balthazar's mind was only just beginning to sort through everything that had happened in recent days. Flipping through the unfiltered images of blood and betrayal, of walking corpses and dying kings. But he stopped when he remembered one moment in particular: something the old man in his dream had said when he'd asked how long he had to stay with the infant:

'*Until you let him go.*'

It was funny – at the time, Balthazar had assumed that the old man was talking about Joseph and Mary's baby. But now he knew . . . he'd been talking about Abdi. And when the full weight of that realization hit him, the tears returned to Balthazar's eyes, prompting Sela to ask, 'Balthazar? Are you all right?'

He turned to her and smiled, admiring her beauty, which neither dirt nor dried blood had succeeded in diminishing, and answered honestly, 'Yes.'

There was nothing ahead but the flat, calm sea, the whole of the heavens reflected in its shimmering surface.

Balthazar didn't know when they would see land or if that land would be Egypt, or Judea, or even Rome itself. Nothing could surprise him anymore, nor could anything discourage his faith that no matter what storms there were ahead, God, or whatever you wanted to call it, would deliver them.

July 19, AD 64

'When you go into battle against an enemy who is oppressing you, sound a blast on the trumpets. Then you will be remembered by the LORD your God and rescued from your enemies.'

—Numbers 10:9

R ome was in flames.
 In less than two hours, the fire had spread from a single villa until it had consumed most of the city's wealthiest district, where senators, generals, and the merely rich lived in the shadow of Emperor Nero's palace. But the houses were as claustrophobic as they were opulent, crammed tightly together to make the most of precious real estate, and this greedy zoning had doomed the neighborhood. Soldiers and citizens alike ran back and forth along the narrow streets, carrying buckets of water between fountains and bathhouses and the blaze. Owners hurried to pull out whatever valuables they could carry before their homes were engulfed. Many burned alive for their efforts. By the time it was all over, nearly a square mile of Rome would be reduced to ash, and half of Nero's palace with it.

Though he would be famously remembered as the madman who fiddled while his city burned, Nero was nothing of the sort. On the contrary, he'd been so panicked by the sight of the burning city that he'd taken to the streets himself to carry buckets of water and had offered up his own money to those brave enough to fight the flames up close.

In the coming months, as outraged Romans demanded answers and accused the emperor of being behind the blaze, presumably to make room for a bigger palace, Nero would famously and ingeniously scapegoat a small, troublesome cult of fanatics who called themselves 'Chrestians' – burning them at the stake, crucifying them, and throwing them to the lions to the delight of the masses. But this would only serve to make these Chrestians martyrs in the eyes of many Romans and speed up their recruitment efforts. In centuries to come, religious scholars would wonder if the tiny cult could have survived without the Great Fire of Rome and the persecution that followed it.

Some would even call it 'the spark that set the world on fire.'

But the old man had harbored no such ambitions when he set the blaze. He was merely keeping a promise.

He watched the fire spread from his vantage point, high on a hilltop overlooking Rome, the distant glow of the flames making the wrinkles on his face look deeper than they actually were. A camel hugged the ground behind him, waiting patiently for its old master. The man was too far away and too deaf to hear the panicked shouts in the distance, but he could see fire growing by the minute and the people buzzing about like wasps that have just had their hive knocked from a tree. And this brought the faintest smile to his weathered face.

Balthazar was nearly ninety years old. He'd been

blessed with five beautiful children and a long, beautiful life with his one true love. There'd been no more miracles in the six decades that had passed since those two weeks – a time he and Sela would come to think of as the great adventure of their lives. In those sixty-four years, life *itself* had become the great adventure, their happiness the miracle.

He and Sela had built a home in the world's great city, in the very heart of the empire that had once pursued them with everything it had. A city with plenty of pockets to pick and palms to read, although they'd resisted these old temptations and become innkeepers instead – with a rule to never, ever turn any expectant couples away, no matter how full up they were. They'd seen Roman emperors come and go, watched their children grow and have children of their own. *The old man in the dream was right,* Balthazar would often think. He'd become richer than Herod or Augustus could've imagined.

And when the time came, Sela had gone peacefully to her rest. Unlike Herod the Great, who, long ago, had suffered through a slow and painful madness that had stripped away whatever dignity he'd had left before death finally, mercifully overtook him.

Balthazar had mourned his wife quietly, his children and grandchildren by his side. And when night came and they all returned to their homes to leave him to his grief, the man who'd once been known as the Antioch Ghost dressed himself in dark robes and slipped into the night, true to his old moniker. He'd wheeled a small cart through the city and let himself into a vacant villa amid

407

the crowded homes of the wealthy. He'd collected as much firewood as he could find within its walls and built a simple pyre out of it – not in the house's courtyard, but around the wooden table of its dining room. When he was finished, he'd taken Sela's body off the cart, washed her, and dressed her in white robes, as was customary. With tremendous effort, he'd placed her on top of the pyre and poured lamp oil around its base.

Before he set it alight, Balthazar had offered a silent prayer for her soul, leaned over and kissed her forehead, and opened a clenched fist, revealing something shiny and gold in his palm.

A pendant.

The one he'd carried for so long. He'd placed it gently in her hands. The cold, wrinkled hands of a woman who, once upon a time, in the land of golden and forever, had sworn that she would burn all of Rome down.

And here it was . . . burning.

Balthazar watched from the hilltop, his face streaked with tears. He was so old, yet so spry and healthy for his age, almost unnaturally so. Sela had always said that his health was a gift from God, bestowed on him as a reward for all the suffering he'd endured. Maybe it was. Or maybe he was just lucky, though he'd come to doubt the existence of luck.

All he knew was, he'd never been quite the same after those two weeks. Since he'd held that baby to his chest. There'd been an indescribable feeling that had never left him, an energy, like the charge of the air before a lightning strike.

When his boys were little, Balthazar would shepherd them up and down Rome's colonnaded streets, stopping to watch musicians perform or petting the strange animals that came from beyond the Himalayas. Once in a while, he would even splurge on a handful of cinnamon dates to share between them. Some afternoons, they would find a piece of shade on the banks of the Tiber. And while his sons – the eldest of whom he'd named Abdi – napped, Balthazar would sit and watch the men fish until he dozed off himself. Sometimes he would dream of those two weeks, of his fellow fugitives and the journey that ended on the shores of Egypt.

Balthazar never saw Joseph or Mary again, but he'd felt them in his soul in the years that followed. When word of their son's arrest and crucifixion reached him from Jerusalem, he'd wept. Not because he adhered to any of the man's teachings – or even knew what those teachings were, for that matter – but because he'd held him as a baby, because he'd felt him always and still. He'd also wept because he was a father and imagined the pain Joseph and Mary had felt upon his death.

As a young man, when Balthazar had seen that strange star vanish from the skies above Bethlehem, he'd thought, *Nothing that bright burns for very long.* He supposed the same could be said about the infant.

Fate hadn't been quite as kind to the other wise men. After slipping out of the Roman camp, Gaspar and Melchyor had fled to the farthest reaches of the empire, never staying in one place for too long, living from one petty crime to the next. They'd been hard, lonely years.

Despite the efforts of Herod's son to sweep the whole embarrassing affair under the rug, word of Balthazar's escape and defeat of two armies began to spread, and the Antioch Ghost was vaulted from minor infamy to legend. It didn't take long for word of Gaspar and Melchyor's betrayal to spread among the criminal class, either. Everywhere they went, the two men found themselves hunted by authorities and cast out by crooks.

In the end, they'd been caught right back where it all began: in the Great Temple in Jerusalem, trying to steal the same golden censer that had landed them in Herod's dungeons thirty years earlier. This time, with no one to devise a daring escape, Gaspar and Melchyor had gone to their punishment as scheduled – crucified and left to rot in the sun outside the city walls.

As they'd hung there, dying, they'd spoken with the stranger who hung between them: the one with the plaque affixed to his cross: *King of the Jews*. Tears had fallen down Gaspar's and Melchyor's aging faces when they realized who the man was and what it meant that they'd been brought here to die beside him. They'd been waiting, after all, almost hoping to be punished for their betrayal all those years ago. They'd carried its guilt and suffered its consequences for too long. True to form, the carpenter's son forgave them both before he died. Balthazar supposed he forgave them too. They'd been dead a long time.

He climbed onto the camel and watched the city burn below him a few moments longer.

'Forever,' he said to himself, then dug his heel into the

animal's side, just like he had in days of old, leaving Rome and its ashes behind. He would never see them again.

An ibex lifted its sleepy head off the desert floor, roused by the beating of feet. It was the only one of its herd to sense the faint trembling, and while the others slept, unaware, it watched a tiny, moonlit cloud of dust move across its field of view, dust kicked up by a galloping camel carrying an old man on its back. After watching them a moment, the ibex laid its head back down and closed its eyes, convinced there was no danger to itself or the herd. There were only two of them, after all. And besides, they weren't headed this way . . .

They were riding toward that strangely bright star in the east.

Acknowledgements

'Acknowledgements' isn't the right word. Rather than 'acknowledge' the following people, I'd like to send my love and sincere thanks to:

Ben Greenberg – as fine an editor as ever there was, and a gentleman and patient soul to boot. To Jamie Raab, Elly Weisenberg Kelly, and my Grand Central family. To my WME family: the bookish Claudia Ballard and Alicia Gordon; the cinematic Cliff Roberts, Jeff Gorin, and Mike Simpson; and the telegenic Richard Weitz and Dan Shear. Also, I'd like to thank Ari Emanuel, because it never hurts to thank Ari Emanuel. To Gregg Gellman, that paragon of legality and keeper of the sacred 'no.' To the Melissas (Kates and Fonzino), who fight for truth, justice, and ink in a world of ever-expanding Kardashians and ever-dwindling shelf space. To my friend, business partner, and splitter of graham crackers, David Katzenberg, and my adorable little KatzSmith family.

And to my actual family, who have to share me with the long nights and closed doors that come with trying to make all of this work, and deal with the grumblings and panic when it doesn't – none more so than Erin and Joshy. My love and thanks for your patience.

Above all, thanks to you, Dear Reader.

Queen of Kings
Maria Dahvana Headley

Once there was a queen of Egypt . . . a queen who became through magic something else . . .

In 30BC, as Octavian Caesar and his legions marched into Alexandria, Cleopatra, Queen of Egypt, learned that her beloved Mark Antony had taken his own life. Desperate to save her kingdom, her husband and all she held dear, Cleopatra turned to the gods for help. She summoned Sekhmet, goddess of death and destruction, and struck a mortal bargain. And not even the wisest scholar could have foretold what would follow . . .

For saving Antony's soul Sekhmet demands something in return: Cleopatra herself. Transformed into a shape-shifting, not-quite-human manifestation of a deity who seeks to destroy the world, Cleopatra follows Octavian back to Rome. She desires revenge, she yearns for her children . . . and she craves human blood.

'So magical, so dark'
NEIL GAIMAN

'Genre-bending, myth-breaking'
TEA OBREHT, AUTHOR OF *THE TIGER'S WIFE*

'A miracle, a marvel'
PETER STRAUB, AUTHOR OF *GHOST STORY*

'A page turner: an epic historical thriller'
DANIELLE TRUSSONI, AUTHOR OF *ANGELOLOGY*

Out now in paperback and ebook editions.